CW00407811

THE NEIGHBORHOOD

BOOKS BY
MATTHEW BETLEY

STANDALONE NOVELS
The Neighborhood

LOGAN WEST THRILLERS
Overwatch
Oath of Honor
Field of Valor
Riles of War
Amira

MATTHEW BETLEY

THE
NEIGHBORHOOD

**BLACK
STONE**
PUBLISHING

Copyright © 2022 by Matthew Betley
Published in 2022 by Blackstone Publishing
Cover and book design by Blackstone Publishing
Artwork by Anthony Morais

The characters and events in this book are fictitious.
Any similarity to real persons, living or dead, is coincidental
and not intended by the author.

Printed in the United States of America

First edition: 2022
ISBN 978-1-6650-6462-0
Fiction / Thrillers / Suspense

Version 1

CIP data for this book is available
from the Library of Congress

Blackstone Publishing
31 Mistletoe Rd.
Ashland, OR 97520

www.BlackstonePublishing.com

PART I
RECONNAISSANCE

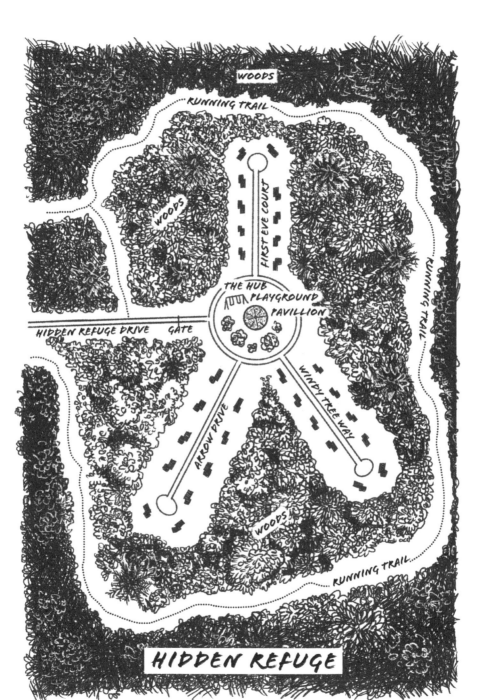

HIDDEN REFUGE

CHAPTER
ONE

The white van drove slowly through the black iron gates, its driver accelerating once he'd emerged unscathed into the inner sanctum of the gated community. The code he'd been provided had worked, as he'd known it would, as it had for the past few days. How these people thought a gate and a code would keep the monsters of the outside world at bay was beyond him. But that wasn't his concern. His job was simple—last-minute reconnaissance of the neighborhood before the operation began that night.

The dark blue Mercedes Amazon delivery van, a mobile fixture in suburbs across America, maintained its twenty-five-mile-per-hour speed as it drove along the shaded, tree-lined road. The woods were still relatively thick, only recently beginning to shed their summer skin of multicolored leaves. A cold front was approaching, and the winds of autumn would soon rattle the trees in relentless pursuit of uncovering the jagged, worn limbs. The street was the only way in or out of the community, although the driver knew a running path wound around the perimeter of the neighborhood, connecting the three residential streets and, in two locations, leading to the main road more than a mile away.

Shards of sunlight broke through the tall woodland canopy glinting off the hood of the van. *It sure is peaceful, though.* He shook his head to himself in a combination of disbelief and resignation at the fact that their target had brought the package to this quiet, secluded neighbor-hood in Virginia. *Whoever had taken it knew that we would come looking for it. Why bring it here? How could someone be this stupid?* These were questions he wasn't paid to answer, and he refocused on the job.

Thirty seconds later, the van emerged into a clearing in the center of the community, revealing the scale of the suburban oasis that was Hidden Refuge, a name selected by the builder precisely because of the isolation, real or imagined, from the outside world and Washington, DC, to the east. The driver smiled to himself at the irony of the name. He knew better. There were no truly safe places in America today, no matter what the occupants of communities like this told themselves. He knew money bought a certain amount of self-delusion, and 99 percent of the time, that delusion would stand against the test of time. Unfor-tunately for the residents of Hidden Refuge, they'd unknowingly found themselves in the 1 percent. But that was their problem, not his.

The driver stopped at the stop sign and flipped on his right turn signal, looking left and then right. Nothing. Luxury also paid for a false sense of tranquility.

The center of the neighborhood lay directly before him, mocking him with its suburban perfection. A wide circle one hundred yards in diameter was the hub of Hidden Refuge. Squarely in the middle stood a white, ornate, elevated pavilion. The front half of the structure was open, welcoming, but the back half was a series of benches attached to a railing that ran around the pavilion. The driver knew it could easily accommodate eighty people based on the size, but he wondered if it was just a decoration. He didn't get the sense that Hidden Refuge was a close-knit community. But he also didn't care.

To the left of the pavilion, a large, complex playground with nets, slides, swings, and bridges stood as if begging for some child to clamber on its empty parts. To the right was an empty field and a pet station, the dark green liner hanging over the sides of the suspended, caged trashcan. *Even the wealthy have to pick up after their pets. At least we have that in common.* Trees were randomly planted throughout the hub to break up the monotony of the flat, expansive grounds.

A sidewalk encircled the area, complete with tall black lampposts every forty feet that stood like sentinels watching over the hub. Jutting off from the traffic circle around the hub were three linear streets arranged exactly like the symbol on the front of the Amazon van, and each street was cut off from the others by a wedge-shaped section of woods, providing a layer of insulation between them. The residents knew others lived on those streets, but they didn't have to see them if they didn't want to. *Must be nice*, the driver thought, having grown up in a dirty apartment in the South Side of Chicago. There'd been no escape from his neighbors or the horrors they'd perpetrated daily. Drugs and murder had been a booming business in the South Side for as long as he could remember.

The entire area put his nerves on edge. He saw the black SUV in his rearview mirror, approaching from behind. *Time for deliveries*, he thought, and turned right onto Founder's Circle, an apt and self-indulgent name for the roundabout. When he reached the first street, he turned right and saw the first residents of the day on Arrow Drive.

Two teenage boys no older than thirteen chased each other on mountain bikes, open jackets flapping in the wind like streamers, oblivious to the threat that had just arrived on their street. The fact that there were children in the neighborhood troubled the driver, but he compartmented the emotion and proceeded.

The homes had been constructed in an alternating pattern, with four large single-family homes on each side, each house in the center of two acres of land. They were arranged so that no two homes were directly opposite each other, another small touch that added to the privacy of the community. The street ended several hundred yards in front of him in a cul-de-sac with two more enormous homes angled in toward the street as if standing guard over Arrow Drive.

Various SUVs and sedans were parked in each driveway, and he watched as an attractive woman unloaded groceries from the back of her black Audi SUV as her two middle-school-age children chased a black Labrador in the front yard. *Suburban America in all its splendor.*

With a little more than two hours of daylight left, the driver approached the first house on the right, 101 Arrow Drive, and prepared to pull into the long driveway. He turned his head to the left as the two boys sped by him on their bikes, which was why he failed to see the little girl on a pink scooter shoot out of the driveway ten feet in front of the van.

His peripheral vision, though, honed to a sixth sense, caught the flash of movement, and his reflexes kicked in. He slammed on the brakes of the van, even before he fully saw what it was that had found itself in the path of the delivery vehicle. Recognition turned to horror, and he prayed to God that he had enough room to stop, although not completely out of a selfless duty to protect the child. He *was* concerned about the girl's well-being and safety, but he was more concerned about his own.

As the van skidded across the pavement toward the girl, he gripped the steering wheel tighter, and he realized there wasn't enough time. He was going to hit the little girl. *If I hit her, this operation is over, and he'll kill me.* The man in charge would not tolerate mistakes, not ones like this, when the stakes were so high.

CHAPTER
TWO

Zachary Chambers—Zack to everyone he introduced himself to—kept walking toward his neighbors' driveway, the Thomases' mail in hand. It was an inevitable annoyance of suburban life that mail was occasionally delivered to the wrong address, but it felt like it had been happening more frequently. *Maybe a sign of societal decay? As goes the Post Office, so goes the world.*

The cool fall late afternoon felt refreshing, and he inhaled deeply as the Amazon van turned the corner onto his street. *Another sign of societal decay, for sure.*

As the driver approached, Chloe Thomas shot down her driveway toward the street, triggering alarms inside Zack's calculating mind. An old habit, he took a mental snapshot instantaneously—Chloe on the scooter, the boys on bikes, the distracted driver—and he realized the imminent danger. *Oh no.*

He dropped the mail and broke into a sprint. The Thomases' driveway was only twenty feet away, and he prayed he'd started running in time.

A woman's screams assaulted his ears, but he blocked it out, focusing on his objective—the girl.

The Amazon van kept coming, its driver distracted by the boys on bicycles. Zack ran straight toward it, engaged in a game of chicken, man versus vehicle, with Chloe Thomas stuck in the middle.

Chloe shot out into the street as the driver finally spotted her, and he slammed on his brakes.

Zack reached her a split-second before the skidding van and hooked her with his right arm around her waist as he turned toward the curve. With the van looming like a monster right next to him, he wrapped Chloe in his arms as she shrieked, and launched the two of them into the air. As they sailed over the curb and toward the Thomases' lawn, Zack rotated his body so that his back was to the ground. His feet cleared the curb as he watched the Amazon van slide across the space he and Chloe had occupied a moment ago. He smiled to himself in relief, at least until his back slammed onto the grass, expelling his breath, and slid to a stop, Chloe secure in his arms.

He looked down at the adorable girl, who seemed to be taking it all in stride, and he felt his breath come back, inhaling deeply, which seemed to amuse Chloe, who smiled up at him.

Sherry Thomas was screaming, even as Zack asked Chloe, "Are you okay? Sorry about that."

"Can we do that again?"

Zack sat up and placed Chloe on the ground next to him. "Maybe another time. That was exciting enough for one day."

Sherry Thomas reached her daughter and wrapped her up with both arms, shouting at the African American Amazon driver, who now stood on the street, concern written all over his face. "How could you not see her? She was on the driveway!"

"It was the boys on the bikes. He got distracted by them as they approached him. I'm sure he was just being careful," Zack stated, intentionally calm, momentarily ignoring the driver. He stood up, ignoring also the dull pain in his lower back.

Zack's presence seemed to calm her, and she shifted her eyes from the driver to him. Sherry paused, exhaled, and said, "Thank you, Zack. Thank God you were there."

"Thank the Postal Service. I was bringing you some mail that got delivered to us by accident." Zack turned to the driver, whom he found staring at him in an unusual way, as if assessing him with a purpose. The driver was no older than thirty, clean cut, light-skinned, with a short, faded haircut. His deep brown eyes shone with alertness and intelligence, *more so than the last Amazon guy we had in here.*

For two weeks during the summer, an Amazon driver had terrorized the residents, delivering his packages as if the neighborhood were his personal raceway. Several families had captured his aggressive driving maneuvers on camera, but it wasn't until an executive who lived on another street had nearly lost his son when the driver had tried to pass a car doing the speed limit on the traffic circle. The driver hadn't seen the boy on the bike, and he'd missed him by inches, causing the boy to crash into the grassy hub. Unfortunately for the driver, another resident had captured in HD the entire ordeal on the latest iPhone. Several phone calls to Amazon had ultimately landed on the desk of one of the executive customer service representatives at Amazon headquarters. One of the homeowners had even emailed Jeff Bezos at jeff@amazon.com, his publicly available email. He hadn't responded—"Probably too busy dealing with a mistress and a divorce," Zack had commented at the time—but the video had sealed the deal, and the driver was gone within days. There'd been no issues since, but Zack understood why Sherry was quick to react the way she had.

"Am I right about what happened?" Zack asked directly but without accusation in his tone.

"I swear to God, I didn't see her. I wasn't speeding. I know what happened over the summer with the other driver." And he did, as it had been included in the target-package brief on Hidden Refuge that each team member had received. "Just like you said, I got distracted by the kids on bikes as they passed me. I only took my eyes off the road for a split second, just to make sure they didn't swerve toward me. It's happened before." He turned to the girl and her mother. "I'm so, so sorry. It won't happen again. I swear."

The young, fit man's apology seemed sincere, and Zack watched as Sherry softened. But there was something about it that felt calculated, as if he *knew* the right words to say. *Stop it, Zack. You're being paranoid, even for you.* Yet he couldn't shake the sensation, even as he spoke.

"What's your name?"

The driver turned back to Zack. "Aaron. Why? Are you going to report me to Amazon? I *really* need this job, sir," he pleaded.

Zack hesitated. His instincts were almost always right. They had to be because of what he did, who he was, but this was just a kid doing his job, *wasn't it?*

"Okay, then, Aaron. No. I'm not going to call Amazon. This seems like it was an honest mistake. Just be as careful as possible. While we might have nice homes and things, all of that is replaceable—but our kids aren't. You know what I mean?"

The man calling himself Aaron *did* know what the stranger meant. He'd felt that way about his little brother before the army, before the streets of Chicago had stolen him from those that had loved him. *But you can't keep the streets on a leash, not always.* "I understand. Believe me," he said, thoughts of his brother adding a level of sincerity to his voice that he knew was unmistakable.

"Good. Now, let me help Mrs. Thomas and young Chloe, and you can finish today's run. Have a good one—and be safe," Zack said, clapped Aaron on the shoulder, and bent down to pick up Chloe's scooter as her mother lifted her from the grass.

"Thanks, Zack," Sherry said, moving off the grass to her driveway. "How are Steph and the kids?"

"They're good. Unfortunately for me, they left me alone and went to Steph's sister's place down in Richmond. It's my fault, though," Zack said, and laughed as he followed Sherry up the driveway. "I told her I had some work to do this weekend, and she told me she was leaving me . . . to visit her sister."

"Ha! That woman is never leaving you, nor you her. While we all have families here, Zack, you have a very happy one, and everyone knows it. I might be a little jealous, in fact."

While she wasn't flirting with him exactly, it wasn't totally innocent. Sherry was an extremely fit brunette with blue eyes who loved her Peloton bike, and it showed. At five feet eleven inches, Zack was a trim, fit man who used the gym in his basement on a regular basis, ate well, and ran when he could. The dad bod was for those with excuses, of which he had none. His brown hair was worn longer on the top, combed up slightly, and short on the sides. His eyes were a deep, dark blue, completing the profile of a handsome man who looked like a daytime soap opera star. He was aware of the impact he had on women, but he was deeply in love with his wife and his kids, and while he appreciated the comment, it had no real impact on him.

"Chad might be too, if you keep talking like that," Zack said, and put the scooter down. "I'm glad you're okay, Chloe," he said to the five-year-old little girl and ruffled her black hair. "I'm sure you'll be stopping and looking both ways from now on, won't you?"

The girl only smiled up at him. Zack had a way with almost all children, which endeared him to their mothers—a fact of which he was also acutely aware.

"Oh. She'll be all right. Kids usually are."

"I dropped the mail back there. I'll grab it and put it in your mailbox."

"Sounds good. Thanks again. And I'll definitely *see* you around."

See you around. It sounded so innocuous, but still. *What's wrong with you? Work got you spooked?* Between the driver and Sherry, he was starting to think his imagination was getting the better of him. He envisioned one of his former coworkers, Charles Davis, laughing at his paranoia. *"Zack, my man, you need to re-lax." Uh-huh. Easier said than done.*

At least he was alone to deal with the issue at work. Without Ethan and Addison running wild in the house, he'd be able to focus on the problem at hand.

Once he'd returned the mail, he walked back up toward his house, watching the Amazon delivery van pull up the street and stop two doors past his. *Just a guy doing his job. Nothing more.* He compartmentalized his concerns, something he was exceptional at doing.

A minute later, he walked up the driveway to his single-family home, his personal oasis from work and other pressures.

A two-story, modern home, the six thousand square feet—without the finished basement, he reminded himself every time—comprised a three-car garage; an upstairs with a master bedroom and four other huge bedrooms and a balcony overlooking the main, two-story family room; a formal dining room; a living room; his office; and a kitchen that seamlessly connected to the spacious family room. A sunroom with a back wall of eight extra-wide, tall windows jutted out of the back of the kitchen and opened onto the screened-in back porch, which only added to the footprint of the house. While more than two-thirds of Hidden Refuge had pools, his backyard contained a sixty-foot-long pool complete with a diving board and curved slide for the kids. A huge play set was set back behind the pool. Beyond the play set, at the back of the property, the woods served as a natural barrier, providing a sense that they were close to nature, although not too close.

Zack was grateful for the material aspects of his life, but he knew they were fleeting, like all things, which only heightened his appreciation for them.

He longed for the hugs that welcomed him every day when he returned from work, yet knew he'd have to wait until Monday afternoon, when his family would come home. He once again inhaled the crisp air of fall. It might have been his imagination or a romanticized longing, but he was certain that the air was cleaner the farther he was from the capital. *It's good for your soul too, no doubt.*

"What's up with the Amazon guy, Mr. C?" Samantha Hawkins asked from her front porch next door in her typical dry, direct manner. A seventeen-year-old junior at the local public high school—one of the top blue-ribbon ones in Virginia and ranked nationally—Sam was an anomaly, as well as their babysitter. "Trying to take over our neighborhood the way they're taking over the world?"

Zack wasn't sure if the bright track star with blue streaks in her blond hair was being serious or sarcastic, which was often the case. He knew from previous conversations that she wasn't a fan of corporate America and distrusted the government, which seemed to be a common theme of her generation. But he didn't think she'd gone full-blown social justice warrior. Sam was more complicated than that, and Zack was one of the few people that recognized it and treated her accordingly.

"He mentioned something about building a corporate office for five thousand people just outside our community. Sounded like a good idea," Zack replied with a straight face.

Sam studied him for a moment. "Hope so. Maybe they'll bring drones. I'm sure the residents here would love to have a drone army buzzing about all day and night."

Such a perfect delivery. A world-class expert in reading people, Sam always eluded him. "You know I'm kidding, right?"

"And you know I already knew that, right?" Sam shot back. "You know, for a defense contractor, you're pretty gullible."

"Got me again, Sam," Zack said. Changing the subject, he asked, "What kind of trouble are you getting up to this weekend?"

Sam smiled. "Parents went to the lodge for the three-day weekend," she said, referring to the three-thousand-square-foot "lodge" in the Appalachian Mountains that her father, an executive with a major bank in Crystal City, had purchased right after moving to Hidden Refuge. "They gave me a choice—a quiet weekend trapped with them and nature, or stay home and survive on my own. Guess which one I picked?"

"You think you'll make it to Monday? If not, text me, and I'll send help."

"Thanks. You're a real stand-up guy, Mr. C. And I figure I'll have a raging party with a lot of illegal narcotics and alcohol. But don't worry—I'll keep the guest list to under two hundred."

"Sounds quaint," Zack replied. "Have fun." He turned toward his front steps and paused. "And Sam, I don't work for the defense department. I run a company that develops new technology. The DOD is just a customer."

Sam seemed to ponder the question, her mistrust of the behemoth Defense Department on her face. "Is there a difference?"

"Definitely." *If you only knew the half of it . . .* "Have a good night, Sam. And seriously, call if you need anything. Steph and the kids are gone, and I'll be working all weekend."

"You got it, Mr. C. See you soon."

Zack waved, climbed the steps, and put the key in the top lock, his mind already reviewing the steps he needed to take over the next several hours. Tomorrow had to go smoothly, or there'd be problems—lots of problems.

CHAPTER
THREE

"And you're sure there are no surprises, Thomas? No one's having a party? Nothing out of the ordinary that could throw off tonight?" Griffin Huntsmen asked Thomas Cartman, the Amazon impersonator who'd been driving the neighborhood for the past two days. His brown eyes—so dark they almost appeared black—bored into Thomas, as if the strength of his gaze would pry any remaining secrets from the team member. While he spoke softly, there was nothing soft about the operation's intimidating leader.

At six feet one inch, Griffin was built like a world-class boxer—all sinew and muscle—but he moved with the speed and grace of a dancer, a fact that no one mentioned, lest they incur his wrath. He was physically intimidating, with stern features that rarely broke into a smile, but he had one redeeming feature that set people at ease: his long, thick, blond hair, which hung just a few inches above his shoulders. When he parted or pulled it back in a short ponytail, he looked like an angry surfer, just as ready to hang ten as to beat someone to death with a surfboard.

Griffin Huntsmen was the owner and CEO of Huntsmen Enterprises, an intentionally innocuous name. His background remained a mystery even to the few dedicated employees he had, except one—Barrett Connolly, an eccentric Irishman who'd been with Griffin since the inception of Huntsmen Enterprises. While Griffin was the CEO and face of the company, Barrett was the chief of operations, responsible for day-to-day planning and execution of the contracts.

For those in their circle, Huntsmen Enterprises had become known as one of the most successful private military and security contractors in and around DC. They didn't operate in the open like some of the other major companies. Their area of expertise lay in the shadows of covert and clandestine operations, and their success was a direct result of how they conducted their affairs. While Griffin and Barrett were the leads on every job, they hired different former operators for each, based on specific criteria, objectives, and skill sets. They'd used some personnel on multiple jobs, but they tried to limit their overall exposure. The less their subcontractors knew, the better it was for all involved. The fact that they also doled out some of the highest fees in the business helped ensure discretion.

The rarely whispered rumor was that Griffin and Barrett had been part of the Central Intelligence Agency's Directorate of Operations as paramilitary operations officers in the agency's covert Special Activities Division, amusingly monikered SAD. Whether they'd been Navy Special Warfare Development Group, 1st Special Operations Detachment Delta, a different unit from Joint Special Operations Command, or just college kids with a desire to deliver justice to the enemies of America before joining the CIA, no one was certain, and more importantly, no one was brave enough to ask.

Thomas never faltered. He'd made his decision even before leaving the confines of the gated community. There was no need to mention the incident with the girl or the man who'd saved her. He wasn't sure what Griffin's response would be, and uncertainty with his current employer was potentially dangerous. Better to keep his mouth shut about the near miss.

"No problems or surprises, boss. With Columbus Day on Monday, I think at least a third to half of the residents might be out of town. Who knows where these people go, but I know they can afford it. I dropped off the packages, waved at the residents, saw some kids on bikes, others walking their dogs, but nothing out of the ordinary."

Griffin nodded approvingly. It had been a stroke of genius on Barrett's part to have Thomas go in for the past two days as an Amazon driver. Griffin had been able to secure the route and the van from an old classmate of his at Penn State who'd become an executive with the e-commerce giant.

"Very well," Griffin said, and turned to the rest of the assembled team inside the school's cafeteria. With the long weekend and the separation of the school from the small town of Falling Rock, Virginia, Griffin was certain that they'd have the facility to themselves for the next twelve hours, which would be more than sufficient. *By this time tomorrow morning, I'll have the package, and we'll be long gone.*

"Michael, do all the terminal guidance systems have full batteries, and are they ready to go? The last thing I want when we get inside is to have our gear malfunction. You're one hundred percent certain they'll pick up the RFID tag, even once we turn on the jammers?" Griffin used his tech's full name, a habit he had with everyone.

This was the one part of the operation he couldn't control—communications—and it maddened him. Like all special operators throughout the world, he knew that sometimes mission success was determined by the quality of the gear used. If that gear failed, then chances were the operation would go sideways. For a man in total control, the thought was fundamentally offensive to his core being.

"I am," Michael replied. "Once our man at the phone company shuts off the landline switch outside the neighborhood, the jammer here and the ones with the vehicles will take out all cellular and satellite communications up to two gigahertz. No one is making a call out of that neighborhood once we flip the switch."

"And you're sure our internal radios will be unaffected?" a young man in a Falling Rock Police Department uniform asked.

"Absolutely. The frequency for the radios is below the jamming frequency for the cell phones and satcom. We'll be fine. The repeater on the roof of this school and the ones on the vehicles will ensure we have continuous comms the entire time."

Griffin felt more comfortable by the minute. *This was going to work.*

Michael looked at the six-man search team that would be responsible for locating the package once the neighborhood was clear. Each member of the team held a specially designed device that looked like a pistol grip with a yellow solid trigger. A smartphone was mounted on top of the device, and in front of the trigger was a black rectangle that was the device's omnidirectional antenna. "Just remember, those modified RFID readers will pick up the tag under ideal conditions at one hundred and ninety-six feet. But these aren't ideal conditions. I really don't know how much interference the structures, wireless signals, and God knows what else will cause. That's why you have to enter every house. The closer you are, the better your chances of finding it."

This was another aspect of the mission that Griffin didn't like. *Too many unknown variables.* "I'm trusting this to you," he said to Barrett, who stood next to him in the middle of the cafeteria.

Barrett was smaller than Griffin, lean and wiry, with a sense of humor that bordered on the sadistic. He maintained his black hair in a neat, classic taper that allowed him to blend into almost any situation, corporate or military. Blue eyes that were neither too pale nor too deep added to the impression that he was a clean-cut executive, just one of the countless hundreds of thousands in DC.

"I got this. If it's there, we'll find it. No doubt about it," the Irish operator said.

"The buyer says it's in the neighborhood, and I trust the validity of his information." This was the first time in all of their jobs together that Griffin had kept the identity of the buyer a secret even from Barrett. It was too sensitive—even for his closest ally and right-hand man.

"Well, then, there won't be any problems, will there?" Barrett said to the assembled team.

Six searchers. Six police officer impersonators in six Ford Explorer police SUVs with communications equipment. One angry Irishman. And a target package worth $100 million to Griffin and his company. *What could possibly go wrong?*

"Roger that," Griffin said. "Men, check your gear one last time and then get some sleep. And remember—no shots fired unless you have no choice. The last thing we want is a dead suburbanite. It's not good for business," which for Griffin, was always the bottom line.

PART II
INCURSION

CHAPTER
FOUR

Sam tossed and turned in her bed, acutely aware of the emptiness and the vast space of the house. It wasn't that she minded being alone in her home. The alarm was set, motion-sensor lights activated, and her father had given her a code to a safe in his office that contained a loaded shotgun he'd trained her to use. It was that she hadn't been able to reach Ben all night. *What could he be doing?* There'd been no text. No call. Nothing. It was completely unlike him.

Benjamin York lived on Forest Edge Court, the first street to the left of Arrow Drive on the other side of the main road into the neighborhood. She didn't consider him her boyfriend, not yet, but they were much more than friends. But like all things with Sam, it felt complicated, mostly because of the way she viewed the world. And she was acutely aware of it and afraid it would derail the blossoming romance.

While the other girls on her track team liked Sam and included her in everything, they sensed that she was different, but none of them could put a finger on it. While she was pretty, smart, funny, athletic, and socially aware—everything a girl trying to survive high school in the modern age had to be—she was occasionally distant, as if she were waiting for something to come, something only she saw. Every time one of her friends felt like Sam was about to reveal her true nature,

Sam would suddenly act like a typical teenage girl, commenting on the popular boys or the latest fashion trend.

The truth was Sam *was* different, and reverting to the role that her friends expected was the act. The real Sam was more mature and more philosophical than even her neighbor, good-guy-personified Mr. Chambers, suspected. She was an old soul, one that somehow felt the weight of the world. To her, seventeen felt like thirty—although she admitted she didn't know what thirty really felt like; it was so far away—and while she couldn't exactly explain why, she knew it set her apart from everyone else at her high school. Moreover, it was why she expended so much time and energy trying to fit in. Because the one thing she did know and have in common with her friends and other girls was a simple truth—high school was easier in numbers.

While she managed to fool her friends, she couldn't lie to herself, and she didn't have a burning desire to deceive a boy just for a meaningless teenage romance. But when she met Ben, she realized she didn't have to. He was a kindred spirit in a teenage world of detachment and technology, and their connection had been forged in the most innocent of ways, like something out of the old '80s high school romance movies she occasionally watched on Netflix.

In the middle of the summer, she'd been on a run, working the wooded path that wound around the neighborhood, her feet striking the pavement in tempo with her thoughts, when a black Labrador had shot out of the woods from her right, nearly scaring her out of her Brooks trail-running shoes. She'd managed to skid to a stop when the dog had leapt up onto her chest, licking her furiously on the chin, before its owner had emerged from the woods.

"Percy! Percy! Get off her!" a boy with longish black hair that hung above his eyes shouted. He had kind features, a nice smile, and was only slightly taller than Sam. He wore a Scoops Ahoy T-shirt and khaki shorts that covered his lean athletic frame, which set Sam, a religious *Stranger Things* fan, at ease.

"Percy?" Sam asked, the big dog now held up by her arms. "As in Weasley or Jackson?" she said, referring to the J. K. Rowling series and

Rick Riordan series. "And please don't tell me your name's Steve," she added for good measure. *Let's see how he responds.* Sam had a way of testing other people when she met them. It was an automatic response that allowed her to categorize people as friend, potential foe, or acquaintance.

The boy studied her for a moment, as if assessing whether she was making fun of him or asking honestly. His blue eyes danced in the shadows of the woods, and he said, "Riordan, of course. Don't get me wrong. I love the Harry Potter books, but I was always more into mythology than wizardry. But that's just me."

Sam studied him for a moment before replying, scratching the grinning Percy behind the ears as he tried to lick her face. Maybe it was the heat, her quickened pulse, the affection of the dog, or some other unknown variable, but she was attracted to the boy, strongly.

"I agree. And I can't remember which one it was, but Harry was a bit of a whiner in it, while Percy has a much better sense of humor, which I prefer."

Before he could control himself, the boy had blurted out, "My name's Ben, and I'm pretty funny too."

Sam had seen the terror in his eyes as he'd said the words. She imagined his angst and smiled. Rather than repelling her, his awkwardness had the opposite effect: charming and disarming. In the moment, she was a girl on a run, and he was a boy with a dog, and all felt right with the world.

"Well, Ben, I'm Sam, and I know *I'm* hilarious. So that makes two of us." She looked at Percy, pools of brown staring up at her in unconditional adoration. "And I'll bet Percy is too, aren't you, boy?"

And that was all it took—a simple young adult fantasy reference, a chance encounter, and they'd quickly become close friends, spending their weeks together until it had naturally evolved into something more. It turned out that while Ben wasn't into school sports, he was passionate about martial arts, and he studied Japanese Shitō-ryū karate three nights a week and Saturday mornings at a dojo in what passed for downtown Falling Rock, Virginia.

Ben, like Sam, was smart, funny, athletic, and incredibly thoughtful. But it was his natural ability to fight that had put the school on notice that while he didn't fit in with any of the traditional cliques, he was not a boy to be trifled with.

For reasons known only to them, two football players had targeted him when he was a freshman. They apparently hadn't done their research and didn't know that Ben had spent the last six years rigorously training in karate and had already obtained his third-degree black belt by the time he was fourteen. Trying to pin him against a locker between periods, the two juniors had thought it would be fun to scatter his belongings across the hallway. It hadn't gone so well for them.

The altercation had lasted less than ten seconds and ended with a broken nose and a dislocated shoulder, which Ben later felt bad about, as he explained to the principal, "I was only trying to get him off of me. I think I hip-threw him too hard, but he was trying to choke me. I'm sorry."

And that was it. The two boys were suspended, and the football coach, a man who despised bullies, had spent an entire month reinforcing through pain and practice the notion that bullying had no place on his team. The next time the two boys saw Ben, they were so polite to him that he'd thought maybe he'd inflicted brain damage.

As for Ben, word circulated throughout school like a California wildfire in summer—the friendly freshman was a wolf in sheep's clothing. Beware. No one had challenged him since, and his reputation had allowed him to wander the halls of high school, effortlessly navigating the factions and cliques.

It was why they were perfect together—two teenagers who didn't quite fit in but were popular enough that it didn't matter. But in each other, they saw what others only grasped the edges of: a maturity, wisdom, and soulfulness well beyond their years. Their romance had escalated quickly and naturally, and their parents were surprisingly positive about the match.

But where is he? Sam depressed the button on the Cobra push-to-talk radio. "Ben, are you home? Is everything okay?" she asked, sounding concerned but not desperate like some of her friends did over their boyfriends.

No answer.

Everything is okay, Sam. You know him. He's as reliable as you are. He'll have a good explanation. He loves you, and the sudden thought both terrified and filled her with a warmth and comfort she hadn't experienced with other boys.

She placed the Cobra radio on her bedside table, rolled over, and pulled the Pottery Barn Harry Potter–themed duvet over her shoulders, smiling as she did. While it was true that she liked Percy Jackson more, she still loved the Boy Who Lived.

CHAPTER
FIVE

Zack sat up on the side of his bed, acutely aware of his wife's absence. He grabbed his iPhone, pressed the screen, since the new phone had no home button, and saw the time. He wasn't going to be sleeping any time soon. The weight of what he was about to do was keeping him from his dreams. He knew it was the right thing, morally, but he also knew that the US government didn't care about his interpretation of morality. He'd learned that lesson before. The only thing that mattered to the power brokers in the bureaucracy of DC was the US Code and how it could maintain the status quo—specifically, *their* status quo.

A sudden wind buffeted the second floor, coming in from the west over the Appalachians and rattling the downspout on the corner of the house. *Need to stop putting it off and get that thing secured. Just one of many things they never tell you when you build a house,* he thought, recalling the insulation problem they'd had in the attic when they'd moved in. The installers had failed to thoroughly fill several spots with the blown-in insulation, resulting in the kids' bedrooms being noticeably warmer in the summer and cooler in the winter. Like Indiana Jones, he'd traversed the attic with a headlamp, the beam arcing across the empty space, wondering how soon it would be before he crashed through the ceiling below, hoping he wouldn't land on one of his children before he found the low spots. A few pictures on his iPhone and one call the next day to the builder had the situation resolved within a week. He was proud of himself for discovering the issue, just one of many that the builder hadn't mentioned.

He opened an encrypted chat application and typed, "Can't sleep. How close are you? Want to do this earlier? No one will be there at 0400." The sooner it was over, the sooner he'd be able to relax. Then again, it was his software. But he knew the Department of Defense wouldn't see it that way, as they'd already purchased the program for a significant amount of money. Not that budgets really mattered when it came to DOD programs, or the government in general.

Zack hit Send and waited. Moments later, three dots appeared in the text window. *Here we go.* But just as suddenly as it had appeared, the screen turned black, and the words "No Service" appeared at the top of the phone. *What? How could that be?*

Zack stood up, walked over to the wall, and hit the light switch. *Might as well get dressed.* He knew he'd pay for it by early afternoon when his eyes would hurt and the feeling of fatigue would set in, but he didn't care—he and his wife had successfully raised two kids so far. He knew what true sleep deprivation was like.

As he walked into the bathroom, the voice-over-IP phone he had on the nightstand caught his attention. "No Service" was displayed in gray digital letters, and Zack's pulse quickened. *No way. No cell service and no internet?* He was not a completely paranoid man, but the chances that both would suddenly go down in the middle of the night had to be incredibly rare.

Once he finished in the bathroom, he dressed quickly in dark gray sweatpants and a black Under Armour hoodie. He felt more secure in dark clothes at night—a holdover from his former career.

Once in his office, he fired up the outrageously expensive desktop iMac that he used for programming and was unsurprised to see the pie slice of curved lines grayed out. The internet was still down. Another burst of wind rattled the office windows, a sign of the impending cold front. A chill passed through him, but not one caused by the cold.

Zack walked to the office closet, opened the door, and bent down to enter a five-digit code on the front panel of a two-drawer floor safe. He told his family that it contained their personal documents in case of a fire—which was true—but it also had several work-related items and one piece of equipment that might have raised the eyebrows of his beautiful wife—an Iridium satellite phone.

Zack grabbed the handset, powered it up, and walked toward the kitchen and the back of the house. He stopped at the kitchen island, picked up a small fob remote, and disarmed the home's alarm system. Three beeps sounded and he slid the back door open, walked through the screened-in porch, and exited to the back deck, an expansive area that contained his smoker, grill, and a luxurious set of patio furniture.

He looked at the phone and stopped dead in his tracks. *No service.* A creeping sensation of dread spread throughout his gut. *Something's happening. There's no way they can know.* He'd been careful to the point of fanatical paranoia in planning tomorrow's event, but still, his mind played tricks on him, especially at three in the morning.

He turned back to enter the porch when he caught a flash of lights through the woods between his backyard and the main drive into Hidden Refuge. He heard several vehicles moving along the road. *What now?* Whatever it was, he knew one thing—it wasn't good.

CHAPTER
SIX

2:40 A.M.

Barrett Connolly led the procession of Falling Rock police SUVs down Hidden Refuge Drive, stopped at the gate, entered the code, and proceeded into suburban Indian Country. As a boy, he'd enjoyed old westerns more than cartoons, the prospect of a different time and an adventurous place more alluring than the streets of the Mary Ellen McCormack public housing project in South Boston. Since his mother had died when he was six and his father, broken after her loss, didn't care what Barrett did, one saving grace was that he was allowed to watch pretty much whatever he wanted. And westerns were what he wanted— and needed—to escape his dreary existence in Southie.

The years between his mother's death and his teenage years were a blur of dark memories, ones he knew were there, just under the surface, waiting to pull him down if he dwelled on them. But it was when he turned thirteen that the Irish gangs of his housing project claimed him as one of their own.

His father was a semi-employed mechanic who bounced around from one run-down garage to another. While the elder Shawn Connolly drowned his sorrows in cheap beer and Irish whiskey, the younger Barrett allowed street violence and petty crime to soothe his raging soul—at least until three days before he turned eighteen.

While the McCormack had been built for the poor predominantly Irish Catholic working class in 1938, decades of disrepair, the civil rights movement, and the Housing Act of 1949 had transformed the waiting list from white to poor Black families. With a slow integration came racism and conflict to the point that by the 1990s, 20 percent of the population was African American.

Barrett never blamed the Blacks for organizing into gangs, just the fact that a group of five Black teenagers had taken to calling themselves the "MC Hammers" because they lived in the Mary Ellen McCormack and used ball-peen hammers on their victims. Their gang's name would've brought derision on them had they not been violent to the extreme—just shy of murder.

Coming home from one of the local bars—South Boston didn't enforce the legal age of consumption—at a little past 1:00 a.m., Barrett and his best friend James Shaughnessy were ambushed by three of the MC Hammers.

While their willingness to use blunt instruments had instilled fear in their previous victims, in the case of Barrett and James, it only angered them. The bigger problem for the Hammers was that they didn't know how to use the flat-end weapons, at least not as well as Barrett and James.

Barrett would later reflect that had he been sober, he might've been able to contain the constantly simmering rage within him, but under the angry catalyst of whiskey, the dark monster within was immediately triggered and unleashed. Two of the Hammers had landed in the hospital; one, in the morgue—the result of an excessive number of blows to the head once Barrett had disarmed him.

While he'd had a love-hate relationship with Boston's finest, he'd never killed. What surprised him was that he felt no emotion about it, no empathy for the fallen boy. An epiphany soon followed—*if killing causes me no remorse, maybe I can use it to escape this life.* While not an overachieving academic, he was smart enough to know there was no real future for him in Southie. If he stayed, he'd end up like most of his friends—unemployed, poor, angry, and violent. Later in life, he'd be glad to have removed just two of those prospects.

After three days of wondering and wandering in panic, waiting for the police to arrive at his father's apartment, on the morning of his eighteenth birthday, he'd walked north through Southie to the US Marine Corps Recruiting office near the piers on Summer Street, enlisted, and never looked back.

Whether the God that watched over all wayward Catholics had been protecting him or not, he didn't know, but the police never identified him or James as suspects in the beatings and murder.

He'd spent fifteen years in the Marine Corps with two-thirds of his career as a critical skills operator with the Marine Corps Forces Special Operations Command, commonly referred to as MARSOC, in Camp Lejeune, North Carolina. But it was a chance encounter with a street-clothed lethal operator in Kabul who recognized the moral fluidity of Barrett's nature that truly changed the course of his life. Barrett had transitioned into the private sector, but the anger never dimmed, and it still fueled him forward on every mission.

In the few introspective moments that he allowed himself, Barrett viewed the boy's death at his hands as the entry fee to a life he'd never have been able to experience had he not killed. He'd learned a valuable lesson—only through strength and violence were one's goals achievable. The Marine Corps had honor, courage, and commitment; Barrett had strength and violence. He preferred his code to theirs.

The convoy of police vehicles were the tip of the spear of the operation, which was broken into four phases—clear, contain, search, and Barrett's personal favorite: "get the fuck out of there with minimal chaos." If the first three phases didn't go smoothly, then the fourth wouldn't matter. Plan B was not something he truly wanted to entertain, but the mission was the mission, and if need be, he'd execute it. He figured his soul could bear more collateral damage. He was damned already, and he hoped the devil might look a little kindlier upon him with a higher bar tab in human misery and devastation. Hell was reserved for the real overachievers.

Barrett's lead Explorer reached Founder's Circle, barely decelerated, and took the turn to the right quickly, the tires gripping the pavement, squealing the way he intended them to. *There's no going back, now. Time to pay the piper, people. One of you screwed the pooch, and now the whole tribe gets to pay for it.*

A wave of calm washed over Barrett. It was an emotion he'd experienced just before combat on several occasions. A mixture of focus, determination, and confidence, a feeling that he was exactly where he was supposed to be at this moment in time and space, spurred him on. *This is going to work, and then we can figure out what's next for Huntsmen Enterprises.* He knew it would likely have to be international after the buzz of the hornet's nest they were about to kick.

He reached for the bank of switches installed between the two front seats—exactly the way they were installed in real police vehicles—and flipped two of them. Lights and sirens erupted on top of his vehicle, shattering the dark quiet of the night. The other five SUVs followed suit, and the cacophony of sound mixed with the wind so that the vehicles' cries seemed to fade in and out, mournful mechanical souls wailing hopelessly against Mother Nature.

He spotted the three vans—one parked on the roundabout at the opening of each street, its tail end facing the street, antennas on top—and kept going. In addition to the jamming equipment, the vans contained the six operators with the unique handheld RFID detectors. They'd made the decision to pre-stage the vans and the men so that they'd be in place before the chaos and confusion began. *Comms had better be out by now, or this whole charade is over.*

The convoy hit Arrow Drive, and Barrett's and the second vehicle turned onto the street. The four remaining vehicles sped onward toward Windy Tree Way and Forest Edge Court. Barrett noticed several houselights blossom into white spots of illumination on upper floors as he pulled alongside the edge of the lawn in front of the driveway to the first home on the right. He stopped, put the vehicle in park, and turned off the sirens, the lights still flashing.

The second Explorer passed him and sped toward the cul-de-sac to start with the flag lots and work backward toward Barrett.

Barrett turned to his passenger. "You know the deal. Stay in the vehicle and maintain comms with the COC," he said, using the old military term "combat operations center" that he and Griffin had decided still applied in this case.

"Understood," said a young man around thirty who'd seen enough combat in the army to have matured him by at least a decade, which was why they'd picked him. They needed operators who could remain calm and collected under intense scrutiny and pressure, ones who wouldn't fold like the young and immature soldiers and junior officers he'd seen cave in during combat.

Barrett nodded, left the vehicle, and dashed up the driveway, withdrawing a heavy flashlight as he did so, the blade of light cutting back and forth across the black surface as he moved. He liked the feel of the Falling Rock PD Nomex flight suit instead of the shirt and trousers. The Kevlar vest fit well, his push-to-talk radio attached to the front, and the rigger's belt held up the thigh holster that was tight around his upper leg, the Glock 9mm 17 Gen5 secure. It reminded him of MARSOC.

He hit the front steps and prepared to knock—just as a light illuminated the porch and the door suddenly opened. A tired man in his late thirties appeared, a gray T-shirt and dark blue pajama bottoms adorning his figure. His black hair was disheveled, and he rubbed his eyes even as Barrett saw the look of concern in them. *Good. The more panicked they are, the easier they'll be to control.*

Before the man could open his mouth, Barrett beat him to the punch, speaking in a series of rapid-fire sentences that landed like body blows. "Sir, I'm sorry to disturb you at this time of night, but we have an emergency, and I need you and your family to get dressed and leave the neighborhood. There's been a train derailment on the commercial line out of DC a few miles southwest of here. Unfortunately, the entire train was carrying commercial-grade chemicals, and three cars that fell off the tracks are leaking some kind of toxic substance used in manufacturing. Has a long name I probably couldn't pronounce even if I had it written in front of me. Because of the winds and the cold front and God knows what else, they're having a hard time putting out the blaze. And they're concerned that if the winds are strong enough and shift, it could send a cloud of toxic smoke and fumes your way. We're setting up a shelter at Falling Rock Elementary School right now, which they're telling us will be completely safe since it's four miles to the north. And that's where we need everyone in this community to go. We're leading people out in convoys. Once you're ready, you can hop in your car and line up at the traffic circle. Sir, do you understand everything I've told you?" And like an auctioneer who'd just finished a wild minute of bidding, Barrett suddenly stopped talking, allowing the man to process everything he'd just heard.

Brian Thomas—husband to Sherry and father to little Chloe, the girl that had nearly been struck by the fake Amazon driver—was a pilot for United Airlines and flew both domestic and international routes. He was also a former C-130 Hercules pilot in the United States Marine Corps. And while the officer spoke, his brain flipped the switch on the military mindset that was always present, even if idle and running in the back of his brain like a computer subsystem.

"Got it, officer. We're going now. And thank you," Brian added, as he closed the door.

As Barrett hustled down the steps, he heard the man yell to his wife, muffled through the front door. "Honey, we need to get the kids and go! There's been a train accident!"

Less than a minute. One down. Four more to go on my side. Barrett thought that with a little Irish luck, they might clear the entire area within fifteen minutes.

His push-to-talk radio erupted, and he heard the other teams report similar success from the first homes. *No one suspects the cops, at least not out here in the suburbs. In the city? Forget it. We would've been made within minutes.*

He chuckled to himself and moved through the grass toward the next home.

CHAPTER
SEVEN

Esli Flores struggled between wakefulness and a semiconscious dream state as the screaming caused him to toss and turn. *No. Not again. Please*, his tangled mind pleaded. *No more screams.* The battle between lucidity and Alzheimer's waged on, and he wasn't certain if he was awake or asleep. *Just no dead babies. PLEASE.*

A survivor of the Salvadoran Civil War, Esli had been a happy and simple ten-year-old boy when the elite, US-trained Atlacatl Battalion death squad had swept like a cemetery wind through his village in northern Cabañas Department. With orders from the military, the soldiers operated under rules of engagement that all civilians in that area were guerrillas. Early in the morning, they'd pulled his parents from their home and shot them in the dirt as they screamed for him to run. Miraculously, he'd dodged the gunfire and fled into the bushes and forest under a surge of fight-or-flight adrenaline that had replaced his grief. The grief and all that it carried would come later.

As his village of Santa Cruz was systematically slaughtered with mortars, gunfire, and aerial bombs, he'd fled north through the jungle, surviving horror after horror, mothers and children dying together from violence, starvation, and pure evil luck. He was discovered by a group of soldiers, spared execution for a reason he still couldn't fathom to this day, and placed on an army helicopter. He was flown to an orphanage in Santa Tecla, where he would remain, a boy with no family, until he turned eighteen and fled north to the United States.

The immigration crisis hadn't reached its full peak yet—that would come during the 1990s—and he'd been able to apply for a green card and claim political asylum under the Refugee Act, which had been passed only a year before his family had been murdered. He'd lived with a third cousin in San Antonio, worked as a day laborer in construction, and waited for his hearing.

Whether the judge had sympathized with his situation or just wanted to push his case through the beleaguered system, Esli would never know. All that mattered was that the judge granted him his asylum and a green card, and four years later—since the green card was back-dated one year, per the process—he naturalized and became a US citizen. It was still one of the proudest days of his life.

Not many of his village had escaped, but he had, and he'd made every moment count. He'd become a tailor—a trade his mother had taught him as a young boy—and built a small chain of combination dry cleaner and tailor shops. He'd met his wife in Houston, after he'd been injured at a Custom Tailors & Designers Association convention. A drunken attendee had bowled him over from behind, driving him headfirst into the corner of a display booth and splitting his head open. His wife had been a triage nurse at St. Joseph Medical Center, and he'd been overwhelmed at the sight of her, unable to breathe or speak. He'd pretended it was the head wound, but she knew, and she'd felt the instant attraction as well.

Decades later, with two beautiful and talented children—a professor of American history, which amused Esli as an immigrant, and an incredibly successful investment banker—his wife had succumbed to cancer, and Esli found himself struggling to get through the days on his own. He'd thought it was just the grief, the painful hole in his heart that had been wrenched open, physically manifesting itself in insidious ways. But he wasn't that lucky. A doctor's visit had resulted in a battery of tests and a diagnosis of early-onset Alzheimer's. As soon as he'd told his son Stephen, the banker, there was little to no discussion, and Esli found himself living in a luxurious guest bedroom with his son, his wife, and their two children.

While most Americans might have paused at the prospect of taking care of an ill parent, that was not the way of his son, who knew the full story of Esli's childhood—the grandchildren would learn it when they were older—and his wife had supported the decision completely. Three years later, he'd fully assimilated into the daily life cycle of the family, playing with his grandchildren, helping when he could—no one could fix a tear or handcraft a princess costume better than Grandpa Esli—and trying to minimize the burden that he felt he placed upon them. He knew his family didn't view him through that lens, but the helplessness and confusion that came with Alzheimer's made him feel that way.

In recent months, the symptoms had grown worse—the forgetting, the wandering, the in-between, where he thought he was in a dream but was physically manifesting it in reality. The last was the most terrifying, for it was after those fugue states where he would find himself in another part of the house than he last remembered being, the journey a black hole of lost memories.

It was where he found himself when he heard the screams, imagining that he was being pulled up from his bed and dressed in a rush, his thick gray hair askew as his son pulled his shirt over his head. In his dream, he stumbled down the hallway, his son leading him—to where? He had no idea. But he knew it couldn't be real, as he heard the sound of children, one crying in confusion.

Blackness and nothingness—and Esli was in the left rear passenger seat of the dark gray Infinity QX80 luxury SUV. *How did I get here?* He wasn't panicked, just concerned. The children—one next to him and one in the third row, as they no longer needed car seats—had calmed down. Their mother, Victoria, was speaking to them quietly. He looked around the interior of the vehicle as the three-car garage door opened. Two oversized duffle bags had been thrown into the rear seat with him, neither fully zipped, clothes sticking out as if trying to escape.

Motion—and the vehicle lurched backward out of the garage and accelerated toward the street. Esli turned and was surprised to see most of the homes on Windy Tree Way partly illuminated. Two other vehicles raced by the driveway toward the central traffic circle. Esli's concern rose incrementally. *Why are we leaving? What's happening?* Unfortunately, the dream state felt like a weight, pressing him into the back of the seat, and he couldn't speak. *I'm dreaming. I have to be.*

The QX80 reached Founder's Circle, turned right—and stopped. A line of SUVs and sedans blocked the way forward. When Esli saw the nearest van in the grass and the men in uniform around it, his concern rocketed into a full-blown panic. His damaged mind recoiled at the shock and sight of men with guns, and his lucidity was blown away in self-preservation.

Esli Flores's mind split, flashing between his past and his present, his childhood and his now, his only thought, *No. Never again. These men will not hurt my family.*

The panic turned to rage—rage against the soldiers that had slaughtered his parents, rage against the government that had ordered it, and rage against the God that had allowed it to mercilessly unfold. The power of the dream magnified his emotions and strength, and Esli Flores, an old man losing his battle with Alzheimer's, dependent upon his family for everything, was transformed into a young man full of purpose and strength. In the dream, he knew what had to happen, and the hesitation of the old was replaced by a need to act, to make things right, to undo a horror that couldn't be undone.

As traffic began to flow, and the first line of cars moved down Hidden Refuge Drive to leave the neighborhood, Esli opened the door of the QX80 and felt the cool air of fall whip around his head. He heard his son speak to him, but the words were muffled like those of Charlie Brown's teacher. The dream had no purpose for the words, as there was nothing that could prevent Esli from his solitary objective—to stop the men with guns.

Esli began to run, building speed with each purposeful step. He heard shouts from behind him, but he paid them no heed. In this dream, he was the one with the power, and *his* will would be the one imposed. He would not be a victim again. He ran harder and saw the men with guns react. *This time, you will be the ones that suffer, and the village will be saved.*

And with each stride, Esli Flores ran toward his destiny.

CHAPTER
EIGHT

Sam stirred in her bed, the push-to-talk radio squawking loudly. She'd left it on as she'd drifted off to sleep, hoping that Ben would let her know everything was okay. His parents had been fighting lately, arguing about something they'd been keeping from him. The arguments hadn't been personal or vindictive, and he'd told Sam he didn't think they were getting a divorce. It was something else, something more fundamental, and he figured they'd let him know in due time. His unnatural patience, especially for a teenage boy, was another trait that she respected and admired in him.

"Sam! Sam! Where are you?" Ben asked urgently, penetrating her semiconsciousness with immediate effect.

Sam opened her eyes and looked at the ceiling and then grabbed her iPhone. *3:05 a.m.? What's going on?*

"Sam! They're evacuating everyone. Please tell me you're somewhere in this car line." A pause. "Sam!"

Evacuation? What's he talking about?

She grabbed the radio and spoke, still trying to shake off the cobwebs of sleep. "Ben, where are you? What's going on?"

"Sam!" he exclaimed with palpable relief in his voice. "Thank God! I was worried sick. Did the police come to your door? Where are you?"

Police? She stood up from her bed and moved quickly to the door, flipping on the light switch as she did. "Ben, I'm fine. I was worried when I didn't hear from you. What happened?"

Whatever it was, it had to be serious, and she needed to get dressed. She tossed the radio onto her bed and started grabbing clothes from her white Pottery Barn dresser.

"I'm sorry. I was exhausted after martial arts and collapsed on my bed after showering. I lay there for a second, planning to radio you, and the next thing I know, my parents are waking me up. I forgot to turn on the radio before I passed out."

Internally, Sam breathed a sigh of relief. *Told you there was no reason to worry. He's one of the few very, very good ones.* "That's okay, Ben. I understand. I figured it was something like that. But what's going on?" She already had a hoodie and yoga pants on and was moving toward the door, the radio in her hand and the iPhone with no service in her hoodie.

"There's been a train accident of some kind, and the cars are leaking some kind of chemical, and they're worried about the wind pushing the fumes our way. You need to get out. We all do. We're in the car, at the circle," he finished, referring to their Cadillac SUV as a "car" the way most Americans still did.

As if on cue, a gust of wind rattled her window, the sound sending shivers up her spine. Sam enjoyed the cool fall air, and she'd left open the window that faced the front yard to enjoy the breeze while she slept. She felt the air pour into the room and ignored it. *Time to leave.* Sam rushed down the main stairs, flipping on lights as she went. *Have to remain calm. Keys, purse, and a bottle of water. Go.* Everything else could wait here. "I'm leaving now. Where are they taking us?" Her parents weren't going to believe this when they found out about it. She reconsidered her choice and wondered if the mountains might've been the smarter option. *Live and learn, Sam. Live and learn.*

"Falling Rock Elementary. They've set up some kind of shelter. I've even got Percy with me." A loud *whoof* echoed from the background.

"Okay. I'm walking out the door right . . . now," Sam said, and turned the knob on the front door. She stepped into the cool, crisp night and pulled the door closed behind her. A large gust of wind hit her, shoving her silently backward, as if urging her to seek refuge inside. "I'll see you—"

A loud *crack* erupted from the woods to her left, followed almost immediately by a much louder *boom* from the traffic circle. *Gunshot*, her mind recognized even before she processed it. She heard it both outside and from the radio, as if in stereo, and she froze.

"Ben? Ben! What's happening?"

Then the screams began, jolting Sam from her sudden terror, and she turned back toward her front door.

"Sam! Get back inside! They're not cops!" Ben pleaded.

Already on it, Ben.

"Get help!" Ben yelled through the radio, as louder voices sounded in the background. "Be careful!"

She thought she heard a man yelling at him, and a wave of panic hit her. "Are you okay? Oh my God, Ben. Please tell me you're okay!"

"I have to help him. I love you, Sam," Ben said, and the radio went dead.

Help who, Ben? Oh no. Please don't do something stupid, you beautiful boy. Her emotions roiling, she stepped inside, closed the door on the sounds of chaos, and turned off the lights. She needed to calm down, to think, to plan.

* * *

Zack stood twenty feet inside the woods near the section of Founder's Circle between the main drive and his street. He waited and watched, the night-vision monocular scanning the scene before him. The entire situation felt *wrong*, especially the police vans that were parked on the grass of the central hub. His fleeing neighbors seemed oblivious to them in their haste to escape, but Zack knew better. He also recognized next-generation communications equipment when he saw it, and the multiple antennas on their roofs screamed at him, echoes of a former life. These were not police vehicles, no matter how hard they'd tried to disguise them.

Once the sirens had announced the police presence, Zack had fled back inside and waited. He'd had a choice: ignore the police or wait and see what they wanted, praying they weren't after him. He hadn't committed any crimes—yet.

The officer that had finally come to his door several minutes later had looked and sounded like a sheriff's deputy, but there was something *off* about him, an underlying menace just below the surface that Zack had once been trained to detect. Without that training, he never would've suspected the man was an impostor. It wasn't obvious, but it was there nonetheless. *He's a killer, not a cop.* But he also knew that none of his neighbors would see it. That's not who they were. *Hell, it's not who I am, not anymore.* So he'd played along with the officer, responding exactly the way any startled civilian in suburbia would in the middle of the night at the sudden appearance of law enforcement, especially in a community like Hidden Refuge. He'd only thrown one curveball at the impersonator, just to see how the man would react.

"Real quick, officer, before you go—do you have any idea why the phones and internet are out? I can't get any kind of signal." No urgency, no suspicion, just a question.

The officer hadn't responded immediately, studying Zack's face for a tell that the resident standing before him was a threat. Zack had felt that kind of intensity before, but he remained motionless and calm, as if standing before a coiled king cobra, waiting for the strike.

The moment passed. "Could be the cell phone towers are overloaded. Could be the wind. As for the internet, I don't know, sir. Seems like all the carriers have outages from time to time." Changing the subject, he added, "Please just get yourself ready to leave with everyone else. I'd hate to have to come back and find you here if the winds do change." The last words had such hostile undertones that Zack was certain the impostor didn't have the self-awareness to hide it. *He's borderline psychotic*—Zack had flashes from years past, but he suppressed them.

"Will do, officer. And thanks for notifying me. I'm going to go wake my wife and two kids and get out. Be safe out there," Zack had lied with a straight face. His instincts had screamed at him not to let the impersonator know that he was home alone.

The man had only nodded and turned away.

The moment he was gone, Zack had gone to his office, grabbed what he needed, and exited by the back porch, silently entering the woods at the back of the property. He'd worked his way toward the street and assumed an overwatch position from behind a towering, thick tree. He'd remained standing since he knew there was no way they'd be looking in the woods. They knew they had the element of surprise, and they were taking full advantage of it.

As he watched, he admired the efficiency of the assault team, which is how his mind registered them and their actions. Whatever they were doing, it was bold and ambitious, and he had to tip his figurative hat to them—at least until the old man charged them and changed everything.

CHAPTER
NINE

Kevin Oliver was amped up to the edge, inches from giving in to his emotions and losing control. His impulse control had always been his problem, and it was why he'd been dishonorably discharged from the air force after only seven weeks at the Pararescue Emergency Medical Technician Basic course at Kirtland Air Force Base in New Mexico.

It wasn't his skills, which had placed him near the top of his class during his assessment phase and in the combat dive, airborne, and SERE (survival, evasion, resistance, and escape) courses of the elite United States Air Force Pararescue jumper pipeline. No. It was his overzealousness, a raging storm inside that propelled him to be better than everyone else. Unfortunately, that also included authority—specifically, those with authority over *him*, which wasn't a trait valued by the military.

He'd been able to keep his temper in check, at least until one of the instructors had seen something in Tech Sergeant Oliver that he didn't like. And like a wolf on the scent of its prey, the master sergeant had decided the Air Force would be a better fighting organization without Oliver in it.

Weeks of torment at the paramedic school had wound him tightly, the psychological tension coiled to the breaking point. And broke he had, unfortunately for the master sergeant's face when the altercation was over. A wired jaw, a broken nose, a fractured cheek, and a quick investigation later, and Tech Sergeant Oliver was just Kevin Oliver. He was just as furious with himself as he was with the master sergeant.

Out of the military with a dishonorable discharge attached to his name, his options were limited. If it hadn't been for his close friend and active-duty PJ, Staff Sergeant Raymond O'Shea from Boston, he might still be wandering aimlessly, a modern-day ronin with strong skills but nowhere to use them.

Raymond was friends with the chief of operations for a private contractor firm called Huntsmen Enterprises. A phone call had been made, a meeting had occurred, and a year later, he felt like he was part of a team, one of the regulars that were called by Barrett Connolly when they had an especially sensitive job. Kevin had a fluid moral compass, and it worked to both his and his employer's benefit.

For the Hidden Refuge operation, he had one job: maintain crowd control at the traffic circle and ensure the residents left as directed. He'd been doing just that, with more than half of the population evacuated to the school. The operation was going as smoothly as any he'd participated in, right up until the old man rushed him.

If it hadn't been for the wind, everything might have been fine, but Mother Nature was a force to be reckoned with, and she had a mind of her own.

Kevin was forty feet from the road, standing near one of the vans, when he heard a door slam, followed by yelling. By the time he identified and faced the commotion, the old man was halfway to him. Instinctively, Kevin withdrew the Glock he wore on a gun belt as part of his Falling Rock uniform and raised it toward the approaching threat. His senses heightened, and he saw an old man in a gray T-shirt, khakis, and wild gray hair under a navy-blue hoodie running toward him at full speed.

"Sir! Stop! I said stop!" his partner standing next to him yelled.

Come on, man. Don't do this. Are you fucking crazy? Kevin's finger was straight and off the trigger, watching as the man held his right arm down and out of view. *You've got to be kidding me.* The man kept running, and he raised his arm.

And then the wind blew, and the night turned to chaos as Murphy, ever the saboteur, took control over the cascading events.

Crack!

The tree snapped in the woods beyond the man just as he extended his hand toward Kevin. Even though Kevin didn't see a weapon in the low-level illumination of the central area's lights, the reverberating crack tricked his mind for the briefest of moments, which was, unfortunately, all it took.

Kevin Oliver squeezed the trigger of the Glock 17 and struck the man squarely in the center of his chest. He knew it was a kill shot even as the echo reverberated across the neighborhood.

The man's momentum ceased, and his run turned to a slow walk, a look of confusion on his face. Less than ten feet from Kevin, the man looked down, took one more step, and looked back up at Kevin.

"I'll wake up soon," the old man muttered, sending a chill across Kevin's back, and collapsed face-first to the damp grass.

The screams of agony and loss erupted immediately, as the man's family members rushed across the lawn, their panicked cries of concern louder than the wind.

"Oh shit. You just killed a civilian, dude," said Kevin's partner.

"Shut the fuck up. I know," Kevin replied, and grabbed the radio off his vest. "Whiskey Six, this is Whiskey Four. We have a problem."

More car doors opened and closed, and Kevin felt the confused gaze of people directed at him. He sensed people moving away from the area as well, likely fleeing the sudden violence for the sanctuary of their homes. Train accident or not, he couldn't blame them. "Shit," his partner said. "We have to get this under control, or this whole thing goes sideways fast."

Kevin knew Barrett was going to be furious, but he hadn't had a choice. The man had charged him, and he'd thought he'd had a gun. Even as adrenaline coursed through his veins, he cursed the gods that he'd been forced into this situation.

A calm voice erupted from his radio, and Barrett issued the one order all of the contractors knew but hoped they wouldn't hear: "Understood. Commence lockdown. I say again, commence lockdown."

CHAPTER
TEN

Even as the old man stumbled to his death, a mental switch flipped in Zack Chambers's head. A call to battle, and suddenly he had shed his civilian skin, revealing the warrior within. *No way you get away with this. Not on my watch.* There was one constant in Zack's complex personality—his moral compass and the physical yearning to protect the innocent. It was that fundamental truth to his nature that had altered his life previously, and it was that truth, once again, that spurred him into immediate action. He didn't care who or what these men were. All that mattered was that they be stopped, and he was likely the only one in the entire subdivision that had a chance of doing it. *Jesus Christ, who murders an old man?* But he'd known others who'd done worse, and he pushed it out of his mind.

The tree that had cracked in half like a rifle shot was just to his left. It had startled him, but he'd remained in position until the impersonating officer shot the old man. As the horrified shrieking intensified, Zack crept forward and unslung his SIG Sauer semiautomatic MPX submachine gun. He preferred to have a full-size AR platform, America's semiautomatic long gun of choice, but the folding stock of the MPX made it a better choice. While he would never in a million years have thought that he'd have to engage in close-quarters combat at home,

Zack still lived by one motto above all others—It's better to have a gun and not need one than to need one and not have one. Some habits die hard. *Or don't die at all.*

The scene before him was chaos. A few people ran back toward their homes, a few tried to start their vehicles to escape, but most stood in shock and fear, transfixed to the ground. He'd seen that reaction before also.

He moved next to a tree a few feet shy of the edge of the woods, standing to ensure he could shoot over the stopped cars in the circle. He braced the MPX against the trunk and placed the red-dot reticle of the EOTech holographic sight on the impostor who'd killed the old man. At just more than one hundred and fifty feet, he was accurate to within a few inches, and he'd run more than two thousand rounds through the MPX to guarantee it.

Well, there goes the neighborhood, he thought wryly, and began to squeeze the trigger as a teenage boy tackled the impostor from behind, driving the shooter face-forward into the grass. Zack eased off the trigger, recognizing the boy. He'd seen him with Sam but couldn't recall his name. *Okay, kid. Good luck for a few seconds while I take care of other business.*

He shifted the sight slightly and placed it on the closest man wearing a Falling Rock police uniform. With a clear line of sight, Zack exhaled and squeezed the trigger. The MPX recoiled with a loud *smack*, the Octane 9 suppressor diminishing the normally loud gunshot to an audible *clap*, as if someone had dropped a heavy book in a quiet library. His aim was true, and the man fell to the ground, struck dead in the left side of his head by the 9mm round. *One down.*

The boy grappled with the impostor, who'd seen his partner fall while trying to fight off the attacking teenager.

The nearest van doors opened simultaneously, and two armed men with black assault rifles—he assumed these were fully automatic since these were criminals who didn't have to abide by the same laws he did—jumped down from each van. The two that appeared near the shooter's position scanned the woods in all directions. *Looking for me. Probably have a few more seconds before I need to beat feet out of here. Might as well make the most of it.*

Zack lined up the sights on the man on the left first, squeezed the trigger twice, and adjusted the weapon even before the man fell. His fourth and fifth shots struck the shooter on the right, and he collapsed to his left as if impersonating someone suffering a fainting spell, except his act was permanent.

Zack moved the sight picture back to the boy and the original shooter. The man had managed to remove himself from the kid's attempted chokehold, and he now faced the boy. Zack waited for a clear shot, as a couple he recognized but didn't know dashed between him and the two combatants.

The boy stepped in and feinted with a straight left jab, causing the shooter to flinch backward. As he did so, the boy jumped forward, spun to his left, and delivered a back sidekick that landed squarely in the shooter's abdomen, driving him backward so that he cartwheeled his arms as he fell to the grass.

Unsuppressed gunfire erupted from the right half of the hub, and Zack heard the crack of the rounds forty feet to his right. *Dammit. Not much longer, and they'll have me.*

A man screamed in a commanding voice, and Zack recognized it as the voice of the one who'd come to his house. *He's in charge. Good to know.*

His line of sight was clear once again, and Zack watched as the shooter sat up and pointed the Glock at the boy, who froze at the sight of the pistol that had just killed one of his neighbors.

Oh no you don't, asshole. Zack fired a single shot that tore into the man's neck, sending a splash of blood across the grass. The man dropped the Glock from his right hand and brought his fingers to his neck as if to staunch the wound.

Good luck with that. Zack knew the hollow-point round had done considerable damage. The shooter was a dead man sitting, even if he didn't know it yet.

The man looked up at the boy who stared back at him in horror as the blood pumped through the shooter's fingers and down his uniform. He fell over sideways, and his hand dropped to the grass, his life spilling out onto the ground, sanctifying it with dark blood.

"Get on the ground! Everyone, get on the ground! NOW!" The appearance of more men shook the boy from his death reverie. He turned around and saw men with guns. Realizing there were no more fights on the card for him, he held his arms up and knelt on the ground.

Bullets struck the tree to Zack's left, and he realized his luck had just run out. The brave boy would have to fend for himself for now. If Zack were captured or killed, he'd be no good to anyone. *Mission first, Zachary. Mission first. Sure. Whatever you say, boss.*

He held the weapon at port arms, turned, and fled deeper into the woods, praying the increased gunfire in his direction wouldn't result in a lucky shot. *At least you got four of the bastards. That's a force multiplier in your favor. Not bad for a retiree.* He smiled to himself at his handiwork as he evaded his pursuers.

His first point of order was simple—get back to his house through the woods and reassess the situation. He knew that once they'd secured the residents, they'd be going house to house to look for him and do whatever else they'd come here to do. He needed a plan, and he needed one fast.

He moved quickly and quietly and thought about his wife and beautiful children. *I sure hope their weekend has been less eventful than mine.*

PART III
UNDER SIEGE

CHAPTER
ELEVEN

Barrett Connolly was furious. What had been a smooth operation had now turned into a complete disaster, and all because of a man with Alzheimer's, the wind, and a shooter with an itchy trigger finger. He was glad Kevin Oliver was dead. Otherwise, he would've been tempted to publicly execute the man in front of the assembled mass of hostages. To make matters worse, there was some unknown element he hadn't accounted for, some brave or suicidal soul who'd managed to kill four of his men within seconds. Whoever he or she was—it could be a *she*, although it was unlikely; he'd met some lethal women in his days— had to be trained. He'd engaged his men from the woods at night with precision fire. He was good. Very good. Which was also why the rogue resident had ascended to the number one spot on his to-do list.

The aftermath had been chaotic, as hostage situations normally were in the beginning stages. He'd been through them before, and nothing he'd faced tonight had been an overwhelming challenge. The first order of business had been to regain control of the situation and of the residents of Hidden Refuge. The only silver lining was that half of the neighborhood had already been evacuated and was en route to the elementary school, where they would have a rude awakening as to the true nature of the threat to their well-being. At least they'd have time to process it, unlike the people back in the neighborhood who'd had their eyes opened violently. But the shock that many were still processing helped make them easier to manage, and his team had used it to pull them out of the vehicles and corral them onto the pavilion in the middle of the hub. A few individuals had squirted out of the area, but the families had remained, their instinct to stay together overruling their instinct to flee. He knew it was hard to run away with children—they only slowed you down. He also knew his men would find the ones that had fled. They always did.

Two of his most trusted operators now stood guard over the residents, even as they cried in fear and comforted one another. The family of the murdered elderly man had roared at him in fury and sadness, informing him that Esli, the man they'd killed, had Alzheimer's and didn't know what he was doing. He'd felt the briefest pang of emotion for them, but then he'd compartmentalized it. He had a mission to accomplish, and the mission came before all else.

He knew he'd have to address the crowd, but first he had to deal with the unknown. Four men were dead, their bodies lined up next to one of the vans in black body bags the assault team had brought with them. Two of his team had led the first convoy out, which left himself, the four surviving searchers, and four of the initial fake deputies. Minus the two contractors now guarding the civilians, he still had a sizable element to hunt down and eliminate the thorn in his side. *If seven men isn't enough to take out one man, then we deserve to fail.*

His entire team stood before him, and he spoke clearly and quickly so that his orders would be followed precisely.

"We've obviously got a problem that has to be dealt with immediately. I have to stay here and talk to these people on the off chance that one of them has the package and is willing to give it up before this goes any further. First, I need you to keep your emotions in check. We've already lost four of our own, but now is not the time to think about them. We can deal with their loss when this is over." Barrett paused to let his words sink in. They were professionals, and they knew the score before they'd signed up for the job. Confident gazes stared back at him. *Good. Stick to the mission.*

"Whoever he is, he's only got a few options. Since we know where he was shooting from based on the trajectory of the bullets, he can either exfiltrate to the main drive or move right back toward Arrow Drive. My guess is the latter. Obviously, something we did made this rabbit suspicious, and we proved him correct. If he'd wanted to escape, he could've done so without us knowing. I believe he thinks he's a hero and is going to try and help these people, which means we have to get to him first, because he's a threat to all of us."

Now, for the fun part.

"We already know he's armed, dangerous, and very good. But we're better. You weren't hand-selected just because you're okay. You're all exceptional, and I need you to be that way for the next few hours. We've got the manpower and the training. Take whatever additional weapons and gear you need from the vans, including vests, although honestly, this guy's making headshots. But better safe than dead. Here's how we're going to flush this bastard out."

Barrett turned to two of the searchers. "First, you two start searching for the package on Forest Edge Court. Our target has to be heading back to Arrow Drive. You should be fine. Be prepared, just in case. Go." The two men nodded and left the group, moving toward the van to acquire the specially designed RFID readers.

"Next, you three are staying here with me," he said to the three van drivers in police uniforms. "Make sure the jammers are functioning and maintain comms with the base of operations. But *don't* tell them anything. I'll update the boss as soon as we're done." Even though the CEO of Huntsmen Enterprises was his closest friend, it was not a conversation he looked forward to. Griffin did not accept failure well.

"Roger that," the three men said, almost in unison, and moved away to the vehicles.

"And you two searchers are also staying here with me, at least until we put this guy down," he said to the last two men who'd hidden in the van before the shooting started. "You've trained on the devices, and while it doesn't look like rocket science, I'd still rather have you two do it, but you can't if you're dead."

Barrett turned to the four remaining on his sheriff's deputy team. "Which means you four have the top priority of getting that bastard. You up for it?" He didn't wait for a response. "You two grab night vision and push him through the woods. If he's still in there, he's going to have to come out somewhere. Use the NODs to hunt him down. If he's got some kind of night-vision device, at least now it will be a fair fight." Directing his attention to the remaining two team members. "You two, move along the front of the homes on the right side of Arrow Drive. If you see any movement inside, break in, and search the house. All four of you, stay in contact with each other on the handheld radios and update as needed. I'll be monitoring. Are there any questions?"

The men looked at each other, shook their heads, and turned back to their leader. *Just as I thought.* "Good. Happy hunting."

Without another word, the men jogged off, the mission already first and foremost in their minds.

Okay. One last thing before I call Griffin and give him the bad news.

Barrett walked over to the pavilion and up the steps, ignoring the cries and pleas of the residents. He surveyed the crowd—parents, children, the old, the young, even a few pets—placed his hands together, and spoke truth to the people of Hidden Refuge for the first time that night.

CHAPTER
TWELVE

Sam was terrified. Her mind still reeled from the last transmission Ben had sent before she'd run back inside her house. She'd instinctively turned off the hallway lights and sat on the floor of her father's office.

First, the gunshot; then, Ben's declaration of love; and finally, his resolution to help whoever it was that needed him—it was too much for her to process. She had to regain some sort of control over her body and emotions. She wouldn't be able to help herself or anyone else in a heightened state of panic. *But you're just a junior in high school. What are you going to do? You're not exactly Eleven from* Stranger Things. *Control. Get control. It's what Daddy would tell you, Sam. Take a breath, assess the situation, and act.* His calmness under corporate fire was one of the reasons he'd been successful throughout his career and was on the board of his bank.

Sam inhaled deeply and closed her eyes, cementing herself in the moment, feeling the carpet in her father's office through the material of her yoga pants, the rough edges of his weathered desk—designed that way for aesthetics—against her back. *Assess. Okay. Something awful is going on, Ben's in trouble, and whoever did it, they're not the cops. Have to protect yourself.* Her eyes flashed open at the obviousness of her first move. *Get the shotgun. Otherwise, you're a defenseless victim.* And that was one thing her father would never let her be.

Sam scrambled to her feet and moved toward the office closet. She pulled the doors open, her pulse slowing as she acted with the reassurance of a purpose. The tall and slender gun case stood on the left side of the closet, the numbered keypad and silver handle just below, beckoning her to use them. She pulled out her iPhone, a useless paperweight at the moment with no service, and turned on her flashlight app. She didn't want to hit the wrong numbers and risk being locked out after three tries. She didn't know how anyone would get into the steel safe after that happened, but she didn't want to find out.

She punched in 0-6-3-0—her parent's wedding anniversary—and was rewarded with the signature beeps that indicated the safe was unlocked. Her parents had been married at city hall when they'd found out her mother was pregnant with Sam; a full ceremony for their families had come more than a year after Sam was born. Sam turned the handle down and pulled. The door swung outward and to her right, revealing the lethal contents within.

Daddy, what the hell? her mind swore reflexively and uncharacteristically. In addition to the black Benelli M4 12-gauge shotgun loaded with Remington 00 buckshot, there were two black pistols she'd never seen before as well as a new pair of noise-canceling earbuds designed specifically for shooting. She knew the pistols were semiautomatics and not revolvers, but that was about the extent of her handheld firearms knowledge. He'd always trained her on the Benelli. She didn't know if the pistols were loaded, but she also didn't want to leave the two handguns in the safe. She didn't envision herself as Lara Croft, but she'd watched enough movies and Netflix to know that sometimes more than one gun mattered.

She took the two menacing weapons and placed them on her father's desk. She'd leave them there, just in case. She grabbed the Benelli and a nylon pouch that contained twelve more 00 shells. With the shells in the pouch, the five in the tubular magazine, and one in the chamber, she figured she had enough stopping power. She knew it was loaded, but just to be safe—as her father had taught her each and every time—she picked up the shotgun and placed her iPhone on the edge of the desk with the flashlight aimed down. She angled the Benelli away from her with the charging handle facing up, slid the lever backward, and looked inside the chamber. *Bingo.* The back of the shell was visible.

She released the charging handle forward and pressed the triangular safety so that the weapon was ready to fire. *Step one, complete.* She breathed a sigh of relief, turned off her iPhone, and slid it into the front pocket of her hoodie. She was a junior in high school that liked young adult fantasy fiction but was now armed with a shotgun. *Great. What now?*

As if fate had answered her question directly, Sam's heart skipped a beat when she looked out the huge office windows and saw two men moving up the street toward her house. She stood still, frozen in place at the sight of them. *Did they see me?*

The two men dressed as officers left the pavement of the street and started moving through the Chamberses' grass in a line directly toward her house.

Oh no. Have to move. But where? Sam grabbed the pouch of shells and slid the clips over the top of her yoga pants, praying they'd stay in place. She held the power button on the right earbud, waited for the light, and inserted both once they were on. The earbuds would allow her to hear sounds inside the house while activating to protect her hearing if she had to pull the trigger. *Beats the heck out of the clunky earmuffs.*

With the Benelli held confidently in front of her, she left her father's office and turned right to move deeper into the house. *Time to hide.*

* * *

As Zack moved, he processed the tactical choices his enemy could make. He didn't know what else to call a group of armed men who'd just taken over his neighborhood but *enemy.* He also knew that he and the rest of the residents of Hidden Refuge were on their own, at least until it was over. They'd cut off the community from all outside contact, and he had an idea how, at least on the cell and satellite phone side of it. He figured they must have also cut a fiber optic cable to the internet providers. He'd seen a work van on the side of the road on Thursday just outside the entrance to Hidden Refuge Drive, but like all complacent suburbanites, he'd dismissed it as part of normal, everyday life. *Who falls for that, anyways? Come on, Zack. Do better.*

Zack crept silently through the woods, the wind masking his movement. He worked his way through the dark mass of trees and underbrush, but as he grew closer to the back of his property, he thought about the force facing him—trained men with weapons and military-grade communications equipment. There was no way he could successfully confront them head-on. As good as he was, there were too many of them. Even bad shooters occasionally get lucky, and he didn't intend to give them a spin on their wheel of fortune and glory. What he needed was to diminish their numbers to give himself and the rest of his neighbors a fighting chance.

Your old skills are coming back quickly, but are you okay with that? His subconscious taunted him with ghosts of his past. *You don't even know what's going on, and you've already killed four men. Your old boss would be proud.* He shook his head as if clearing his nose of a bad smell, although he knew bad thoughts were much worse. *Enough. No doubts.* He could contemplate his actions and the fate of his soul later. He still needed to level the playing field *and* figure out what their objective was. That knowledge would dictate his actions, if he could manage to stay alive.

He stopped for a moment and looked at the back of his house, contemplating the best choice. He looked back the way he'd come, through the woods and toward Founder Circle. He knew they'd send men in after him. It was the smart play, especially with the strength in numbers they had. Fortunately, he knew how to counter it.

Instead of stepping out of the shadows and into his backyard, he turned away and moved deeper into the woods, cloaking himself in the darkness. With the clouds from the approaching front, even NVGs wouldn't help the enemy if he concealed himself and waited for them to come to him. *Unless they have thermals, in which case you're screwed. Fuck it. You only live once. That's what the kids say, right?* If Steph heard him think like that, she'd be furious. There was life before Steph and the kids, and there was life with Steph and the kids. Fortunately for her, she had only been exposed to a glimpse of the former.

But his mindset was still the right one. He had to focus on the job at hand, not his family. It reminded him of a conversation he'd once had with a former Navy SEAL, a chief petty officer who'd retired after twenty years of service, the last fifteen with SEAL Team Four on the East Coast. They'd had dinner in DC—two former warriors exchanging stories over steaks, the rest of the diners unaware of the heroes in their midst. The conversation had turned to mental toughness, and his friend, Patrick, had put it in simple terms: "It's really easy. We have a job. We train for it each and every day. And when we go out on a mission, that's how we think of it—you just go and do your job. Pure and simple. You might get killed, you might get wounded, but all that matters is that you do your job, because you know your teammates are going to do theirs."

If Patrick had been with him as he stalked through the trees, he would've said the same thing he had at dinner. *Some truths never die.*

Zack stopped moving and used the night-vision monocular, spotting the area he needed ten feet in front of him—a fallen tree that lay horizontally across the floor of the woods. Its three-foot-wide trunk had been shattered at the base by a bolt of lightning, and the tree had collapsed to the ground, where it lay dead, waiting for the forest to one day reclaim it with undergrowth and decay. But before that time arrived, it was the perfect place for a hide site where Zack could engage his enemy before being detected.

Halfway along the enormous tree lay a gap between the ground and the bottom of the trunk, elevated by a few microterrain features. Less than twelve inches high, the gap was enough for him to lie prone and observe the woods and his backyard, which gradually sloped down from him more than one hundred feet away. A slightly elevated position was better than no elevation at all.s

He knelt down, slid forward onto his belly, aimed the suppressed muzzle of the MPX, and grabbed the monocular. Whomever they sent would have to come this way. He was certain of it. It's what he would do.

What he didn't expect was the crashing sounds from his left that exploded through the woods as two men started running more than eighty yards away. *What the hell? They couldn't see me yet. No way. Something else is happening.*

He ignored the sounds and scanned the backyard, which was when he briefly saw two figures dash across the gap between his house and the Hawkinses' home next door. With horror, he realized their objective. *Sam. She must have stayed in her house, and now they're coming for her, thinking she's me.* He had to do something, and he had to do it fast.

But the moment he moved, he risked revealing his position and ceding the only advantage he had left. He calculated his options and forced himself to remain still. He only needed seven or eight more seconds. Zack just prayed that Sam could hide and stay alive long enough for him to get to her.

CHAPTER
THIRTEEN

Sam lay on her stomach on the thick carpet, the shotgun barrel resting on the floor between the two posts in the upstairs railing. She'd considered all her options, and every one had resulted in her being captured or worse by the men with guns. She figured that if they had men out front, they'd likely be out back as well. She needed to give herself a fighting chance and getting caught before she could escape didn't seem like the best idea. If Ben could fight back, so could she. She just hoped her boyfriend—after the transmission, she'd instinctively and protectively applied the term to him—hadn't been hurt or . . . Her mind trailed off, a sudden swell of emotion slamming her consciousness with ominous foreboding. *You can't think like that. He's fine. He's not going to do anything too stupid, even if he is a teenage boy.*

The second-floor balcony overlooked the two-story family room. The staircase from below wrapped along a curved wall more than thirty feet away. She'd positioned herself at the far end of the balcony, adjacent to the wall that led to her parents' bedroom. From her vantage point, she had a clear line of sight to anyone coming up the stairs. She was still holding out hope that the men would bypass her house and leave her alone to plan her next move.

If she'd had time, she'd have activated her home's alarm system, but she'd rushed up to the second floor. She also figured that if they could cut off the internet and cell phone service, they could hack into the alarm systems. *Who are these people?* Before tonight, her biggest concern was next week's AP Chemistry exam on intermolecular forces and properties. *Pretty sure lethal force isn't one of the properties.*

The wind continued to batter the house in gusts, the siding rattling under the barrage. Sam checked her phone. Still no service.

A loud pounding on the front door startled her, and she dropped the phone on the carpet, the iPhone landing on its face next to her. As if in tune with her own heart, the pounding continued for several seconds. There was a pause in the relentless beating, and Sam breathed a sigh of relief. *Maybe they got the hint?*

The front door crashed open, and the reality of her situation threatened to shut her down. The terror was paralyzing, threatening to suffocate every thought and action. *This can't be happening. This can't be happening.* While her father had trained her to effectively operate the shotgun, that training hadn't included the horrifying vulnerability that now assaulted her. Sam felt her world teeter on the brink, as if plunging over the edge could somehow make her reality disappear.

Honey, breathe. It will be okay. No matter what, I love you. Just focus on what you have to do. You are strong enough for this. Show them, she heard her father's soothing voice in her head. *Show them all.*

Sam hadn't realized she'd been holding her breath until she heard her father speak to her, trying to save her even in his absence. She exhaled as she heard footsteps moving quickly up the main hallway, and she knew with a final certainty that her time was upon her. All actions, events, relationships, interactions, her entire being, the core of who she was, had prepared her for this one moment. But as her father, the man who had raised her to be the strong, young woman she was growing into, had often told her, *You can prepare all you want, sweetheart. But when the moment comes—and it comes for all of us, one way or another—how you face it will determine your fate.*

The first man appeared below her, and all thought ceased. She suddenly felt detached from her body even as her senses heightened, stretched beyond what she'd thought had been their normal limits. The panic, the fear—all of it—just stopped. She placed her finger on the trigger and waited.

More noises erupted from somewhere outside the front of the house. She ignored them and watched the first impersonator, a slow anger forming in the pit of her clenched stomach.

The fact that they'd used the one thing that all people in the neighborhood valued infuriated her. Not law enforcement. Most people respected that. No. It was more insidious. It was the sense of security and safety that the residents in Hidden Refuge felt, relied on, *trusted*. And these *evil men* had exploited that vulnerability to take the entire community hostage. Already suspicious of the government in general, she was mature enough to recognize tonight's invasion was an affront, and she would not stand for it.

The man swept the downstairs with some type of long, black rifle, like the ones that Sam had seen on TV in the hands of the military or SWAT teams. Attached to the side was a flashlight, the wide beam spotlighting parts of the kitchen and sunroom in bright discovery.

Keep going. Don't come upstairs. Please.

The man turned and moved toward the stairs, satisfied that the first floor was empty. He reached the carpeted steps and started upward. Sam tracked him with the sights mounted on the front of the barrel as he climbed. He moved the rifle up and along the banner and railing, the light mercilessly stalking Sam in her ambush position.

Sam only had one job left to do, and as the light crept quickly toward her, rather than wait for the final illumination, she did it.

I'll make you proud, Daddy, she thought, and pulled the trigger.

* * *

The two figures dashed through the woods toward Zack's kill zone, breaking twigs and small branches as they trampled on the fresh bed of leaves that had fallen the previous week. The men had moved closer to the edge of the woods, which made it easier to spot their dark silhouettes against the ambient light from the backs of the homes. Most of the neighbors had at least one motion-sensor flood light that remained at a low level until it detected movement, at which point it suddenly increased in brightness. Zack followed their quick progress, his finger resting on the curvature of the MPX's trigger.

Wait for it. As if offering themselves up to the gods of suburban war, the two men reached the edge of Zack's property, unaware that the owner was concealed in the woods directly behind them.

Zack squeezed the trigger, and the first three shots took the man on the left in the back, and he fell forward onto the wet grass as if pushed by an invisible hand. Zack shifted the holographic sight to the second man, who'd stopped in his tracks when his partner fell.

Recognizing too late that the threat lay behind them in the woods, he tried to turn, but a second controlled series of shots took him in the upper chest, with the last round drifting upward and striking him dead between the eyes. The man's momentum kept him turning, and he collapsed like a ballerina performing a pirouette, sinking to the grass in a lifeless corkscrew.

Right between the running lights. Good kill. His detached mind appreciated the skill, but a part of him was sickened. He'd just killed six men within the last ten minutes. *This doesn't feel like retirement.* This was why he'd left the job. *That, and your team leader was a bastard, but who's counting?*

Zack leapt up and bounded over the fallen tree, pushing forward as fast as possible to get to the Hawkinses' home. Within seconds, he emerged from the wood line at full speed, sprinting between the two corpses toward his objective.

His left ankle was suddenly pulled backward with enough force to cause a catastrophic fall, but his upper body kept moving. His left foot came free of the obstacle, but it was enough to send him face-first onto his own lawn. He turned to the left to absorb the impending impact and realized with horror what had tripped him. *The first gunman is still alive. You only hit him in the torso. He's got a vest. They all do, dumbass.*

Zack would've excoriated any of his former teammates for such a rookie mistake, as almost all operating forces worldwide wore some kind of protective Kevlar. Even bad guys were smart enough to wear vests.

He hit the ground with a jarring shock but turned to the left, rolling onto his back. The MPX was already muzzle-down as he'd been running, which might've been the only thing that saved his life.

Instinctively aware of where the first fallen man lay, Zack adjusted the MPX even before he saw his enemy look up at him. The man's right arm moved up along his side, a black pistol in his hand.

Zack made eye contact with the man in recognition of his last-ditch effort to save himself, and then he pulled the trigger on the MPX twice. Both rounds struck the man in his forehead, and his head fell limply to the grass, the pistol no longer a threat.

Zack scrambled to his feet and sprinted. Whoever these men were, they'd come prepared. *Headshots. They need to all be headshots.*

Accepting the new rules of engagement like a clinical tactician, Zack accelerated across the lawn, a dark figure appearing to float from one backyard to the next.

He hit the steps to the Hawkinses' back deck and ascended as quietly as he could. Unlike his home, theirs didn't have an enclosed porch, just one long deck that spanned the entire length of the house.

He crept toward the back door, when the thunderous roar of a shot-gun reverberated from inside.

* * *

Even with the electronic earbuds, the explosion of the Benelli inside the home was tremendous. The 12-gauge buckshot caught the man in the chest and face, and Sam was selfishly relieved that the lights were off. A wash of black appeared on the wall of the staircase, and the intruder collapsed to the stairs, his rifle tumbling to the carpet. His body leaned against the wall and then slid before toppling forward in a head-first dive down the carpeted steps.

Sam stared in horror and awe at what she'd done to another human being. *A bad one, Sam. One who came into our home to do you harm. It's not your fault. He did this, not you,* her father's voice said calmly inside her head. *You need to move, princess. There are more of them.*

A second crash of glass came from the back door downstairs, and a fresh sense of panic shook her from her reverie. She needed to move and find a new hiding place.

She stood up from the floor, the shotgun held in front of her just in case the new intruder appeared below.

"Don't move—or teenage girl or not, you're dead. I don't want to kill a kid, but after what you just did, I will," a menacing voice said from behind her, from the short hallway off the main branch that led to her room.

Sam realized her fatal mistake. *The window. Should've closed it.* Her mother would be furious, as she'd reminded her dozens if not hundreds of times over the years to shut the window when she left her room. Somehow, she always forgot, and she was about to pay a very steep price for it. The additional noises she'd heard had been the second man climbing up to the roof over the front porch and to her window.

Sam froze, truly terrified for the first time that night that she was about to die. *I'm sorry, Daddy. I did my best.*

*   *   *

Even as the shotgun shattered the silence of the night from inside the Hawkinses' house, Zack knew he had one chance to save Sam. It was based on one simple assumption—that the man upstairs holding his babysitter at gunpoint thought Zack was one of the two shooters coming from the back to support him.

Zack hurled an outdoor tabletop speaker like a baseball at the left half of the sliding doors. The metallic cube struck the door with a crash that punched a hole in the glass and created a jigsaw puzzle of tiny pieces that held together for an instant before large chunks of it began to fall to the patio and inside the house.

Zack knocked a section away from the handle, carefully reached inside, slid the lever up, and pushed the door to the right. More glass cascaded to the floor, but he ignored it and stepped inside.

He was thankful Sam hadn't turned on the lights, and that his natural night vision remained active. His mind took a snapshot of the carnage even as he moved to his left toward the staircase at the far end of the room.

Sam was above him, frozen, the shotgun held in both hands but her head turned to the right. *Remember, she doesn't know it's you. The only way this works is if you fool them both.*

Zack's footsteps crunched across the shards of glass before leaving streaks of mud across the family room carpet. *Sorry, gang, but the dirt's probably the last thing you'll see when you guys get home,* he thought as he looked at the dead gunman, facedown at the bottom of the stairs, blood thickening on the nap of the carpet. He was pretty sure that luxury carpet or not, the stain protector wasn't rated for blood and bone.

He heard voices from upstairs as he started working his way up. Sam was looking to her right down a hallway to which Zack had no line of sight. *Keep talking, kid. Keep him distracted for as long as you can.* She'd placed the shotgun at her feet and stepped away from the railing.

Zack reached the landing and started moving toward Sam, praying to all the gods that she wouldn't look at him until it was too late. Even if she did, he hoped the darkness might cloak his features. *Only a few more seconds.*

He was only a few feet away from the hallway, and he heard a voice order Sam to turn away toward the railing, which was exactly what Zack had needed. As Sam turned away from him and to her left, Zack spoke up in a muffled voice.

"It's clear out here, but the bastard in the woods . . . got my partner. I took one to the vest . . . in the back. I've got her in my crosshairs," he finished, and waited. Zack Chambers felt a calmness wash over him, and he knew with an undeniable certainty that the ruse would work.

Sam's head turned toward him, and Zack held up his right finger to his lips, hoping she'd see the gesture and hold her tongue. The silence that followed stretched across a dark eternity, but Zack remained still. His hands were empty, and the MPX was slung across his back.

"Roger. Coming out. Secure the shotgun. She knows how to use it."

"Roger that."

Zack stepped closer as if moving toward Sam. The black barrel of the shooter's rifle emerged from the hallway immediately in front of him.

"Get down, NOW!" Zack screamed, as he reached forward and swept upward with an open palm, striking the barrel of the rifle. The impact drove the barrel up and away from Sam, who dropped to the carpet like a limp doll.

The shooter, dressed in a police uniform, reacted to the attack and pulled the trigger, and a series of six or seven shots erupted in blinding flashes in front of Zack, who forced himself to ignore the light and instant absence of sound except the new buzzing in his head.

Sam screamed in terror, but the sound was muffled in Zack's ears.

Zack viciously punched the man's trigger finger and felt several small bones break under the blows. The man screamed, and his hand went limp, the finger leaving the inside of the trigger guard. Zack violently yanked the man's finger with his left hand, snapping it backward with a satisfying *crack* that felt like kindling breaking cleanly.

With the shooter's right hand disabled, Zack solidly punched the man in the jaw, weakening his resistance further. In one fluid motion, he grabbed the assault rifle's stock just behind the charging handle and pulled the weapon toward him to remove or loosen—it didn't matter which, for what came next—the shooter's left arm from the rifle. He felt the weapon change hands, offering itself up to him to do as he wished, and Zack responded by pummeling the shooter several times in the face until the man collapsed in an unconscious heap of blood and uniform on the hallway carpet.

Zack breathed heavily, and his ears rang loudly, drowning out most sound. It wasn't the first time he'd been close to gunfire in a confined space, and he knew it would pass, usually improving noticeably every ten or twenty seconds. The ringing would stay for days, though. That was the cost of doing close-quarters business.

Zack heard Sam call to him. He knelt to make sure the shooter was unconscious and turned to his babysitter. The teenager who'd defended her home and killed a man sat up against the wall, one hand on each bent knee, staring at him.

Zack moved toward her, the buzzing in his head decreasing further. He knelt down and took her hands. "Sam, are you hurt?"

She shook her head, looking quizzically at his face.

She's in shock. She has to be. The first time he'd killed had been hard, and *he'd* trained for it. She was just a junior in high school. *But she's tough, and you know it.*

"Good. Now, I need you to listen to me. We don't have much time. They'll be coming, and they won't make the same mistake twice. First, I'm really proud of how you handled yourself. Most kids—hell, most adults—would've collapsed under the pressure. You did the right thing, and I know your dad will be proud of you too."

Sam was struck with a wave of emotion at the mention of her father. Zack saw her true pain and fear, but they vanished, replaced by a confidence he knew was there. "That's the girl next door I know. Good. That's the game face I need you to have until this is over. Can you do that?"

Her calm replenishing itself with each word, Sam nodded. "You got it, Mr. C."

Zack smiled at the politeness. "Here's the deal. I have no idea who these people are or what they want, but most of the neighborhood has been taken hostage by them. In addition to the one you dropped, I've taken out six of them."

"What? You've killed six people? *Tonight?*" Sam asked awestruck. "Forget about these guys, Mr. C. Who are *you*?"

That was a fair question in more ways than Sam knew. "Listen, I promise, when this is over, I'll tell you some of it, but for now, we have more pressing matters at hand. Like I said, we need answers, and this guy, here," Zack said, pointing over his left shoulder, "is the only one who has them. What I'm about to do, you're not going to like. Honestly, I don't like it, but if he doesn't start talking, we can't help any of our friends and neighbors."

At the mention of the neighbors, Sam's eyes widened. "Oh my God. Ben—he called me on the handheld radios we use to talk instead of cell phones. Do you have any idea if he's okay?"

Zack heard the desperation in her voice, the need to know that the boy she cared about was safe. "That's his name. *Ben.* I couldn't remember it earlier. And yes. He's safe. He's a brave one, Sam. He fought and beat one of the hostage-takers, but then they outnumbered him, and he gave up, which was the smart move. He's okay. We just need to figure out how to help him and the others stay that way."

Sam nodded, shook her head, and looked at the unconscious gunman. "Mr. C, this is seriously messed up. What are you going to do to him?"

"Whatever it takes, kiddo," Zack replied. "Whatever it takes. Are you with me?"

"Hey, you're the adult. I'm just following your lead."

"Good. Now, let's get him up against the railing." He yanked white plastic zip ties off the man's vest.

"Here's the deal. Get your shotgun, and if he wakes up before I get him secured, shoot him in the knee. Just don't hit me. And be glad you have those earbuds in," Zack said, pointing to her hearing protection. "My head is still ringing."

"That's because guns are loud, Mr. C. *Very* loud."

Tell me about it, kiddo, Zack thought, and started to secure their captive's wrists to the wooden railing, reflecting on the recent years of civilian life that had just been swept away like the remaining chess pieces of a lost game. *Except this game is just beginning.*

PART IV
COURSE CORRECTION

CHAPTER
FOURTEEN

With a population of nearly half a million and a land area just less than twice the size of Washington, DC, the rugged Republic of Malta lay in the middle of the Mediterranean, its location a strategic military asset throughout its colored history. An archipelago comprising three main islands and several smaller ones, its terrain consisted of mostly rocky, dissected plains that resulted in sharp coastal cliffs along the perimeter of the islands. The country had been conquered by one nation after another for centuries until the British gave the island state its independence in 1964, allowing it to join the Commonwealth of Nations, the UN, and most recently the EU and Eurozone, which allowed Malta to prosper as a financial center and tourist destination.

The first time Zack Chambers had flown into Malta International Airport, he'd had the strange sensation that he was flying backward in time to some ancient medieval period where he might need a sword instead of a Glock. Within the first week, after tours of the ancient walled city of Mdina, Fort Ricasoli, the Red Tower, and several free-standing megalithic temples, he was certain of it. It was also why over one hundred movies and several episodes of *Game of Thrones* had been filmed at various locations on Malta.

While time had changed the island, its traditions steeped in religion had blossomed and were still a critical part of the daily lives of the Maltese people, who were almost all Roman Catholic.

One of the critical facets of daily life that Zack had learned almost immediately was that there were over 360 churches, and each one was the focal point of its parish, as evidenced by the festivals, special masses, and even fireworks displays. The second fact that had struck Zack was that most of the population spoke English—officially the second language of the country and taught in school—which was a good thing for Zack, who'd only thought of *Maltese* as a cute breed of dog barking above its weight class.

But it wasn't the history, the architectural splendor, or the warm, inviting culture that had drawn Zack Chambers and a team of CIA Special Activities Division operators. It was the online gaming industry, which was introduced on the island in 2004 when significant tax breaks had transformed the economy of Malta and led to one of the highest concentrations of online-gaming licenses in the European Union. As a result, it was now home to over three hundred online, invisible casinos that served customers all throughout the EU and attracted all sorts of elements, including organized crime. With that amount of cash flowing in and out of the banks, the casinos were the perfect place to launder large amounts of money.

In addition to the reported criminal element, the online gaming industry attracted wealthy financiers from all over the world, and it was one such financier that had drawn the attention of the US government. The worst part about it from Zack's perspective was that he was a US citizen who had betrayed his own country.

Raymond Moretti, known as "Ray-Ray" to his friends, had existed as a relative nobody for six years, slaving away on the trading floors of Wall Street, futilely attempting to make a living with a business degree from Wharton. While the six-figure income was nice, it was New York City, not Cincinnati, and the cost of living barely kept him in the black. He was a natural at identifying low-risk stocks, but he spent the few hours he had to himself away from work trying to devise a way to earn money with little overhead and almost no effort. And it was e-commerce that presented the perfect opportunity. The trick had been determining the right products to peddle, and he'd landed his first big sales with inflatable lounge chairs. Next, he'd stumbled upon fidget spinners and fidget cubes, and before he knew it, after setting up agreements with producers in China to direct-ship his customers and prevent himself from taking on inventory, he was earning tens of thousands of dollars. Within one year, he'd earned his first million, and he'd walked away from Wall Street.

But Ray-Ray wasn't content with just e-commerce. An avid online gambler, he'd heard about the licensing opportunities on Malta before they'd been publicly announced, and he'd pounced on them, opening Big City Limits in honor of New York City, which had quickly earned him more millions. Even then, had he just remained in the online gambling business, he would've never entered the spotlight of the US government.

Unfortunately for Ray-Ray, on a trip to Malta to inspect the servers of his company, tour the country, and lose real, hard cash in one of the nation's four physical casinos, he'd become close friends and business partners with Aleksei Belyekov. The *real* problem was that Aleksei was a Russian oligarch, the kind with ties to the Kremlin at all levels.

Aleksei had earned his fortune during the privatization period after the fall of the Soviet Union, accumulating great wealth through private holdings in the oil sector. While several oligarchs had fallen out of Moscow's favor throughout the years amid public outcry, Aleksei had weathered the storm. While his fortune had grown, so had his greed, and he'd ventured into another market: private security companies.

In the wake of the US invasion of Iraq and the continued occupation of Afghanistan, Russia had learned several lessons from observing Western forces and military doctrine, but the most important one had been simple—privatizing the military through the use of contractors was tremendously profitable and allowed a country to covertly exercise its foreign policy objectives with somewhat-plausible deniability. Like Ray-Ray, Aleksei was a self-proclaimed pioneer, and he'd founded the Patriotic Sons of Perun, named after the Slavic mythological god of war.

Within three years, the Sons, as they were colloquially referred to in the private-military-and-security-company community, were the largest

Russian private fighting force, operating in Africa, the Middle East, and South America. Aleksei was eager to increase both his wealth and his personal reputation, and while he was simultaneously spreading the foreign policy objectives of the Kremlin, he was also turning a handsome profit by engaging in business ventures that he'd identified on his own. It was the latter activity that had landed him squarely in the crosshairs of the CIA, quite literally.

The trend in African countries plagued with civil strife was to outsource personal security for entrenched dictators or even so-called democratically elected leaders, which made the Democratic Republic of the Congo an ideal deployment for more than one hundred of Aleksei's finest Sons. In addition to serving as security advisers to Congo's president, the advisers also secured exclusive gold- and diamond-mining rights from the resource-rich nation.

While all of this had gained the attention of the international press, it would have just raised eyebrows had it not been for the murder of a freelance reporter and his thirty-six-year-old cameraman. While the reporter—a British journalist who'd written bylines with the BBC, the AP, Reuters, and Sky—was legitimate, the "cameraman" was a CIA case officer and the nephew of the deputy director for counterterrorism at Langley.

Even while his mutilated body, hacked to death by machetes in an "attempted robbery" was in transit home, an unofficial investigation conducted by a JSOC team out of Camp Lemonnier on the Horn of Africa had unearthed the truth. The Russian Sons had been ordered by Belyakov to make both the reporter and the story disappear. The primary goal had been to protect the diamond mine that had been producing millions of dollars in uncut gems for months. On orders from DC, the four Russian contractors that had executed the assassination had been disposed of directly by the JSOC team, while the rest of the world remained unaware that a small conflict between the East and the West and broken out in the Congo. The murder of an American clandestine officer on African soil would not stand, which was how Aleksei Belyakov found himself the unknowing target of an international manhunt headed by the CIA.

But Aleksei wasn't alone in his culpability. His partner in the mine was none other than Ray-Ray Moretti. And to make matters worse, Ray-Ray had actually been present when the reporter and CIA operations officer, Henry McCall, had been executed. The CIA had obtained a special presidential finding on Ray-Ray Moretti, and in an aggressive move, DC had declared him persona non grata in the US and green-lit an operation to assassinate him.

The fact that Ray-Ray Moretti was unaware of all this mildly troubled Zack Chambers, but that wasn't Zack's problem—his only focus was successfully completing the mission, which meant Ray-Ray had to die in a spectacular fashion. The solution that Zack Chambers; Griffin Huntsmen, his SAD team chief; Charles Davis; and Noah Anderson had devised was exactly that—spectacular and deceptive. There would be no international blowback for the US. When it was over, the people who needed to receive the message to prevent further hostile acts against US personnel would get it loud and clear through unofficial means.

Griffin had used a contact in Afghanistan to smuggle two Iranian-made explosively formed penetrators, referred to as EFPs by US soldiers in Iraq, where the evil devices had been delivered to the insurgents to wreak havoc on Americans. The IEDs retained Iranian markings that would positively link the attack to Iran's Republican Guard Force. The fact that Iran had no connection to Ray-Ray was inconsequential, as they *did* have ongoing business negotiations with Belyakov for potential operations in Yemen. In the aftermath of the attack, Zack and his team knew that the link to Iran would create a plausible-enough smoke screen that the real culprit, the US, would never be discovered.

In less than thirty minutes, both Ray-Ray Moretti and Aleksei Belyakov would die in a fiery explosion on their way to lunch at the most unique of locations—Popeye Village, the film set built in 1979 for the Robin Williams movie *Popeye*.

Located on the northwest part of the main island of Malta in Anchor Bay and built into the craggy, curved landscape, all twenty buildings and their contents remained untouched, frozen in time. The set had evolved into a prime tourist attraction and amusement park, complete with tours, cast members that sang and interacted with visitors, sunbathing on the beach, multiple restaurants, and even a large hall called the Rough House. It was the last building that was the location for their luncheon, as Aleksei had reserved the entire hall due to its view of the cove that opened into the Mediterranean beyond.

But you're not going to make it there, Zack thought, staring at the US Navy ScanEagle UAV feed on the HD monitor. The UAV belonged to the Arleigh Burke–class guided-missile destroyer USS *Carney*, which coincidentally was on a port call in Valetta and also happened to be their exfiltration from the country once the operation was over.

Zack and the team had been in Malta for the past month, establishing a base of operations in a rural farmhouse in the northern part of the island. All four men had also grown short beards and absorbed enough sunlight—except Charles, the only African American of the four—to reasonably pass for native Maltese. Zack, Griffin, Charles, and Noah had all explored the island, mastering the main roads, the back roads, and even the narrow streets of Valetta. Within two weeks, they could navigate without a map from the densest urban centers to the expansive plains on the western half of the island.

The farmhouse itself was owned by a wealthy CEO with ties to the gaming industry and a brother who was a senior executive and lifelong diplomat at the US State Department. Once he'd understood why, the ask had been an easy one for the CEO to oblige.

Ironically, the farmhouse no longer resembled a farmhouse but a luxurious, spacious building with multiple bedrooms, an open main-floor plan, and an external second-story balcony that wrapped around the front and side of the home to provide a stunning view of the ocean less than a quarter mile away. Near the end of Triq Tad-Dahar Road, it was also within two miles of Popeye Village.

The large family room had been transformed into the operations center, and Zack looked up as Griffin came down the stairs, outfitted in his tactical gear, complete with khakis, a gray long-sleeved shirt to blend in with the rocky terrain, tan Oakley tactical boots, and a tan Kevlar vest with multiple pouches. Even without a weapon, Griffin was a fearsome individual. While every member of the team had a month's growth of beard, Griffin's made him look like some kind of ancient Norse warrior. *At least we'll be wearing tan balaclavas made of neoprene.*

"Everything running like clockwork, Zachary?" Griffin asked as he walked over to the table and stared at the monitor.

"Really? After two years, you're *still* going to go with my full name? You know I can't stand it, right?" Zack said, mock outrage in his voice.

"Oh. I do. But I *don't care*, which is half the fun."

"You're a real charmer." Even though the gibes were in jest, there was a part of Zack that was still cautious around Griffin Huntsmen. The team leader did everything *right*, but even after multiple operations, there was a quality about him that troubled Zack. No matter how hard he tried, he couldn't shake the sensation that Griffin had a compartmented section of his personality that *no one* saw, ever. What was inside was anyone's guess. Zack knew all men had their inner demons, but a man like Griffin? What those might be was alarming, to say the least. There was a side of him that was ruthless in its determination to see a mission to its definitive conclusion.

"But to answer your question, we're just waiting for Ray-Ray and Aleksei and their unfortunate security team to leave the villa for lunch. The ScanEagle will stay on station at twelve thousand feet until the operation's over."

"Good. No room for error. It's nearly ten thirty. Their lunch is at eleven," Griffin said.

The sound of footsteps stomping down the stairs echoed throughout the main floor as Noah and Charles, the two junior men on the team, carried the team's duffel bags to stage them near the front double doors. Once the targets were down and they'd vacated the farmhouse, a follow-on team would sweep the residence and remove all evidence of their presence. All personal items would be destroyed at the US embassy, and their surveillance equipment and other gear would be shipped home.

"We set to jet?" Noah asked, a slight Texas accent in his words. A good-looking thirty-two-year-old with short, neat brown hair, Noah was an anomaly for the CIA and SAD since he hadn't matriculated to the agency via the military or the college recruitment program. Instead, he'd been a San Antonio police officer with a college degree from Texas A&M, but when his brother, a Special Forces Green Beret and his idol, had been killed in Afghanistan years into the post-9/11 occupation, his focus had changed, and a raging storm inside him had been triggered. He focused the anger into a singular purpose, honing himself into the best shape of his life, and two years later, he'd applied to the CIA and been accepted within a month of his application. Three years into the agency, and he'd deployed to Afghanistan for the first time, teaming with JSOC to kill a Taliban leader who'd been terrorizing US forces in Kabul. That mission had slightly calmed the internal storm, transforming him into the highly capable operator that he was, committed to capturing or killing the enemies of his nation.

"Easy, Tex. Why you always in a hurry? It'll all sort itself out soon enough. It *always* does," said Charles Davis, the remaining operator on the team and Noah's best friend. Whereas Noah was intense, driven, and aggressive, Charles was as cool as a summer breeze, to the point that Noah was convinced the African American from Atlanta had been raised by a Zen master from the Tibetan monks. Unlike Noah, Charles had found his way to SAD by the traditional route—the military via the Navy SEALs as a chief petty officer.

It wasn't Tibetan monks, but an honest, decent, and hardworking man named Earnest Davis who'd actually raised Charles, ensuring the smart, athletic boy had every advantage that Earnest could afford from his high-paying blue-collar job as a welder. Charles had never met his mother, who'd died in childbirth, but his father considered him a blessing for surviving the delivery. He'd provided a steady, nurturing environment, moving from an apartment in the Old Fourth Ward to a blossoming suburb and better schools. Charles had thrived, excelling at school and sports, particularly wrestling and basketball, although he was only five foot ten. He'd always intended to go to college, but plans—as he'd later learn in the SEAL teams—never unfolded the way they were visualized at inception. His father had died of a sudden heart attack, a widow-maker that he'd had no chance of surviving, the week after Charles's high school graduation. He'd been devastated, and he'd stayed with his wrestling coach, who'd been one of his father's closest friends. Hours of informal mentoring and talking had led Charles to make a decision he'd questioned initially but eventually would be convinced had been the right one—to forego college and join the navy. He'd felt lost without his dad, and the military structure called to him in his darkest hours. Nine years later, after multiple tours in Iraq and the Philippines and an encounter with a case officer hunting Islamist terrorists in the Philippines, Charles had left the teams for the clandestine world of the CIA with no regrets.

"Give me a break, brother. We've been here a month, and we're minutes from showtime. Are you seriously telling me that after weeks of preparation, you're not a little bit eager to get this show on the road and take these two down?"

Charles smiled as he put four duffel bags down on the hardwood floor. "Did I say that? That's what you *heard*. I'm ready to go, but there's no rush. The bullets and Band-Aids always come in due time. Enjoy the ocean air while you still can."

Zack just shook his head at the banter as he studied the UAV feed, early-morning sunlight glinting off the two black Mercedes SUVs await-ing their passengers. Belyakov's villa was just north, past the outer edges of the urban sprawl of Valetta. Situated along the eastern coast, the villa was a multitiered stone fortress with a view of the ocean at the bottom of short rocky cliffs.

"Playtime is over gentlemen," Griffin stated, ending the back-and-forth between Noah and Charles before it really began. The two men were known to exchange witticisms on random, esoteric subjects in such a rapid fashion that it often resembled the dialogue of a Quentin Taran-tino movie. "Gear up and be ready for final confirmation."

The team's weapons were laid out on the dining room table, which could seat twelve comfortably. Each member of the team had carved out a small area for his gear, and they'd checked and double-checked each magazine, smoke grenade, medical kit, and radio to ensure that it would function when the time came. They all understood one truism: *If you take care of your gear, your gear will take care of you.*

Laid out above each man's gear was an oiled eleven-inch version of the HK416 A5 5.56mm assault rifle with an assault grip under the barrel and an EOTech holographic red-dot sight above the barrel. A newer version of the assault rifle that ended Osama bin-Laden's life, the HK416 A5 was a lethal precision piece of weaponry.

"You got it, boss," Charles said in his smooth manner.

"Time to cowboy up," Noah responded, and both men started affixing the tools of the trade to their Kevlar vests.

"How much longer?" Griffin asked. A former national champion wrestler from Penn State, Griffin was a precise man, and he loathed being late. If an operation didn't start exactly when planned, he felt a surge of negative energy course through his body as if threatening to short-circuit his senses. "Time stands still for no man," his father used to preach at him, and as much as Griffin loathed the abusive alcoholic and self-centered lawyer who'd ruined his childhood, Aaron Huntsmen had been right about the finite quality of time: there was never enough of it.

"Any . . . minute . . . now," Zack said as if willing the targets into existence on the screen.

From the angle of the orbiting ScanEagle, they had a clear shot of the ornate, double doors, and Zack felt a sense of relief as figures poured out of the building toward the SUVs. *Wait a second. There's too many of them. There's only supposed to be six—four security, Belyakov, and Moretti.* He studied the picture and instantly recognized with horror what the other four figures were—two women *and* two children.

"We have a major problem. Somebody screwed the pooch on the intel. We have four civilians getting into the SUVs. Two women and two kids." Zack said.

Like rugby players attacking the ball, the entire team assembled around the HD monitor as the figures neared the SUVs. The silhouettes appeared small on the monitor, but Zack could see that one of the female figures wore a red dress with a wide-brimmed hat; the other was a brunette with a white dress. All he could discern about the children, who trailed the woman with the hat, was that they were at least half their mother's height. As they watched, Moretti, the brunette in white, and two security personnel entered the first Mercedes, and Belyakov, the lady in red, and the children approached the second SUV with the remaining two security members.

"Jesus," Noah said. "She's Belyakov's wife, and those are his kids, which makes the other woman Moretti's girlfriend or something."

Zack looked up at his team chief, and the thing that he had wondered about—the true, merciless nature of Griffin Huntsmen—stared back at him, the essence of the man beneath the mask revealed. Zack's blood ran cold, and he felt his pulse pound a little harder. Before Griffin could speak, Zack declared, "No. No innocents. That was the deal. No civilian casualties, *especially* women and children." But something had changed, and Zack knew the answer even before he'd finished speaking.

"Listen to me, Zachary," Griffin said, a hard resolution in his liquid brown eyes. "This is happening, no matter what. I can call back to HQ, but—after what happened and how hard it's been to track these two, let alone the odds of getting another opportunity where all of our resources and stars align—this is it. And they're going to say the same thing: to remove these two players from the board, that the collateral is acceptable. We stick to the plan. The IED takes out the first vehicle, no matter who's in it, and then we only shoot to kill Belyakov and Moretti. We try to avoid hurting the women and children. We can even try to spare the security detail. I don't care about them. But the primary targets *have* to die. I just need to know one thing: Are you with me?"

Noah and Charles had been watching the exchange. The tension in the room ratcheted up several notches. No one spoke, and the question lingered, begging to be answered.

There it is, Zack, and he suddenly felt his world teeter as if he were balanced on a pinpoint of morality that had physically manifested into existence. The choice was clear, and what had moments before been a straightforward operation had turned into a battle for his soul. He felt the weight of it threatening to pull him under. *"Go along to get along" has never been your style. And killing kids? Not when you know they're there.*

But the powers that be were not in the field. They were back in their windowed offices in northern Virginia, drinking Keurig coffee, and watching the world go by. It was easy for them to make decisions that they personally didn't have to enforce or live with. They sent operators like Zack, Griffin, Noah, and Charles to do their bidding. *And I'm okay with that, but this is too much.*

Zack had always asked himself one question before every mission— *Can you live with what you're about to do?* It was really that simple. And for the first time since he'd been a member of SAD, the answer that came back, resounding in his head like a jackhammer, was no.

"No. I'm not. Not like this. No matter what Langley says, we have to abort." Zack turned away from the monitor and started moving with purpose toward the door, the keys to one of the armored black Range Rovers magically appearing in his hand. "I'm going to disarm and retrieve the IED, and we can—" was all he had time to say. He never heard the powerful blow that struck him viciously in the back of the head. He felt himself falling, and he thought, *I should try to catch my fall.* But then the edges of his vision closed in on him like shutters, and all he saw was darkness. He never felt the floor as he crashed into it.

PART V
BALANCE OF POWER

CHAPTER
FIFTEEN

"First," Barrett began, his eyes moving across the face of every person in the crowd as he spoke. While he didn't have the physical stature of Griffin, he commanded—no, *demanded*—respect naturally, and even though the residents of Hidden Refuge were his hostages, they still responded to his charisma. He was one of the rare people on the planet who made an excellent first impression, only to ruin it once those around him began to understand his true nature. "I am sorry about what happened earlier. I can't take it back. I definitely did not want this to go down this way. You don't have to believe me, but it's true. When this is over, we will make restitution."

Stephen, Esli's son, glowered at Barrett, fuming at the words. He shouted, "How can you 'make restitution' for taking away my father? A man who survived a massacre in El Salvador, only to be gunned down in his *own neighborhood*? Take your restitution and go fuck yourself, you murdering bastard." Stephen lowered his head, his verbal ammunition spent.

He's right on every count. Don't blame him for it, or this will go harder. "You're right, and I'm sorry. I won't bring it up again." Barrett turned his attention elsewhere. "And since I don't want this situation to drag on any longer than it needs to, I'm going to ask you, one time, for your help to end this."

Confused murmurs rippled across the pavilion. A good-looking man in his early forties, holding the hand of his wife, asked, "We didn't ask for this. I'm just a dentist. How can I help you get out of here any quicker? You need a root canal?"

Barrett's gaze fixated on the man, ignoring the sarcasm. "Easy. One of you, a resident of this lovely community of Hidden Refuge, took something that does not belong to you. It's because of that one act that we are here tonight. Had the person responsible not done that, you would all be home asleep in your beds, blissfully oblivious to the existence of me or my friends. But instead, someone made a very bad decision, and you're all paying for it." Barrett let the words sink in, watching as the residents looked at one another as if they suddenly had the deduction powers of Sherlock Holmes.

"Here's your sixty-four-thousand-dollar question: Who took the laptop that doesn't belong to them?" A hushed silence fell over the crowd, the only sound the wind rushing through the trees or the occasional clicking of a bat using its sonar as it flew just out of sight in the lowest layer of darkness above their heads.

Barrett watched the people. Their expressions of confusion, anger, and frustration all appeared sincere. He hadn't expected an answer. He'd told Griffin that whoever had it would likely stay in their house, too afraid to leave it behind. He counted to thirty in his head and continued.

"That's kind of what I suspected the response would be," Barrett said, and stepped so quickly to his left that there were several startled cries from the captive audience. He began to pace methodically toward the left side of the pavilion. "And that's okay. There's no harm yet, no foul. My men are searching for the laptop as we speak. We'll find it, and then we'll be gone."

Barrett reached the railing, turned perfectly on his heels with military precision, and began to stalk back across the wooden floor. "But please hear this part, and hear it well. If any of you—and I do mean any of you—try to be a hero, we will kill you on the spot. This isn't a game. I don't *like* games. I don't have time for them. They're exhausting."

He kept walking, deep in his own thoughts, unaware of the skeptical glances and concerned looks from those who suspected he might not be completely on the sane side of the tracks.

"As long as you do what we tell you, there will be no problems."

Unfortunately, before the night was over, Barrett Connolly would be proved a liar.

CHAPTER
SIXTEEN

James Donovan—Jimmy to his friends since fifth grade at All Saints Catholic School in Cincinnati—opened his eyes and was greeted with shades of gray and a throbbing face. He was fairly certain his nose was broken, and blood still ran slowly in rivulets down his face, parting around his mouth like a miniature red sea. He tasted the acrid coppery taste of blood on his tongue, and he realized his bottom lip was split where he'd been hit with the buttstock of his own weapon.

This isn't what you signed up for, Jimmy. Unlike most of the other men on the team, while he'd externally expressed enthusiasm and the all-in attitude that Griffin and Barrett demanded, internally, he'd been hesitant about it. Hidden Refuge wasn't a village in the Korengal Valley in Afghanistan or a suburb of Baghdad. This was American soil occupied by Americans, civilians with families that he'd once sworn an oath to protect as a young squad leader in the 1st Brigade Combat Team of the legendary 10th Mountain Division.

The figure of a man, the one who'd killed several members of his team, swam into focus. The man was good looking, fit, but had the look Jimmy had seen in soldiers, Marines, and Special Forces countless times—the look of hard experience.

Jimmy's hands were extended over his head and tied to the banister railing with his own zip ties. His tactical Kevlar vest had been removed and lay on the floor in front of him next to the M4 5.56mm assault rifle he'd been carrying. His shoulders ached from the awkward angle, but he thought that might be the least of his worries, especially once the man started quietly talking to him.

"I don't have much time, a few minutes at the most. So here's the deal. I need some information, and I'm prepared to do whatever it takes to get it. But before we get there, I have an easy one for you—what's your name?"

Jimmy hesitated for a moment too long, and blinding pain shot through his face from the soft punch to his broken nose he hadn't seen coming. It wasn't intended to do more damage, just trigger excruciating agony. He let out a low moan, closed his eyes, and gritted his teeth through it. *This man is not playing around with you.*

"I don't have time for tough-guy games, intentional delays, or unintentional hesitation. Let's try this one more time, or the next punch does more permanent damage. Sound like a plan?"

"Yes," Jimmy blurted out the second his tormentor had finished speaking. "And it's Jimmy. Jimmy Donovan." There was no point in hiding. The operation had gone catastrophically sideways, and the odds were no longer in their favor, at least from where Jimmy was sitting.

"Good. I believe you. Now, let's get down to brass tacks, as they say. And just so there's no misunderstanding between us—I do not *want* to hurt you. I really, really don't. It's not who I am anymore, but if you force me, I'll go back there in the blink of an eye," the man said, and leaned in close to Jimmy's face, as if emphasizing his point by proximity.

Jimmy felt the man study him, and he saw the whites of his eyes inches away, the irises black orbs of merciless accusation. *Tell him whatever he wants. The only thing you shouldn't give him is Griffin's name, because if you survive this stranger and this night, Griffin will kill you for talking, no questions asked.*

"I understand," Jimmy said, the words sounding more like "eh undersand" through the swollen nose.

"I thought so. Let's begin, and I'm cutting right to the chase. What are you guys looking for?"

A simple question with a simple answer. "A laptop. Specifically, a Dell 5500 series government laptop."

There was a slight pause, as if the man were processing the information.

"What's on it that makes it valuable?"

"A list," Jimmy said, preparing for what came next and already fearing it.

"What kind of list?"

"I don't know," Jimmy said. "He's not telling us. I swear to God on my mother's soul. *Please* believe me," he implored. Jimmy's heart pounded harder, dread forming in the pit of his stomach, bracing for the blow he expected to come next. He shut his eyes and waited.

"Who's *he?*" the man whispered directly into his ear.

The closeness, the *intimacy* of it, startled Jimmy so badly that he jerked on the floor, straining his arms, sending bolts of pain shooting down his shoulders.

Here you go. Time to play your only card. "Barrett. Barrett Connolly. He's the man running this operation."

"Would this person have dark hair and eyes that occasionally flickered with crazy?" the man asked.

Well, that's one way to put it. In fact, Jimmy had thought the same thing the first time he'd met Barrett. The Irishman was cunning, lethal, and nearly certifiable. He'd made a mental note to never land on Barrett's bad side, but in the end, while the thought of Barrett coming after him made him nervous and uneasy, the thought of Griffin hunting him flat-out terrified him.

"I see you've already met him," Jimmy said.

Ignoring the reply, the man ordered, "Tell me about him."

"What little I know," Jimmy said. "He's a former Marine, Marine Special Operations Command. Did some spooky stuff with them in the Middle East and Afghanistan, just like everyone else in our line of work. Got out, may or may not have worked at Langley with the paramilitary types over there, and then left to break out on his own."

"When?" was the only response.

"Within the last few years, I guess. I've only been with them for the past two, and only for certain jobs," Jimmy said. "But more importantly, he's a dangerous man. He doesn't care about the hostages, and he definitely doesn't care about the girl. There's something *broken* inside him, something just not right. He's unpredictable and violent. Like I said, he's dangerous."

The man absorbed the information, leaned in again, and said, "What does that make me, then? I've already killed six of your friends. What's one more unlucky Irish guy to add to the list?"

No emotion, no anger, just truth. *Whoever this is, he's as dangerous as they are. We picked the wrong neighborhood.*

The man was about to speak when Jimmy's push-to-talk radio erupted on his vest. "Hunter Two, what's your status? I heard faint shots from your direction. Did you get him?"

Jimmy looked at the man, who turned to the girl and said, "We need to move. Do you have any duct tape?"

"We do," she replied, and dashed down the stairs to the kitchen.

Jimmy seized the opportunity and spoke quickly. "Listen, I never wanted to do this job. You don't have to believe me, but it's true. I was a soldier once. This whole thing is *wrong*. I don't know why or how, but it is. But this job, it's a million-dollar payday to each man, free and clear."

The man studied Jimmy's face before replying. There was a commotion from the kitchen, the sound of a drawer being yanked open, its contents scattered as she searched for the tape.

The radio called to Jimmy once again. "Hunter Two, I say again, what's your status?"

"I don't care what you think," Zack replied. "You may have sworn an oath once upon a time, but you betrayed that once you started working with these men. Like it or not—all of this blood, the old man you guys killed—you're just as responsible for it as they are. If I hadn't shown up, you would've captured her, and God knows what that crazy bastard would've done to her." The man's voice grew stronger with each word, and Jimmy heard the girl's footfalls moving up the stairs.

"Just between us, let me tell you one last thing. Personally, I'm tempted to shoot you in the head, right here, right now. But she's seen enough bloodshed for one Friday night, which means you get a pass. I'm going to duct-tape you to this railing, make sure you can't escape, cover your mouth—don't worry; I'll punch a hole in the tape so you don't suffer; I'm not a monster—and then I'm going to do everything in my power to stop this madness, no matter what I have to do or whom I have to kill."

The girl returned and handed the roll of thick, black tape to Jimmy's interrogator. "Here."

The third call from the radio grabbed their attention, and the man and the girl stood in silence as Barrett Connolly spoke. "Is that you, Mr. Citizen of the Year? Are you causing more problems out there in the big bad woods? Did you take out *more* of my men?" Silence. "You're there. I can *feel* it. Whatever you think you're doing, you're doing the wrong thing. You're not a white knight. You're only going to get more innocent people killed." His voice was sinister and syrupy, threatening in the extreme. "And I'm going to prove it to you. You have five minutes to come my way and surrender. If not, someone dies. You know where we are. The clock starts now."

"What now?" the girl asked, fear and concern in her voice, as she handed Zack the tape.

"Thanks. Give me a second," Zack said, and turned back to Jimmy. "Before we go, one last question, and maybe it will buy you a little credit with the man upstairs or whatever god you worship. Where are they taking everyone?"

"Falling Rock Elementary. It's where the cops and FEMA would go for a real emergency. Because of that, we're using it as a base of operations and to secure everyone once they're there."

Zack nodded in the gloom, yanked a long stretch of tape off the roll, and tore it, the sound raising the hairs on the back of Jimmy's neck.

"Well then, Jimmy, it's been a blast," Zack said, and placed the tape on his mouth, pulled out a knife, and cut a slit in it so Jimmy could breathe. Within a minute, he'd used enough tape on Jimmy to guarantee he was going nowhere for the foreseeable future.

Zack grabbed Jimmy's vest, the Commando assault rifle, and the radio and stood up. "Let's go," he said, and the team of two—one operator and one teenage girl, both killers—disappeared from sight.

God, please let me get out of this alive, and I swear I'll change. There was no response, and Jimmy focused on breathing through the small slit in the tape, his nose swelling shut by the minute.

CHAPTER
SEVENTEEN

Griffin stood in the hallway outside the entrance to the gymnasium. The residents of Hidden Refuge had just had their safe worldview shattered minutes earlier. Once they'd followed his contractors in their SUVs and parked their vehicles in the back of the school, out of sight, the frightened people had been herded into the gymnasium. Griffin had personally broken the news to the residents that they were hostages.

Their initial disbelief had been dispelled when one of the husbands, a father to twin girls no older than six or seven, stood up to leave with his family. He'd made it three steps toward the double doors before one of Griffin's men slammed him against a wall, zip-tied his hands behind his back like a professional cowboy, and sat him down on the floor. The use of violence had been a psychological sort of blunt-force trauma, beating the rest of the civilians into immediate obeyance.

Between the two Falling Rock PD impersonators; the four contractors armed with M4 assault rifles; Michael, the comms magician; and Thomas, the Amazon impersonator, there were more than enough armed gunmen to keep the fifty-three men, women, and children under control. But while Griffin and his headquarters element had the situation in hand, Barrett had just finished updating him on the unfolding chaos inside the neighborhood. The two had long-range push-to-talk radios encrypted in a closed network just for the two of them. The conversation had ended with a simple directive from Griffin: "Use the rest of the civilians as bait. I don't care what you do to them, but you *have to regain control.* Do you understand me?"

Barrett had assured him he would, informing his boss that he had a plan. He'd told Griffin he'd call him back in fifteen minutes, and Griffin had started the chronograph on his black and silver Omega Seamaster dive watch. He appreciated the irony of the watch, the only timepiece worn by James Bond throughout his endless battles against iconic supervillains. He was definitely *not* one of the good guys, nor did he want to be. His ambitions were too large to be curbed by something so meager as altruistic intentions. He had a goal, an objective, a quantifiable end state, and he would not be deterred, no matter what obstacles fell across his path.

Griffin leaned over, his back against the wall, his hands on his knees, breathing deeply to minimize the red wave of frustration and rage he felt rush toward him. He was reminded of his wrestling days at Penn State, when the anger he felt welling up inside him, a dark rage whose source was a motherless childhood, threatened to overtake his actions. *Keep it in check. It will work out. They'll get him.* He knew Barrett would hunt the man down until dawn if Griffin let him, but he needed Barrett to expedite his operations. It was nearly 0315, and time felt like it was accelerating, slipping further and further out of reach until there'd be none left.

He straightened up, looked at the iPhone, waited for the facial recognition to unlock the phone, and found the number he needed. It was a DC area-code number with no associated picture. *Time to make the call. Be calm, cool, and confident. Three Cs, Griffin. You got this.*

Once the civilians had been locked down in the gym, Griffin had ordered Michael to turn off the jammer for the school. They'd collected all cell phones, and the only ones using the airwaves for the foreseeable future would be Griffin and his team.

He hit the number and placed a set of Apple EarPods in his ears. The number rang twice before his buyer answered. "Yes. Do you have it?" The voice was alert, and Griffin realized that the man was as wide awake as he was.

"Negative," Griffin said, concisely explaining the situation. "We're searching, but we've run into a problem. There's a rogue element on the board, and he's killed several of my men. We have no idea who he is, but we're about to force him into a corner. I expect him to be neutralized within the next ten minutes. One of the teams is searching for the device while we deal with this issue." He finished and waited, slightly concerned, not for his safety but for the prospect of upsetting the buyer. He was the man who held the purse strings to the $100 million payday, and he didn't want to jeopardize that at any cost.

"I thought you said your men were the best. That's what you're getting paid for, because of your reputation as the best." It was a question in the form of a statement.

"They are, and I assure you, we'll have this variable off the board soon. My chief of operations is overseeing it as we speak. My word is my bond, and I don't take it lightly," Griffin said.

There was a pause on the other end, and the man replied, a trace of his accent evident for the first time in the conversation, a fact that Griffin chalked up to the stress of the situation. He'd met more than one operative in his time who subconsciously slipped back into his native tongue under extreme duress. His buyer, while powerful and backed by a small fortune, was no different. "Very well. Call me as soon as you have an update."

Griffin responded with a question, a mannerism he detested in other people, which only emphasized the gravity of the situation. "You're absolutely positive, beyond a shadow of a doubt, that the laptop is still in the neighborhood?"

A reluctant and frustrated sigh met his query. "As I told you before, there is a motion-activated GPS inside the laptop. It's concealed to look like a component of the motherboard and draws power from it. We lost the signal, for whatever reason—could've been a technical issue, the computer was jarred, who knows—but our tech people tell me it will reactivate without question. Just between us, if it were still working as it should, we never would have lost it, but we have to assume it's still there—for *both our sakes.*"

"Okay. Then, we'll get it back to you before the end of the night."

"Good, but know this: if you fail, you don't just fail me. You fail my employer. And they are not tolerant of failure—not in the least." The call ended, the not-so-subtle threat lingering long after the connection was lost.

Griffin breathed deeply once again, his pulse decreasing by a few beats, and his thoughts turned to the events that had transpired thus far. Something had gone wrong, but things never went wrong without a good reason.

Griffin moved away from the wall and toward the doors to the gymnasium. He needed to see something for himself, if only to ease his mind. *What did you miss, Barrett? What did you miss?*

CHAPTER
EIGHTEEN

"Mr. C., what are we going to do? That monster just told us he's going to kill someone, one of our friends, our neighbors. While our families are safe, we can't let that happen. It could be Ben. *Please. You have to do something*," Sam pleaded.

The two of them stood outside on the deck, the lights of the central hub magnified by the parked vehicles and the vans, flashes flickering through the woods. She was right. His babysitter continued to impress on all counts—maturity, bravery, and intelligence. Sam Hawkins was going to be a formidable woman someday. Zack just needed to keep her alive for the rest of the night so she could survive being a teenager first.

The situation was deteriorating so quickly that the tenuous hold he had on it threatened to disintegrate in his fingers like wet newspaper. The harsh reality was that there was no good move for him. None at all. There was no way he could turn himself over to the psychotic Irishman, but he loathed the thought of another innocent life lost, a soul forfeited at the altar of these evil men. But before he could do anything, he needed Sam to get clear of the battleground.

"Sam, I need you to listen to me. There is no way they're going to kill Ben or anyone else. I won't let that happen. I need you to do something, and it's going to be really scary, but if I didn't think you could do it, I wouldn't ask. I swear to God."

Sam heard the concern and urgency in his voice, and replied, "When this is over, I expect you to tell me who you were in your former life. I feel like I just found out that my neighbor is Jack Bauer."

Zack laughed, glad that her sense of humor was still intact. She'd need it once the night was over. He knew there was a part of her still in shock, a part that would need time to process the fact that she'd taken a life. Justifiable or not, it was no easy task, and he'd been trained to do it, coldly and with the utmost calculation. She was just a suburban teenager thrown into the literal line of fire.

"I promise you this—I don't work for CTU. Always too much drama there, you know what I mean?" Zack said with a sly grin.

"Plus, it's the government, and you know what I think about them," she declared, her smile faltering, semi-serious.

"I do. Now, here's what I need you to do, as we're all running out of time," Zack said, and paused before delivering his request. "I need you to run."

"Say what?" Sam said, taken aback.

"How familiar are you with the running trails that weave in and out of the neighborhood? You've run them what, hundreds if not thousands of times, correct? You think you can navigate them at night, on your own, in the dark? I wouldn't ask if I didn't think you could."

Sam hesitated, acutely aware that time was imposing its will on them, a force and concept as real as the shotgun in her hands. "I can. Where do you want me to go?"

"For help. You're the only one who can. I want you to work your way to the other side of the neighborhood and pick one of the paths that leads to the main road outside the subdivision. They're jamming our communications, and once you get outside their range and get a signal, you call for help. Tell them to send everyone they can. Tell them about the school too. Just keep running, Dory-style, and don't stop," Zack finished.

"Did you just reference *Finding Nemo*?" Sam asked incredulously.

"I have kids, remember? We're a Disney family. One last thing—do you want to take the shotgun or a pistol? I'm not sending you unarmed. Pistol will be lighter and has more rounds. That Glock is a good weapon, accurate and reliable." They'd retrieved the pistols from her father's office before leaving her house.

"The pistol," she said. "I can handle it if I need to." Her confidence had grown in the last few minutes, and the sense of panicked urgency she felt added to it.

"Good. Your father was smart. Somehow got fifteen-round magazines. The gun is loaded, and there's a round in the chamber. I checked. There's no traditional safety on the Glock. It's built into the trigger, and the first part of the pull takes it off. Just keep your finger straight and off the trigger until you need to fire. It's a nine-millimeter, but it will kick, although not like the twelve-gauge. Just try to control it. Most people think you need to line up a perfect shot with the rear and front sights on the target. Under the circumstances, consider it an extension of your hand—point at what you want to hit and pull the trigger. Also, take one of the push-to-talk radios. Keep it on but turned down. You can monitor the communications network they're using, although they'll likely change it. Any questions?" Zack asked as he handed Sam the Glock 19 and the handheld radio he'd taken from Jimmy.

"No. But what are you going to do?"

"I'm going to have a conversation with an Irish psychopath and play a little game of psychological chicken with him."

"Do you think it will work?"

"I hope so," Zack answered honestly. "Sam, there's no more time. I need you to go."

Sam Hawkins caught Zack completely off guard as she leaned in and wrapped both arms around his waist, the Glock in her right hand. "Thanks for saving my life, Mr. C."

The display of gratitude elicited a strong affinity for the girl, a sudden desire to protect her at all costs. He was humbled by the gesture, and he loathed himself for what he was asking of her. But it needed to be done, and he had a war to wage.

"It was my honor, Sam," Zack replied, the emotion of the moment threatening to overwhelm him. He stepped back, and she released her grip. "More importantly, do you know how hard it is to find a good sitter these days?"

Sam laughed. "Anytime, Mr. C. Anytime."

"Good. Now *run like all of our lives depend on it.* Because they just may. I have faith in you."

Sam spun on her heels, leapt down the stairs from the back porch, and sprinted across the damp grass toward the tree line and the pathway that lay hidden beyond.

Zack heard her footfalls fade as he moved down the steps and toward the front of the house. He needed to buy some time, and he had less than a minute before the Irishman's deadline. His options were limited, and there was only one real tactical course of action—Zack Chambers had to find the laptop before the Irishman's army of phony officers did. It was the only leverage that might save the residents of Hidden Refuge from a violent end.

Zack grabbed the push-to-talk radio he'd taken from the dead man on the staircase and depressed the talk button as he stood beside the house and observed the abandoned street of Arrow Drive. *Here goes nothing and everything. Better make it count.*

CHAPTER
NINETEEN

Barrett Connolly stared at his watch. There was less than ninety seconds until he had no choice but to send a message he didn't want to send, but like Griffin said, mission first. *And these people are nothing more than bargaining chips. Don't forget that.*

He sighed, put his left hand down, and moved to the crowd, scanning petrified faces as he drew closer to his potential victims.

There was a young couple that caught his eye, and he stopped. There were no children with them. The man, in his early thirties, was average-looking, with ruffled, curly brown hair and a pair of stylish glasses with dark brown rims on the upper half that faded to clear on the bottom. The arms of the glasses were a bright blue, which was what grabbed Barrett's attention. Even more noticeable was the fact that this average man was with a stunning brunette with bright green eyes, a straight jawline, and chiseled features straight out of a fashion magazine. *How does a guy like that end up with a woman that beautiful?*

In Barrett's world, it was the strong alpha males that won trophy wives like the one before him, not some suburban schmuck with glasses. It was an affront to his misogynistic and out-of-date worldview. While most of America had evolved along the lines of *Modern Family*, albeit slowly, Barrett had regressed to a version of America more suited to the 1950s and *Mad Men*.

"You," Barrett said, pointing at the man with his Glock 17 Gen5. "Stand up and come over here." He was cold and calculating. He had to be. He was a killer, not a monster.

The suburban joe stood up, but his wife tried to hold on to him, terror forming on her face as her husband was pulled away from her. "No!" she cried, as the man turned back to look at her.

As if preternaturally sensing the end of his time on earth, that his time with his soul mate, whom he adored, and all other experiences were about to end, he bent over, placed his hands on her face, and kissed her firmly on the lips. "I love you. You're the best thing that ever happened to me. No matter what happens, it will be okay. I promise."

"I love you always," the woman said, and released her grip on his arms, tears already falling down her cheeks. There was nothing else to say.

The man straightened up, looked at Barrett, and started walking toward him, a condemned man moving forward under his own power to his demise. Barrett had to give him credit. The man knew what was likely coming and was facing it like a man. *I promise I'll make it quick.*

He looked at his watch. Forty seconds to go. *The coward wasn't going to show. Well, I guess he can live with more blood on his hands*, which made Barrett wonder, for the very first time that night, exactly what kind of man they were facing.

Suburban Joe reached Barrett, stopped in front of him, and waited. They studied each other for a brief moment, and Barrett saw a combination of fear and anger in the man's hazel eyes. The man broke the silence first.

"First, you're going to burn in hell for this—for all of it. No matter what you do, you're a condemned man and a coward," the man said quietly, careful that his words didn't carry back to the assembled mass of hostages. "Second, make it quick and then move my body out of the way. These people shouldn't have to see it."

Barrett smirked and nodded. "Fair enough." He looked at his watch. Fifteen seconds. He looked up one last time, and said, "Turn around. This will be over before you know it."

"Go fuck yourself. Have fun in hell," the man said, turned around, and stared at his wife, fighting to stoically control the panic he felt gripping him.

"Oh. I'm well aware of my divine fate. Trust you me, my friend," Barrett replied in a smooth, hushed voice. "Now, say goodbye to your wife."

The man, Jeff Simmons, stared at his wife, Claire, the most beautiful woman he'd ever laid eyes upon. He was a genius computer programmer who'd developed several unique health-monitoring applications, including the first heartbeat monitor app for smartphones. Claire was a professional singer and dancer, currently performing at the National Theater in *Jersey Boys*, which was on a hiatus due to a stage reconstruction issue. Jeff had been in DC for a meeting with a software company, and he'd stopped for a cup of coffee at a Starbucks. The beautiful, angry woman in front of him had been furiously struggling with her iPhone, looking for the display brightness setting, which Apple kept hidden from its customers, and Jeff had offered to help. For reasons unexplained, the woman had struck up a conversation with him, and they'd shared a cup of coffee, bonding over the nuances of smartphone technology, as well as Broadway show tunes, which Jeff loved.

But all of that was about to be over. *At least Claire will live.* "I love you, baby," Jeff said out loud, his words echoing as a commitment to her that would live on long after he ceased to.

Barrett stepped to the side of the man, straightened his right arm, and aimed the Glock at just above his ear. There was no need to traumatize everyone with an exit wound to the face. The people gasped in horror, cries and whimpers catching fire. He moved his finger off the trigger guard to the trigger and started to squeeze.

"I wouldn't pull that trigger, not if you ever want to see the laptop again," a disembodied voice said from his radio.

Barrett stopped the increasing tension in his finger and held fire, the Glock still pointed at the man's head. He raised the radio to his lips. "Well, well. I thought for sure that our Good Samaritan wasn't going to make an appearance. Cutting it a little close, aren't you? This poor man was about to make his gorgeous wife a gorgeous widow."

"Lower the weapon, or I destroy the computer. I don't care what's on it, but obviously, you do. And if I do an *Office Space* number on it, then you no longer have a reason to be here. You have until the count of five." There was a brief silence, followed by, "Five . . . four . . . three . . ."

A swelling rage threatened to blind Barrett to reason, but the voice of his employer, his friend, brought him back to the periphery of what passed for sanity in his mind. *If you do it, make it count. Make them remember what happens if they don't comply.*

Barrett lowered the weapon.

And just as quickly, he raised it back up and fired point-blank into the back of his hostage's head. The man's body fell forward as a shriek of pure anguish rose from his wife.

She collapsed to the gazebo floor, her body shaking uncontrollably in a state of pure torment, shattered cries pouring forth like a wounded animal. The sound was awful, and others broke down into tears, adding to the mournful wails.

But Barrett didn't care about them anymore. Their purpose had been fulfilled, including the man he'd just killed. *It served the greater good*—our *greater good.*

The real object of his affection had just established communications, and Barrett's only focus was on the Samaritan and the target package. "You don't dictate terms. *Ever.* Talk, and make it count, or I'll kill not just this poor guy, but *all of them.*"

CHAPTER
TWENTY

Zack watched Barrett through his zoom-lens monocular, a wrath begging to be unleashed. His pulse pounded, and he wanted to *hurt* the executioner, to make him pay, slowly. He closed his eyes and inhaled, held it a moment, and exhaled deeply, calming his raging soul. He'd tried to save the man, but the monsters in charge had just sent a message—one sealed in blood: *You are not in charge.*

In order to retain the temporary freedom that he needed to maneuver through the neighborhood, he had to buy time. And to do that, he had to play the only card he had—one printed with information, not royal figures made of diamonds. He'd made the only move he could— he'd bluffed with the information Jimmy had provided.

It had worked, but for how long, Zack had no idea. His street was clear, and they obviously hadn't found the laptop. *Or they would've left. That's the only way this thing ends.* By means of elimination, that meant he had to find the teams that Barrett had dispatched to Forest Edge Court and Windy Tree Way. If one of them found it first and reported back to the evil leprechaun, Zack's ruse would be up and people would die. He was certain there would be blood for retribution. That was the kind of man Barrett Connolly was.

Zack moved along the front of the houses and toward the cul-de-sac.

His first destination was Windy Tree Way, where he assumed he'd find the closest enemy team. As he moved, he spoke, maintaining the best noise discipline that he could, the wind providing an additional layer of auditory concealment.

"Barrett, that's a good strong Irish name. I'll bet your mother thought you'd go far, and look at you now. Taking an entire neighborhood hostage, killing an innocent elderly man, executing a hostage, and threatening more people. You've really hit your stride." Zack was baiting him, testing the waters to elicit some kind of emotional response. "By the way, I'm going to make you pay for what you just did. Somehow, some way, you're going answer for it."

He had already reached the cul-de-sac and jogged quickly around the back of the two end houses.

There was silence, and then laughter. "Why don't you come on out and give it a shot? I'm right here, Mr. Suburbia."

Zack heard the cries of the residents in the background, but he heard the woman's wails of agony in the air.

"Regardless of what you think, this isn't personal. It's a *job*—a very high-paying one, at that. And you're doing your all-American best to muck it up. Fancy yourself a hero? Is that it? Trying to prove something to yourself? Are you some kind of weekend warrior looking to go full-time?"

Zack had reached the woods on the other side of Arrow Drive. There were at least three hundred yards between his street and Windy Tree Way. At night, it would take him several minutes to traverse the terrain. At least the wind was on his side.

"Could a weekend warrior kill all of those guys you hired? If so, you'd be out of business pretty quickly," Zack said as he slipped into the trees and was enveloped by the suburban forest. He stood still, allowing his eyes to adjust ever so slightly to the intense darkness. The coming cold front and clouds had blotted out the waning crescent moon, and illumination was next to nothing, although the night-vision monocular helped. "But let's not talk about me. Rather, let's talk about what I want."

"Let me guess—and it's rather boring, I might add—you want me and my friends to release the hostages, *your friends and neighbors*, and be on our merry way. Does that sound about right?"

"A boy can dream, can't he?" Zack shot back.

"No. He can't. Not on this night," Barrett said, his voice taking a serious, flat tone devoid of emotion. "It's 'adults only' at this party. No matter what—and I really mean this—we are not leaving without that computer. I don't know if you really have it, but if you do, I'll make you a deal. You bring the laptop here, and we'll leave. No questions asked. You get to be the hero, and we get what we came for. A simple trade: your lives for that laptop."

Zack pushed deeper into the woods, the flickering lights from Windy Tree serving as his personal beacons.

"Can I call a friend? Maybe get a second opinion?"

"I don't think so. The terms of this deal are binding. It's a real take-it-or-leave-it, one-time-only kind of a deal." Barrett paused, waiting for an answer.

"You drive a hard bargain, Barrett."

Another pause, another wind-driven shudder of the trees around Zack as he stalked through the woods.

"You keep saying my name like it matters. Trust me. It doesn't. The only thing that does matter is *this deal*. Last time I'm going to ask—Do we have one, Mr. Hero?"

Zack considered, truly, for the first time. Had he had the laptop already, he might have turned it over. He thought that Barrett would kill him, no matter what assurances he gave, but if it saved the lives of everyone else? It was something he'd have considered. The problem was that he didn't have the laptop, and it was all moot speculation.

He was two-thirds to Windy Tree Way. *Better answer the man.* But that was when the screaming started, and Zack's only thought was, *What now?*

"I need some time to think about it," he said in a rush to Barrett. "Talk to you soon. Toodle-oo."

And then he started sprinting through the underbrush, breaking twigs and crushing leaves, creating a noise that was like an emerging storm, furiously laying waste to everything in its path. Zack didn't care, because the screaming was loud enough to mask his movements.

CHAPTER
TWENTY-ONE

Barrett was stupefied at the audacity of his prey. The man was obviously trained, confident, and deadly. The fact that he knew about the laptop was problematic, but as to whether he had the prize in his possession, Barrett wasn't convinced.

While events were unfolding on Arrow Drive, his search team had come up empty on Forest Edge Court, and he'd dispatched them to Windy Tree Way with an extra warning to be cautious. Until they'd captured or killed the guerrilla in their midst, every other resident not at the pavilion under guard was to be treated as a hostile. No exceptions.

But he still struggled with the fact that the man had just hung up on him, albeit with a handheld radio. *He's up to something. You know it. But what? I've still got more firepower than he does. What can he really do?* If Captain America really did have the laptop, there was no course of action other than to hunt him down and take it back. Hidden Refuge was on lockdown for the next few hours, with no way in or out. Their quarry could try to hide, to wait them out, but the search teams would eventually pick up the signal, and then they'd have both the laptop and him. Plus, there was the question of the hostages. Whoever he was, he was not about to let more civilians die, if he can help it. *He waited until the very last second to respond before you were about to execute the husband.* And then it hit him, and he smiled at the boldness of it.

Barrett appreciated aggression and action. He respected those who were willing to take what they wanted. Life was too short, too fleeting—a lesson he'd learned young. The man had to know help wasn't coming, which meant he also knew that he was on his own. But he had the skills to operate that way, with no support. He was trying to force the situation to a resolution. Of that, Barrett was now certain, but the only way to do it was with the laptop. And if he was trying to buy time, as evidenced by the way he'd just ended the conversation with Barrett, it meant that while he knew about the laptop, he was still trying to find it.

It's now a race. We have to find the laptop first, no matter what.

Barrett reached for the radio and switched the channel to the alternate frequency. Once his men had heard the interloper on their channel, they would've recognized the network was compromised and switched channels the way they'd been instructed. *You can never have too many contingencies*, he thought, and lifted the handheld to his mouth just as the second radio on his gun belt for Griffin and the base of operations came to life.

"This is Hunter Actual, I'm on the way to your position. Take no further action until I get there. I say again, take no further action until I get there. Be there within seven or eight minutes."

Barrett sighed and released the talk button. If Griffin was on his way, something had changed, something that had a direct impact on the cat-and-mouse game playing out in Hidden Refuge.

He lowered the team radio, raised the command push-to-talk to his mouth, and replied, "Roger, Hunter Actual. Standing by. Out here."

There was nothing more to add. The team could keep searching until Griffin arrived. But for the first time that night, Barrett felt the balance shift, like a children's seesaw, in favor of the neighborhood's last action hero. *There are just too many variables, and with each man that you lose, they start to stack up in his favor. You know this. You need to make Griffin understand.*

Something drastic needed to be done, something that would force their prey out into the open, no matter what. If this man was some kind of former Special Forces operator or worse, he only understood force, and he had to be shown that resistance would be met with overwhelming violence, even if it wasn't directed at him.

Come on, Griffin. Get here soon so we can do what needs to be done. Mission first.

CHAPTER
TWENTY-TWO

Griffin was furious with himself. It wasn't Barrett's fault. The responsibility was all his. He trusted Barrett like a brother, and in Barrett's defense, there was no way he could've known who the residents were. They were names on a list, but *who they were*, that was the critical information that had been missed. He should've studied that list himself, rather than delegating it to his chief of operations. But he'd been distracted because of the buyer and the enormity of what they were acquiring. The information on the laptop was power, pure and simple, and a shadow balance between nations depended upon it. He didn't consider himself a traitor; he was just balancing the scales of power—*and* getting paid a fortune to do so.

He accelerated around the curve, the tires of the Ford Explorer gripping the pavement as if it were a racetrack. The planning for the operation had been so thorough that he'd even had the Explorers pursuit-rated like real police vehicles.

There were always unknown variables, no matter how hard they tried to avoid them. It was inevitable, part of the business. But something like this? He gripped the steering wheel tighter and drove.

As soon as he'd seen the name on the list, he'd frozen, a statue stuck to the gymnasium floor, oblivious to the world around him. And then he'd put the several sheets of paper back on the table and informed his team that he was heading to the neighborhood. His instructions to them had been simple: Maintain control of the hostages until he returned. Do not hurt them, and *absolutely* do not shoot anyone. Griffin would be the only person making life-and-death decisions for the rest of the night.

Griffin Huntsmen would not be denied what was rightfully his. He *knew* that he really was the smartest person in the room, no matter the room or its occupants. He'd proven it again and again, one mission after another, for God and country, yet America's premier intelligence agency had fallen into bureaucratic disrepair, handcuffed by presidential directives.

It seemed the US government had decided that a progressive agenda, diversity, and social justice were more important than national security. He'd seen it coming. They all had. The daily agency-wide emails that focused on inclusion and feelings more than pursuing the enemies of the state. In his worldview, complacency and political correctness were just as dangerous as any violent extremist groups. One could be killed, while the other was an insidious ideology that preyed upon the young, naive, and institutional bureaucrats who only cared about their retirement pensions.

The fact that the agency was now on the chessboard would make his success that much sweeter. He'd made his decision to resign when he'd seen the writing on the proverbial wall—not even he could fight CIA city hall. But tonight, he could at least exact a little personal revenge, even if most of the agency's personnel would never find out about it.

Small victories are better than no victories, he thought as he closed the distance to Hidden Refuge.

His past had caught up to him on the night of his most ambitious operation. And if he could acquire the laptop *and* cross that name off his list, well, that was equivalent to winning the Super Bowl of mercenary clandestine operations.

CHAPTER
TWENTY-THREE

Sam ran along the paved path, her Brooks running shoes softly landing with each stride, striking the ground with a barely audible *thwup*. She was a sub-five-minute miler on the track team, which made her the fastest girl in her high school and one of the fastest in the region. Her best time was 4:51, which placed her in the top 1 percent of girl high school runners in the country. Even the world high school record was only 4:33.27, which made Sam fast—very fast.

But the conditions weren't exactly track-meet ideal, and there was the small matter of her carrying a loaded handgun. *If Ben could see me now*, she thought, and then she prayed that no one *could* see her.

She was still processing the fact that her attractive, suburban, all-around-good-guy neighbor was something much, much different than he projected to the world. What that was, she planned to uncover, but first she had to make it out of the neighborhood, and the only way was the path that ran through the woods and encircled the entire subdivision.

There were three ways to access the running trail from the outside world, and two were off the main road that Hidden Refuge Drive intersected. The third was from a large pond about a mile south of the community. She and Ben had taken leisurely strolls along it nearly every day, coveted private time for the two of them as they grew closer. While it was a literal memory lane, it wasn't the one she needed.

Her target was the entrance approximately a half mile north of Hidden Refuge Drive, where the path emptied onto the shoulder of the main road, generically named Bypass One because it circumvented the not-so-bustling mecca of Falling Rock several miles to the west. There were no homes near the entrance and no reason for anyone to be near it at this time of night. It was just a dark opening in the woods, beckoning runners to enter like the mouth of a modern fairy tale—or horror story, depending on the inclination of one's imagination.

Once she hit Bypass One, there would be a street less than a quarter mile away that had four or five homes on it. These were considered "blue-collar" homes, smaller and older than those in her neighborhood, but Sam didn't care. There could be meth-dealing felons living on the street, but all that mattered was finding a safe place to hide while she called the police.

Sam's heart pounded in her chest as she traversed the path, subconsciously aware of every step, the cushioned soles springing her forward. She kept her arms at a ninety-degree angle, pumping up and down to add momentum as she ran. The only variables detracting from her perfect form were the gun in her right hand and her iPhone in the left. She was fairly certain they would disqualify her from competition.

She estimated she had run at least three-quarters of a mile, with another three-quarters to go, having circumnavigated Windy Tree Way and Forest Edge Court. The remaining part of the path was a straight shot with one curve to the left about twenty yards before the road.

She tried not to let her mind wander, but the wind, the dark, and her fears conspired against her. *Please, please, please, let Ben be safe.* Teenage love or not, she cared deeply for him, felt a physical compulsion to be with him.

The world was a cruel place, and the ugly realities that were broadcast into each home every day through twenty-four–seven global news coverage took a psychological toll, even on kids in high school just beginning to figure out who they were. Add the constant pressure that lingered in the back of each student's mind about school shootings, and high school was a stressful time.

But Ben made all of it better. *Which is why you need to run faster and stop letting your worst fears get the better of you.* It was her dad's voice again, the silent sound of reason. She would tell him everything, every detail, because he would want to know and because he would be proud of his little girl. She allowed herself a small smile at the thought and ran harder.

The wind continued to rush around her, swirling leaves across the path that stuck briefly to her body, as if clinging for life, before being whisked away. She knew the actual front was forecasted to blow through later, during the night, but she couldn't recall exactly when. When it did, the temperature would plummet by ten to fifteen degrees within a few hours. Sam hoped the hostage situation at the pavilion would be over by then. Otherwise, there were going to be some very angry residents—not that they weren't already furious, terrified, and praying to survive the madness of the night.

The final curve in the road blurrily swam into view, a dark tunnel of gray surrounded by the blackness of the woods that turned to the left. *Almost there.*

She held up the iPhone. Still no signal. *How far do these jammers work?* Mr. Chambers had told her about the vans, as well as his intention to disable them if he could. But if he wasn't able to, the burden was on her.

She hit the curve and flew around it, increasing her speed in hopes of escaping the dark embrace of the woods. Her mood soared slightly at the sight of the road, natural illumination, and a light pole, out of sight, guiding her way.

A few seconds later, she stood on the side of the road, putting her hands over her head to catch her breath, careful to make sure the barrel of the Glock was pointed away from her—which was when she saw the darkened Falling Rock SUV parked thirty feet away on the left side of the path, facing her. *Oh no.*

Movement to her right, from behind her, stopped her dead in her tracks and froze her blood, panic gripping her stomach tightly.

"*Do not move.* I see the gun and the phone. If you make any sudden moves, I *will* shoot you, and since my weapon is suppressed, no one will hear it, not that it will matter to you, as you'll be dead." The voice was calm, clear, and confident, which told Sam that the man who had been lying in wait at the end of the path would do exactly what he said.

He had her literally dead to rights. *That's twice in one night.* Then again, being some kind of assassin wasn't exactly her full-time job. She'd only been doing it for less than an hour. There was nothing for her to do but comply.

"What do you want me to do? You're one of them, aren't you? Just don't kill me, please," she said, and then for no rational reason, added, "I'm only seventeen."

Her hands were still on top of her head. She wasn't foolish enough to make any sudden moves. When her father had been teaching her to drive, he'd said to her in terms clear enough that even a teenager enthusiastic to get her license could understand: "If you ever get pulled over, do *exactly* what the officer says, no matter what. Do not argue. Don't move quickly. Nothing. Do you understand?" And she had. While the man holding her at gunpoint wasn't someone whose job was to serve and protect, the same rules applied.

"Smart girl," the man said. "You may get out of this just yet. But first, turn around, *slowly.* Like I said, one wrong move, and your young life is over. I don't want to shoot a girl, but you're holding a gun, and until *I'm* holding that gun, you're a threat. So please go slow."

She couldn't fault his logic. *Which is probably why he's some kind of mercenary and you're a high school student.* She did as he asked, turning slowly to her left as an irrational fear came over her, as if she were about to come face-to-face with the incarnation of evil. She stopped and found herself less than fifteen feet from her ambusher. She could make out gray features, dark clothes, a Kevlar vest like the other impersonators wore, and the gun that was pointed directly at her. His eyes were his most visible feature. She could still see them—at least their whites and the black holes that punctuated them like periods on his soul. He was a man in shadow—but then the shadows around him moved, and Sam's terror ascended to a whole new level.

An arm drenched in blackness snaked around the man's left shoulder and reached under the man's left wrist, grasping the pistol under the barrel near the trigger guard. Simultaneously, a hand reached up from the man's right side and plunged something into his neck below his jawline. The man issued a cry of shocked pain, and his neck turned dark black with blood. Sickened from the sudden violence, Sam turned away and instinctively dropped her iPhone, holding the Glock in front of her.

The sounds of the man's dying struggle elicited a gag reflex, and she found herself wanting to throw up. *Don't do it. He was going to kill you and, at best, was holding you at gunpoint.* She fought the urge and then looked back as the impersonator's killer lowered the dying man to the ground, the man's pistol now in the hands of its new owner.

The dying man's right hand tried to press against the wound, but it was useless. Whatever his killer had done, it was permanent—there was no stopping the flow of blood. He fell onto his back and stared up at the night sky, a blanket of darkness looming over him. Within seconds, his existence was consumed by it and he was no more.

Sam stood in shock, pointing the Glock at a spot between the dead man on the ground and the figure standing before her. After a very brief moment, the shadow raised its hands and spoke.

"Are you hurt?" a young voice asked.

What? No. I'm fine. Who are you? her mind responded before she realized she wasn't voicing her words aloud. She took a deep breath, exhaled, and replied, "No. I'm fine. But before I tell you anything else, who the *hell* are you and why are you here? I need to know if you're a friend or foe." And she raised the Glock directly at the figure's chest. This was no time to lower her guard. People seemed to be dying all around her tonight, and she didn't want to be one of them. "Talk," she commanded in a voice she hoped sounded confident, not terrified, the way she felt.

"I'm pretty certain I'm a friend. My name is Nicholas Chambers, but my friends—and people I save, I might add—call me Nick. My brother lives in Hidden Refuge, which appears to be under the control of people pretending to be the police. It's impressive you made it out," he added almost absentmindedly.

"It wasn't easy. Trust me," she said, an image of the dead man slumped on her carpeted steps flashed behind her eyes.

"I bet. You have that look that someone your age *shouldn't have*, but life isn't always fair," he said somberly. "Anyhow, I received a text from my brother, and then we lost communications. Thought maybe it was just his cell, but when all communications went dead, including his voice-over-IP line and satellite phone, I decided to show up early, only to find his neighborhood on some kind of lockdown. There was a convoy of cars led by a police vehicle that I passed earlier, and when I did, my cell phone stopped working. I tried to enter, but a cop—or at least someone who claimed he was a cop—stopped me halfway down Hidden Refuge Drive, told me the neighborhood was being evacuated, and asked that I meet them at the elementary school, where the convoy of residents was heading. Something about him set off alarms. So I lied and told him I was lost, and before he could do anything, I rolled up the window, slammed the car into gear, and did a U-turn right there in the middle of the road."

"Wait a minute. He didn't try to stop you?" Sam asked, somewhat incredulously.

"Negative. I didn't think he would. He was probably too concerned with what was going on inside. Also, if he tried to shoot me and missed, he'd have to assume I was going to go get real law enforcement. Better to play it safe. It was the right call for him."

He had a point. *Why risk further complications?* Sam was pretty certain that the bad guys had already started taking losses by then. No need to make a bad situation worse.

He continued. "As soon as I got out of there, I turned right on Bypass One, drove a short distance, and saw *another* SUV on the shoulder, as if he were trying to hide from traffic. There was something way wrong about all of it. I drove for another half mile, parked, and checked the police scanner app on my phone. There was nothing out of the ordinary. No news of an evacuation or anything. Just an accident west of Falling Rock, fifteen miles from here, which makes me think someone set that up to keep law enforcement and emergency responders away from this area. Regardless, I decided to work my way back here on foot and conduct my own reconnaissance. I'd only been here for a few minutes, hidden in the woods, observing, when you emerged. I was close enough to hear the conversation, which told me all I needed to know—this guy was not an officer of the law, since I'm fairly certain real cops don't threaten to kill seventeen-year-old girls after sneaking up on them. And I didn't have a suppressed weapon, at least until now. I did what I had to do, and I'm sorry you had to see it."

He stopped talking, allowing the information to register in Sam's shocked brain. "Well, that's my story. What about you, kid? What happened to you?"

Wait a second. What did he say? I have no idea. She'd heard everything and was grateful that the man—older than she was but only somewhere in his late twenties, by the sound of him—had saved her life. But one fact had hit her like a sucker punch, as if the unfolding violence and terror weren't enough. Suddenly, she found herself rambling in staccato, as if purging the information would make it less painful. "You're Mr. Chambers's *brother*? I had no idea he had one. I'm his babysitter, and he saved my life tonight. He's in trouble, although he's killed a bunch of them. Actually, the whole neighborhood's in trouble."

The shadow moved forward. Dark features transformed into gray ones, and Sam realized she'd been right about his age. A young man, clean cut, good looking, with a lean, honest face materialized before her. Unlike his brother, his dark hair was cropped close on the sides and spiked up in front, the rest of it laying down neatly.

"Wait. He's *killed people*? Tonight?" Nick shook his head. "I want to say I'm surprised, but I'm not. My brother has a bit of a hero complex— justifiably so—and well, if there's something bad happening, then that sounds about right. I guess you thought you were living near a nice family man next door. But tonight you got to meet Zack Chambers for real: the man, the myth, the legend."

How could he be so calm after killing another human being—with a knife no less? Her curiosity about the Chambers family had reached a level that demanded answers. *There's two of them?* "What is it with you guys? Is your whole family some sort of secret team of superagents working for the government?"

Nick let out a genuine laugh that startled Sam, given the circumstances. "Not exactly. In fact, that's about the last thing you'd find us doing. But first, can you lower that gun, please? And I'll tell you all about the Chambers brothers."

Sam realized she had no choice but to trust the man who'd just committed murder on her behalf, although she wasn't sure it really was murder, considering the man had held her at gunpoint. She lowered the Glock. *Whatever. Semantics. The judicial system is messed up to the max. Let them sort this out later.*

"Thank you," Nick said, and lowered his hands. "Now, does this path take us back to the neighborhood? If so, we need to move because I need to go help my brother."

She watched him wipe the knife on his dark pants. *He's cleaning the man's blood off of it!* When he folded it, and put it in some kind of pouch on his belt, she realized that in addition to the dead impersonator's weapon, he had a holster with a pistol of his own. *Jesus. Who are these guys? And now he wants to head back into the dragon's lair?* "Mr. Chambers told me to get help. Why not stick to the plan, find a place to call the police, and wait for them to arrive?"

Nick looked at her for a moment, understanding her hesitation, especially after what she'd been through already. "Because whatever is happening inside is likely happening fast, and by the time the police arrive, it might be too late. I can't take that chance. I know you don't know me, but I'm really good at this, although maybe not as good as my brother. But no matter what you choose to do, I have to go, and I have to go now. You can obviously handle yourself, and I could use your navigation to get me back there safely, but I'll do it alone if I have to. It's your call."

Sam contemplated her fate. The man before her was treating her like an adult, not a terrified seventeen-year-old high school girl. It gave her pause, but it felt good—really good—to have someone acknowledge what she already knew: she was stronger than most. *He's right about the police. You have to go back with him, for Ben and for all of them. He'll get lost without you, which will put him and the others at risk.* It wasn't really a decision at all. "Okay. I'm in."

"Let's go. And just so you know, I'm pretty fast. Do you think you can keep up?"

It was Sam's turn to laugh. "I set my high school track record for the mile last year, and I'm only eighteen seconds off the world record. What do you think?"

"I'll take that as a yes," Nick replied with a grin she could see several feet away.

"Good," Sam said. "Now follow me, and *you* can try to keep up."

Without another word, she turned on her heels and fled back into the mouth of the woods. For Sam, it was neither a fairy tale nor a horror story. It was just a Friday night in suburbia.

CHAPTER
TWENTY-FOUR

As Zack broke through the barrier at the edge of the woods along the backyards of Windy Tree Way, the source of the screaming revealed itself, and Zack took a mental snapshot of the scene before him as he adjusted the suppressed Glock 17 he'd taken from Jimmy at Sam's house. During the run through the woods, he'd slung the SIG MPX over his back.

A teenage boy around Sam's age was scrambling away from one of the hostiles, which was how Zack categorized them, since he knew they were all likely former operators—military and paramilitary types from the DOD or Intelligence Community. The gunman in Falling Rock PD fatigues and a Kevlar vest was nonchalantly walking behind the boy, as if taunting his prey with his casual attitude. The boy wore a hoodie— *didn't everyone these days?*—dark jeans, and a midsize backpack that Zack would've considered a tactical day pack in his former life.

The slow-motion chase was unfolding near a large play set that was an interconnected maze comprising a long slide on one end, jungle gym bars, an elevated platform with a green A-frame canopy and a rock wall on one side and a rope net on the other, and a series of swings on the other end. Addison and Ethan had one just like it, as there were only so many companies in America that made high-end, commercial play sets. Between the play set and the back of the house, a couple in their fifties or sixties screamed at a second gunman who held them at gunpoint as he casually watched his partner stalk the boy like an '80s horror movie killer.

For the second time that night, Zack was grateful for the chaos and commotion, as well as for the fact that he'd emerged onto the property at a spot on the left half of the yard that was out of the line of sight of both men. He moved quickly, the screams and the wind masking his footfalls on the damp grass, the backdrop of the woods providing a dark canvas into which he blended, but not for much longer. He needed to close the distance before he took decisive action to end the confrontation. He only had a clear shot at the hostile holding the terrified couple at bay, as the boy had scrambled under the elevated platform near a hanging tire swing.

Just a few more seconds. Zack moved at a hard-jog pace, the Glock tracking the gunman. He was equidistant from the gunman and the play set, and he slowed his speed to line up a clean shot on the hostile with the couple. Anyone who thought running and gunning was a sound tactical technique watched way too much TV or thought *Call of Duty* was the height of realistic warfare. A good shot required control and accuracy, and jogging was not conducive to either. There was a reason operators used a combat walk, where one slowed down to a fast walk with knees bent to prevent the muzzle from rising and falling with each stride, and even then, it wasn't perfectly accurate.

Zack transitioned into a hasty version of it and aimed the Glock at the gunman. The good news for Zack was that the couple was to the gunman's right, and any wild rounds wouldn't strike them.

Zack unleashed three shots in quick succession. One or two missed, but the odds were in his favor. He heard a grunt of pain as one round struck the target. He fired two more times and was rewarded with the sight of the gunman beginning to crumple straight to the ground, although he didn't watch long enough to see him hit. *Head shot. Good.* And then he focused his attention on the next enemy and the boy under the play set.

He didn't have a clear shot, as the two figures had merged under the shadows of the platform. *Oh well. Plan B.* Zack ducked his head under the edge of the platform, as the space didn't have enough clearance for him to stand at his full height. It was made for children, not grown men engaged in close-quarters combat. He was pretty sure this wasn't one of the approved usages in the play-set manual.

Zack accelerated, covered the remaining distance in three quick strides, and lowered his left shoulder, the Glock still in his right hand.

The gunman looked up at the last moment and saw a dark shape rush at him from under the play-set clubhouse. He had no time to react as he was struck with a tremendous impact that moved him sideways, knocked the breath out of him, and slammed him into the back of the steps that led up to the clubhouse floor. The Glock he held had been knocked out of his hands, and he tried to wrap his arms, to no avail, around his attacker.

The tackle would've made Zack's college football coach at the University of Michigan proud, but it wasn't enough to end the fight, and Zack wasn't about to risk the boy's life. He wanted to end the confrontation immediately. As the two men bounced off the wall, Zack pressed the suppressor against the man's chest and fired. He felt the impacts, momentarily forgetting the gunman was wearing a vest but reminded of it when a blow caught him in the right jaw. *Was worth a shot*, he thought, and felt another strike catch him in the ribs. The two punches were enough to stop his momentum. *Fine. Have it your way.* Zack raised the pistol to the man's head, but his attacker regained his situational awareness, grabbed the pistol, and moved it aside as Zack fired.

The bullet tore chunks from beneath the play-set clubhouse, spraying the two men with splinters, although the gunman caught most of the debris due to his proximity to the muzzle. The Glock wouldn't move, and Zack found himself in a struggle with an opponent who matched his strength, if not his abilities. *Okay, sport. Deal with this.* Zack fired several more shots, pulling the trigger until the weapon emptied, and he felt the slide lock backward. Each shot sent a spray of sharp, wooden shards down upon them, but it was the gunman who took the worst of it, as Zack had closed his eyes and looked away.

Zack was rewarded with a loud and genuine shriek of pain, and he smiled inwardly. *Must have caught him in the eyes. Too bad for him. Good for you.*

Zack released the useless weapon and delivered an uppercut that landed squarely under the man's chin. He felt the jarring blow and heard a hard *thump* as the top of the gunman's head was driven into the bottom of the platform. The man started to fall forward, and Zack grabbed the edge of the Kevlar vest at both armholes. He pivoted to his left and flung the man to the ground. He hit the side of the hanging tire and bounced off it like a pinball, crashing to the dark earth, yet somehow still had a little fight left in him. He scrambled forward, escaping the underside of the clubhouse.

You've got to be kidding. I'll give him credit for that, Zack thought. Before the man could go any farther, Zack leapt forward and launched himself into the air. As he passed over the wounded gunman, who was now on his hands and knees, Zack slipped his left arm under the man's chin and around his neck. His right hand locked under his left wrist as it crossed in front of the man's neck, and Zack pulled hard. His momentum and strength yanked the man off his hands and knees, and Zack landed on the ground with the man lying on top of him, staring up at the black sky.

Zack locked his legs around his waist, immobilized him, and pulled his left arm tighter, ensuring his arm constricted on the man's carotid artery. The man tried to struggle, but his efforts were weak, and within fifteen seconds, he was unconscious in Zack's arms. *Night night, sweetheart.*

Zack pushed him off, and the man fell onto his face in the grass. Zack pulled out another zip-tie he'd taken from Jimmy, grabbed the man's arms, and put them behind him. Within seconds, he had his opponent incapacitated and secured. *At least you didn't kill him, not that you didn't try.*

Zack was comfortable with the body count he'd inflicted on the enemy force that had invaded his neighborhood and murdered an elderly man. Whoever Barrett Connolly was working for hadn't done their homework or they'd have realized that Zack Chambers was a resident.

And then, well, they might have acted differently, at least removing him from the playing field before they started. But they hadn't, and Zack was showing them that, as throughout history, one well-trained individual with enough resources and willpower could shape an entire battlefield. He thought of Vasily Zaitsev, the legendary Russian sniper who killed more than three hundred Nazis at the Battle of Stalingrad. More recently, there'd been the Marine Corps legend Carlos Hathcock in Vietnam and Chris Kyle, the murdered Navy SEAL, in Iraq. While they were long-range gunmen, it was the psychological damage that they had inflicted on the enemy that was valuable in war. And while Zack wasn't a schoolhouse-trained scout sniper in the military, he was waging a personal war and removing enemy combatants from the suburban battlefield one at a time. If he kept it up and didn't get himself killed, the enemy would have to consider abandoning their plans. *I guess they forgot that a hostile force requires a seven-to-one ratio when trying to take an urban area.* While he wasn't a math genius, he was fairly certain that ratio no longer held. There wasn't an endless supply of former military contract killers, even in Virginia.

Zack looked at the boy, who scrambled to his feet, and he realized he was actually a young man, maybe a year or two older than Sam. The hood had come down, and blond hair that had been pushed up and back fell across his eyes. "Are you okay?"

Zack heard movement, and a woman cried out, "Josh! Josh! Oh my God!" Before the boy could reply, his mother rushed over and engulfed him in a hug, nearly knocking him over. The woman stared over her son's left shoulder at Zack. "Thank you, thank you, thank you."

Josh replied, "I'm so sorry. This is all my fault, Mom. I'm so sorry."

His fault? What did this kid do to unleash an army of private contractors on a suburban neighborhood? But before he could ask, a voice called out from behind him, and he froze. "Zack, I guess I owe you a debt of gratitude, even more so than the agency."

The voice was familiar and sent a rush of blood to his head, but he hadn't heard it in years. *It can't be.* Zack turned as Josh's father appeared next to him, holding the first dead gunman's M4 assault rifle in the ready position, comfortable and confident enough to use it at a moment's notice. The man was in his late fifties and trim, with black hair peppered with streaks of gray. He wore a short beard but kept his neck clean, but it was the look of amusement that caught Zack off guard.

Zack was surprised nearly to the point of shock at the man standing before him—retired CIA deputy director Brandon Harper, former director of the National Clandestine Service.

Zack stared at the man, and his features remained emotionless, but then, uncontrollable to even himself, his eyebrows reflexively lowered and he felt his jaw tighten. "With all due respect, I honestly thought I'd never see you again. At least I hoped not."

The man looked at Zack and then back to his son. "I understand, but here we are. We need to get back inside, and I can tell you what all this is about, but first, are you telling me you had no idea we were neighbors?"

Zack's eyes bored into the man, and he thought he saw Brandon flinch. "Let me put it this way: if I'd have known that you lived in Hidden Refuge, *I would've never moved in.*"

"Son, I'm going to say this one time, and you need to hear it: I'm sorry about what happened to you, but you need to find some way to live with it."

Zack nearly snarled at the man. "I thought I had, at least until tonight. It's been six years, *six years.* I now have two kids and a wife, and *none* of them know the life I lived at Langley. My wife knows parts, but I never wanted her to know it all. Like you said, the past is the past." *How could this be?* Was God mocking him from the heavens for trying to build a new life—one without violence and bloodshed? Zack believed in second chances, desperately, but maybe real ones were never truly given, just various shades of personal growth and forgiveness for the sins of the past.

Brandon nodded. "I hear you. I really do, but sometimes, especially for people like us, the past is *always there.*" He turned to his wife and son. "Please allow me to introduce you to Zack Chambers, our neighbor. Also, he's one of the best operatives Special Activities Division ever had. Now, we don't have much time, and there's plenty to talk about. Let's get back inside so we can figure out the next move. Zack, I need to know what you know, what you've done, and then I'll tell you what this is all about. Better yet, I'll make my son do it, since he's the one who caused it, although unintentionally." Despite the relief that his son was alive and unharmed, the note of accusation was evident.

Yup. That's the Brandon Harper I know, Zack thought as he followed the legendary CIA officer back into his house.

CHAPTER
TWENTY-FIVE

The four Hidden Refuge rebels sat around the Harpers' kitchen table, a large white oval that could comfortably accommodate six. On top of the table were the assorted weapons they'd acquired from the two members of the enemy occupying force, including two M4s and two Glock 17 Gen5s. Between Zack's SIG MPX and the other Glock he carried, they had more guns than people, reminding him of a Texan—one of two—he'd once worked with, whose motto was simple: the more guns, the better. He wondered where Texas Pete, whose nickname created itself, was today. It had to be somewhere better than in a neighborhood under assault.

Zack had dragged the unconscious surviving gunman and zip-tied him to the railing on the back porch, gagging him with the Gorilla duct tape he'd brought from Sam's house. *You could also never have too much duct tape.*

Zack looked at the Harpers, trying to soften the anger he felt for the patriarch of the family, focusing on the son and wife, whom he knew had been terrorized and were frightened by the prospect of what might have happened had Zack not arrived.

"Riddle me this before we begin—how did you know I lived here?" Zack asked. The question nagged at him, as he'd never *once* seen Brandon in the neighborhood, even though he was only one street away.

"Old habit. Call it professional paranoia," Brandon answered, opening his hands wide to emphasize the point. "Once we moved in, I used the wonders of Google and Zillow to pull up the listing for each home, and when I saw 'Z. Chambers' listed at 103 Arrow Drive, I had a friend in the FBI run a background search on the property, only to discover that it was you. I've considered reaching out to you so many times, to try and explain, but then I always talked myself out of it. I figured you'd moved on and I should let sleeping dogs lie . . . lay . . . or whatever the hell they do. One of the great things about Hidden Refuge is that with more than two acres for each home, you can see your neighbors, wave to them, but you don't have to talk to them if you don't want to. Personally, that's just the way I like it, and I figured you did too, after what happened."

Zack had to give it to the retired director and clandestine case officer. He always knew how to assess a situation and make the right decision based on that assessment. *Then again, if he's so smart, what the hell are we all doing here tonight?*

"I guess it was bound to happen, two former agency employees living in the same neighborhood, especially this close to DC. But it sucks that it had to be you," Zack said.

"Come on, Zack. You know the Intelligence Community is one of the largest employers in the Capital Region. Between NSA at Fort Meade, CIA at Langley, and DIA, as well as a host of others, there are *always* multiple spies or analysts living in the same place, even if they don't know it."

Zack sighed. "You're right. More importantly, you were wise to keep your distance. I'm just sad that it's come to an end, but I guess it was inevitable." Zack turned to the son, Josh, and said, "Listen, I know you're young—what, eighteen or so?—but I need you to think clearly and tell me what's going on, and more importantly, what's on that laptop you have in your backpack? No BS. Just direct answers. We don't have much time. The ringleader for this circus and I were talking when I heard your screams. He's going to be reaching out to me soon. Start from the beginning, but as a former boss of mine once said, be quick, be concise, and be gone—although you can ignore the last part. I'll likely interrupt you with questions. Answer them and move on. Good to go?"

Josh looked from Zack to his dad, who nodded at him to proceed. *It's always that way between kids and parents, looking for consent.* And he knew it would be that way for him someday too, if he survived the night.

"I'm a high school intern at the agency," Josh said, referring to the CIA the way that 99.99 percent of the people in America did, employee or not.

"Intern? Since when does the agency have interns?" Zack asked.

"Since always, Zack, especially in the Analysis Directorate. Most of the agencies in the IC have them," Brandon replied, referring holistically to the Intelligence Community. "They can work for us for two summers and then several hours a week during their senior year. When they finish, they end up with a GS offer to come on board permanently, intern with us through college under salary, and then hit the ground running full-time once they graduate," he added, referring to the government General Schedule pay scale all federal employees fell under. "It's a great way to find young talent, and it ensures we groom them *the right way*—no bad habits to break from prior occupations."

"Got it. Keep going, Josh," Zack said to the younger Harper, whose boyish looks were even more pronounced in the warm soft-white light of the kitchen.

"Anyhow, I ended up in the front-office staff of the Operations Directorate, handling random tasks that someone with little experience could manage—creating spreadsheets, tracking actions normal employees didn't have time to complete, travel requests, and whatnot. It's a good place to learn . . . and to see how some of the really spooky and cool HUMINT is done. I loved being there, and it helped that I'm a legacy hire from my dad," Josh said.

"Okay. I get it. It's all going great. You're learning the ways of the Force," Zack said with exasperation. He needed answers, and he felt the weight of time again, pressing him, threatening to pin him down. "What changed? What happened that has us all running for our lives and me killing a whole lot of men in police uniforms on a Friday night?"

Josh was a quick learner, and instead of looking to his father for counsel or approval, he answered quickly and directly. *Like father, like son.*

"One of the things I got stuck with is inventory. It's crazy. We have to account for every computer, headset, monitor, printer—basically every piece of IT equipment the agency has. The system is inefficient and runs on software that desperately needs to be updated, and we always seem to be either missing a piece of equipment or looking for one."

"Government bureaucracy at its finest, Zack. You remember that aspect of it, don't you?" Brandon interjected.

"Not exactly. *I* remember the hypocrisy and bad leadership that focused on the wrong things for political purposes and led to the potential loss of innocent lives," Zack shot back viciously, breathing deeply as soon as he finished. "Now, please let your son finish."

Mrs. Harper, an attractive woman in her late fifties with black, shoulder-length hair and a soft face, a woman that Zack had never met, reached out and placed a hand on Josh's right shoulder, both comforting and encouraging. *No matter what you think of him, they're a close family. He's not a monster, Zack.*

"While doing an inventory for monitors, I found a laptop this past Monday. It had no sticker or barcode on it. I asked around the office, and no one seemed to know whose it was. I even called our IT support folks, but they had no record of it, and there was no profile on it. The Windows home screen was password protected, and even a hard reset wouldn't open it. After getting nowhere, I left it in the cubby, locked away. I figured someone would eventually claim it. I even sent an email to the entire directorate and front-office staff but got no response."

Zack sighed, but before he could speak, Brandon said, "I know what you're thinking, Zack. Whoever is involved in this, Josh's email sent a signal to them that the laptop was about to be discovered or taken by the assets folks."

"Even worse," Zack added, "his email forced them to act. So how did the laptop that you locked away end up in your possession?"

"Like you said, someone acted," Josh answered. "On Wednesday, my internship with that office ended. By the end of the day, after my send-off, I'd completely forgotten about the laptop and figured it was someone else's problem. I'd packed up my personal belongings, and because I wasn't doing the internship next semester, I brought two boxes home with me."

"And you didn't open them until when?" Zack asked, although he feared he knew the answer.

"Late Friday afternoon, just before dinner. I had some time to kill, and I figured I'd go through the box of books and grab something to read, as it had a number of books about the agency. I even had a copy of this thriller about a CIA mole that some female analyst wrote. I asked her to sign it, which she did. She still works there, but the world doesn't know it. It's kind of crazy the regulations placed on her by the agency."

"Josh . . ." his dad said, encouraging him to speed the story up.

"Sorry. When I pulled out all of the books, I found that laptop," he said, pointing to the Dell. "When I saw it, I just stared at it, as if doing so would make it go away. I kind of freaked out."

"Freaked out? Why? You know you didn't take it," Zack said.

For the first time, Josh laughed. "Do you know what the environment is like at the agency these days?"

Zack didn't, and quite honestly, he didn't care. It wasn't his problem anymore, but judging from the tone of Josh's voice, he figured morale might not be as high as it was among people who worked for Google or Apple—or any other large private enterprise other than the federal government. "I don't, but I can imagine."

"One of the things I learned in the front office was that the seventh floor—as in the director—suspects there's a leak of HUMINT operations. DIA had some analyst who was sleeping with a reporter, and he was feeding her reports on several Chinese military programs DIA was targeting. It made defeating our attempts to target it easy. Seems like everyone in DC is leaking something, whether it's the White House, Congress, another agency, or even the National Security Council," Josh said in frustration.

"You know, for an eighteen-year-old who's just an intern, you seem to know a lot," Zack said.

"I'm offended, Zack. Really. He is my son, after all," Brandon said in mock offense.

"There you go again, making this all about you," Zack shot back.

"I pay attention, Mr. Chambers. I may be eighteen, but I *love* the agency—what it does, what it stands for—and to see the things I've seen, even if I'm just a glorified gopher, do you have *any idea* how cool that is for a senior in high school?"

Damn. This kid's a true believer, Zack thought with admiration and respect. *He's what the agency needs, not you and your cynicism. Your time has passed.* "Fair point. And I felt that way too . . . *once.*"

"Good. But what I was saying is that while everyone in the government seems to be leaking, no one knows who's doing it at the CIA. Some sensitive missions have been compromised because our adversaries knew what we were about to do before we did it."

"Wait a second," Zack interrupted. "How did we learn about that?"

"SIGINT from NSA. They were targeting the same people and caught communications discussing our planned operations. Needless to say, people freaked out, especially in security and on the seventh floor. People have been getting pulled for special polygraphs, some more than once, but as of last week, it's still happening. I heard from a friend who works in the director's office that Director Jamieson is furious to the point that he's borderline paranoid."

Jesus Christ, what a mess. If the CIA can't conduct covert operations, it's like benching your star QB indefinitely.

"Like I said, as soon as I saw the laptop, I freaked out. The last thing I want to be accused of is stealing classified material, government property, or worse. My career would be over before it even begins. Security can be overzealous, to say the least, to the point that people are walking on eggshells. I've heard horror stories of honorable and trustworthy people forced out of the agency for all sorts of things, often with no recourse."

"Now you're getting it, kid. The agency has *all the power.* It's one of the reasons I left. At least you know what you're getting into, and you seem like you have a good head on your shoulders. Sounds like the agency could use more of that."

"I believe it's worth it, and it's my decision to make," Josh stated.

Good God, he's a strong-willed one. "I won't argue that, but just to speed things along, let me guess—as soon as you found it, you told your dad about it. What time was that?"

"I got this, son," Brandon said, taking over the conversation. "I was in DC giving a talk at the Press Club on the future of foreign surveillance in an evolving technological world and didn't get home until close to seven p.m."

"Glad to see you parlayed your government service into something lucrative," Zack said accusingly.

Brandon huffed slightly, and said, "Didn't you? Don't you have a little private company that develops software for the DOD, unless my information is wrong?"

Zack sat silently, rebuffed with nothing clever to reply. *Bastard has a point.*

"Like I was saying, I got home, and Josh told me right away. I tried to log in using a few of the admin passwords some of the IT guys showed me at the agency, but none of them worked. I honestly thought the whole situation was odd, but it wasn't alarming. Like Josh said, equipment gets lost, mislabeled, misplaced all the time. It's a fact of government life. After thinking about it, and because of all the leaks the IC has had in recent years since the last election, I figured better safe than sorry, and I called a friend of mine still at the agency. Left him a voicemail, but I hadn't heard back yet."

Like a predatory lion that's just picked up the scent of prey, Zack perked up in his chair. *Who doesn't return a call from Brandon Harper, retired director of the Clandestine Service and legendary superspy of the CIA?* "Whom did you call?" Zack asked.

"Terrence Rockford, the current executive director of the agency," Brandon replied. "Why?"

Zack looked at him perplexed. *What is it with these guys and their country club names? Did they all go to CIA prep schools, Ivy League elites who wanted to play spy?* "You don't think it's odd that someone didn't call *you*, of all people, back? Hell, I don't like you, but I'd still return your call within minutes—even if only to insult you."

"You don't let up, do you?" Brandon asked, a slight tone that possibly resembled a hurt feeling in his voice.

"After what happened?" Zack answered seriously. "No. I don't. I can't."

Brandon only nodded. "If you're thinking that Terrence is somehow involved because he hasn't returned my call, don't. He could've been at work late. You know how that is, even on a Friday night. His cell would've been in his car or one of the lockboxes at the entrances. Not even the number three at the agency is allowed to bring his iPhone into work. Too much of a security risk."

Zack knew this was true. After the NSA's Snowden fiasco, all agencies increased their security to prevent adversaries from using cell phones to infiltrate them.

"No. My guess is he worked late, got my message, and will call me tomorrow."

"Okay. Now that I understand how you got your little treasure here, how did you know they weren't real cops?" Zack asked.

Brandon let out a small laugh, startling his son and his wife. "Seriously, Zack? After *all the years* in this business, you ask me that question? How did *you* know they were lying? Better yet, you even shot one before you knew for certain." Zack had briefly summarized what had transpired before the interrogation-in-the-form-of-a-conversation had begun. "He could've been a cop with a quick trigger finger—and the old man was *running* at him, according to you. No. You just knew a liar when you saw one, which meant the whole lot of them were impostors."

"That's fair. I guess if anyone would know a liar when he saw one, it would be *you*," Zack said, almost regretting the insult the moment it left his lips.

Brandon only smiled and shook his head. "And that's when I thought it might have something to do with the laptop and decided to keep us here instead of evacuating with the rest of the neighbors."

Zack continued. "And you've been holed up in here since they left? Don't you have a weapon or even a small arsenal? After all the covert work you've done? How the hell did they get the drop on you?"

Josh spoke for the first time in several minutes. "It's my fault. I freaked out when they came back to the house the second time. We were in here in the dark, and when the first one kicked down the door, I grabbed the backpack and jetted out the back, only to find the other one waiting out there."

"When he broke through the front door, I grabbed my wife and followed Josh. There was just no time to grab my Kimber 1911 off the kitchen counter. Hell, it's still there, not that we need more guns," Brandon said, sweeping an arm across the weaponry arrayed on the table.

Zack's mind raced. Before they could do anything else, they needed to relocate. He didn't know how many men Barrett had with him, but if he had more at the elementary school, he could call in reinforcements.

"Okay. Here's where we are. We've got what they're looking for. That gives us the advantage, at least in the near term. We don't know what's on this thing or why they want it, but we have it, which makes finding us their number one priority."

Zack checked his watch. It'd been nearly fifteen minutes since he'd ended the conversation with Barrett. He had no idea what the man was up to, but he knew that the more time he gave him, the worse it would be for all of them.

"Here's what's going to happen, unless you have a better idea. I'm taking the laptop, I'm going to exfiltrate out of this neighborhood, get a cell signal, and call in reinforcements, if Sam hasn't done it already." He'd also told them about her exploits and her current mission to escape and call for help. "It gets this thing away from these bastards, and I get to call in the cavalry."

"Exfiltrate?" Josh asked. "Who talks like that?" His voice was a mixture of puzzlement and awe.

"Former operators who never left the life, no matter what they say or do," Brandon answered, staring at Zack.

Zack sighed. "You may be right. I guess that part of me only went to sleep, lying dormant for a night like tonight. But know this—it's that part of me that saved *your lives* and is going to keep you safe. You're staying here. Get your gun, keep the two Glocks and one M4—I'm taking the other one; my SIG is almost out of ammo—and wait here. Take that radio," Zack said, and pointed to the leftmost of the two push-to-talk radios standing next to each other on the table. He looked at his channel. It was set to his lucky number: four. *I'll take any good omen I can get.* "Set it to channel four and monitor it. Barrett will be contacting me soon. If you hear that he's sending men here to find this team, get the hell out. Just leave. Go into the woods. Only fight if you have to. You know the drill. I'd turn off the lights too, just to be safe."

Zack stood up, placed the laptop in Josh's backpack, and grabbed the M4 and two extra thirty-round magazines. "Keep my SIG. I'll be back for it. In fact, feel free to load it with some of the nine-millimeter rounds from the Glocks, although now that we have M4s, I'd stick with that since it's more accurate at longer ranges," he said, handing Brandon the MPX.

His gear secure, the M4 in his hands, and the backpack on his back, Zack looked at all three members of the Harper family. "Any questions?"

"Thank you, Zack," Emily Harper said. "We owe you our lives and our son's. We'll pray for you."

Not an overly spiritual man—although he did believe in God after all the strange, horrific, and beautiful things he'd witnessed—Zack nodded. "Good. I can use all the help I can get."

Brandon extended his hand to Zack, who hesitated but then gripped his former boss's hand firmly. "Thank you," he said, and Zack nodded in reply, acknowledging the gratitude as well as the bridge of bitter time that stretched between them.

Without another word, he exited the Harper house, dashed through the backyard, and never once glanced at the dead man he'd left in his wake. He entered the woods once again, a hunter returning to its natural environment.

CHAPTER
TWENTY-SIX

Ben York sat with his parents and Percy along the railing at middle of the back of the pavilion, waiting and watching the men dressed as police officers, mostly focusing on the crazy one that had nearly executed one of their neighbors. The initial shock and adrenaline surge from the violence and death had worn off, and exhaustion was starting to set in, even with the heightened sense of terror. Fortunately for the group of hostages and Percy, the temperature had only fallen to the low fifties, although it felt cooler with the endless breeze and gusting winds. They all knew the cold front was coming, but Ben also knew that this entire horrific ordeal would be over before morning. It had to be.

Once morning arrived, with it came a sense of normalcy: early grocery deliveries, parents picking up friends' kids for sports, and even landscaping services—all of the Americana you'd expect on a Saturday morning in suburbia. And once that inevitability was a reality, the jig was up, as Ben's dad would've said. He'd been hearing it all his life, but he didn't know where his father had picked up the saying, although he was certain it wasn't from Elizabethan times. Parents always tried to sound cool, even when they didn't.

Percy let out a whimper, the stress and tension affecting the sensitive dog. "It's okay, boy. This will all be over, and then we'll have you back home. I promise." He leaned in and placed his head on top of the dog's as if telepathically transferring some larger cosmic knowledge. "I love you, Percy."

Ben felt his mother's hand on his shoulder. "We'll be fine," he heard Charlotte York say, and he turned to face his parents. He knew she was right, but he wasn't worried about them, even though they were the ones held at gunpoint. He was worried about Sam, about where she was, praying that she'd remained hidden and out of danger. His stomach was knotted, and he felt helpless, just as he'd felt moments after Mr. Flores had been shot and killed by the man Ben had fought, a man that was now dead too, shot by an unseen force in the woods.

"I know. I'm just worried about Sam. That's all," he replied, continuing to scratch Percy behind the ears.

"Son, she's a strong-willed young lady, and I have no doubt she's fine, wherever she is," David York said. He was a relatively fit man at the age of fifty-five, which was surprising, considering he was a highly paid, brilliant, and overworked commercial lawyer for a firm in DC. "All that matters is that she's not here."

Ben was silent, nodding in acknowledgment of his father's statement, although not necessarily in agreement. The fight with the killer had rustled something awake inside him, a confidence in himself that he hadn't fully understood but was accepting by the minute.

A wiser and older man would've realized Ben was transforming, shedding the skin of adolescence, maturing in real-time. But Ben was still a seventeen-year-old boy, only grasping the edges of the emotional process accelerating inside him. He'd been forced into a choice to risk his life for another human being, and he'd instinctively chosen wisely, doing the only thing he knew how to do: the *right* thing. He could feel the change, and it urged him forward to confront another issue that troubled him.

"Are you two going to tell me what's going on? I don't think it's a divorce, but it's also not a small thing, whatever it is. And after tonight, I'd like to know, please," Ben added, looking at his parents directly as he spoke.

"Ben, do you think this is the right time, honey?" Charlotte asked.

His mother was a beautiful brunette with green eyes, with the classic looks of an elegant actress from the 1930s. His father described her as a "version of Michelle Pfeiffer that Michelle Pfeiffer wished she could be." Ben hadn't seen any movies with Michelle Pfeiffer in them, but he trusted his father's judgment, and his mother's beauty was obvious. He was also certain it was from his mother that he'd inherited the soulfulness that Sam had seen in him.

"Actually, I think it's the perfect time, Mom. We're not exactly going anywhere, at least not for the next few minutes," Ben said. He felt emboldened with each word. If he could confront a killer, he could press his parents for an answer that he knew would affect his life.

Ben's dad looked at his mother, who looked back at him in the knowing way that married couples do, a silent acknowledgment unspoken between them. His dad sighed, and said, "First, we're not getting a divorce. Do you think I'd be crazy enough to leave your mother, the amazing and beautiful woman that she is?" Ben saw his mom blush, even in the dim lamppost-lit pavilion. "I've been offered a job, a very lucrative job, one with more money and more prestige. My firm doesn't know about it, and your mother and I have been discussing it. I haven't made a decision, and we planned on talking to you about it first."

Ben felt his confidence falter, his stomach tightening, not in fear of the men with guns, but of one thought, one singularity, or more appropriately, the *absence* of that singularity—*Sam.*

"Where?" He steeled himself for the answer.

"New York City, for a firm that does international commercial law. They're based out of London but have an office in New York, and they want me to run it. It's a hell of an offer, son."

For the first time that night, the possibility of a life without Sam reared its lonely head, and he shuddered internally. He glanced at the Flores family, the parents and the children hugging each other in a tight-knit group of grieving consolation. *I know I'm only seventeen, but however love is defined, all I know is I feel something that strongly for Sam. I want to be with her, no matter what. It feels like it's meant to be, as cliché as it sounds, even to me.*

Ben looked back at his father. "What are the options?"

His father smiled. "Always calculating the moves. I like that. I bet martial arts has taught you to think like that. It will serve you well when you get older, son. Don't forget it. As for options, there are two, and that's what your mother and I have been *disagreeing* about. One—we could all move as a family to the Big Apple, but that pulls you out of school, and I won't do that to you. Or two—I could get an apartment, live up there during the week, and come back down on the weekends. People do it, but then I'd miss out on seeing you both during the week, and I really *don't* like that idea."

Ben instantly thought of two more. "How soon do you have to give them an answer?"

"They want an answer within a month, but after tonight, I'm sure I could get an extension. Why?"

"How badly do you want the position, Dad?" Ben asked, surprising his father with his directness.

"Honestly, I don't know. I've always believed that family comes first, but this is the first time I've considered a change."

Ben understood that even parents, especially once their children had been raised to survive, as Ben had been, made decisions that satisfied their own needs and not just the needs of their children.

"How happy are you at your current job?"

"Actually, fairly happy, although the new job would be a challenge, and I do like challenges, especially when it comes to the law."

"This might sound a little self-serving, but have you considered using the offer to get something more from your current firm? I bet they'd make you a counteroffer to keep you. I've met your partners at the holiday parties. They love you there."

The enormity of the realization that his beloved son was maturing before his very eyes into an astute young man hit him in the heart like a blow, a mixture of pride and sorrow at the loss of innocence. *Not that watching an elderly man get murdered and four other people shot and killed likely hadn't already done that.* The pride outweighed the loss and David smiled, his eyes glinting slightly from emotion. "That's exactly what your mom and I have been talking about. You sure you two aren't in cahoots?"

"There you go again, Dad, showing your age. I'm pretty sure no one says that anymore."

"Well, they should. If it's good enough for me, then it's good enough for everyone." He smiled again, reflective and silent. "Fine. Since this family is a democracy, I guess two out of three votes have it—I'll talk to my partners next week and see what they have to say about it. God knows I've brought them a ton of business and made all of us very well-off."

"So, no New York?" Ben asked, hopeful that the idea of his father in NYC was no longer a consideration.

"No promises, but don't worry. Whatever happens, I'll make sure you'll finish out high school here with your friends . . . and with Sam," he added, grinning like the younger man in love he once was.

Ben felt himself blush, but he didn't care. He looked around at the assembled hostages, feeling positive about his future. *It will all be okay. You'll see her soon. It—will—all—be—okay.*

At least that was what he thought until the Falling Rock Sheriff's SUV pulled into the neighborhood and parked on the grass near the pavilion. A fierce-looking man stepped out, hair pulled back into a pony-tail, dressed in khaki cargo pants, a dark gray pullover, and a Kevlar vest similar to the ones the remaining gunmen wore. Every single person knew immediately that he was the real man in charge, not the one that had threatened to execute Mr. Simmons. The near-executioner moved quickly to greet the newcomer, who'd walked to the back of the SUV and lifted the tailgate.

Ben watched him as he left the rear of the SUV to greet his friend, the menacing psychopath. When Ben saw what he carried from the vehicle, the positivity he'd felt moments before evaporated, quickly transforming into a cold irrational fear. *He wouldn't do that. He couldn't.*

Fortunately for Ben, he had no real insight into the true depths of Griffin Huntsmen's pathology. If he had, the fear he felt would've been a full-blown panic.

CHAPTER
TWENTY-SEVEN

Sam led the way for several minutes, her feet pounding on the trail she'd already run just a short while before.

Nick Chambers followed, maintaining pace with her, although part of him was slightly concerned at how quickly and sure-footed the girl moved. *What the hell have you landed yourself in the middle of, Zack?* Whatever it was, it didn't sound good, although he was confident that his brother could handle it, at least until he arrived as a force multiplier.

He carried the silenced Glock in his right hand and the dead man's handheld radio in the other. Neither spoke, as both understood that the closer they moved toward Hidden Refuge, the greater the chance they'd be detected.

As they ran, Nick formulated their options, and one kept pushing its way to the front of the idea line. *The guard at the gate. He's the way in.*

"Hold up a second," Nick said in a subdued voice, not a whisper, which actually carried farther than talking quietly.

The pair stopped, the only sounds were that of their breathing and the wind in the woods. Nick stared into the trees to his right, but he couldn't see any sign of the subdivision. "How far are we? Better yet, where are we in relation to the main gate? I have an idea."

Sam considered how far they'd run, and said, "It's probably a half mile in that direction. There's a path that intersects this one and spills out about a hundred yards before the gate."

"How far are we from that path?" Nick asked immediately.

"Honestly, I don't know, but we haven't passed it, which means it's close. What's your plan?"

"I'm going to neutralize the gate guard, take his SUV, and drive right on into the neighborhood," Nick said calmly.

It was the calmness that disturbed her more than anything else. "Are you *insane*? Are you trying to get killed?"

Nick actually laughed softly in response. "Not at all. In fact, unless something goes horribly wrong, this will work, and then I'll be able to get inside the neighborhood to help my brother, *and* we'll have transportation."

Sam's mind raced to catch up to the decision that he'd already made, and she realized two things—that there was no point in arguing with him and that he was likely right. She was desperate to get back inside, regardless of the risk, to somehow help Ben, although she knew there wasn't much more she could do. Without the Chambers brothers, she'd be another hostage or dead.

"Fine. Let's keep moving and get back as quickly as possible so you can spring your master plan," Sam said with more sarcasm than she intended. "By the way, you still haven't told me what you do for a living, although I can take several guesses that might be close."

The two started walking down the path, studying the woods for the opening. "I kind of work with my brother, if you must know, but what's more relevant, what you *really* want to know is this—I went straight into the army out of high school. I used to be a Green Beret with Fifth Special Forces Group. Two tours in Afghanistan and one in Iraq sort of soured me. I left that life for a different one and became a US Marshal, of all things."

"But you don't do that anymore? How old are you? You look young— very young," Sam emphasized.

"Thanks. I'll keep that in mind the next time I'm looking to date college girls."

Sam laughed softly. "That's not what I meant."

"I know. I've been getting it my whole short life. I'm actually twenty-nine, the younger of the Chambers brothers."

A dark hole suddenly appeared along the path, beckoning them to enter. "Here we go," Sam said, and stepped off the main path. She felt like she was running in circles, although she knew she was moving forward, always forward, like her track coach repeatedly ground into her head.

"When we get there, you're staying in the woods while I take care of the guard. Is that clear?"

Sam had no desire to face down any more gunmen. "You got it, Younger Mr. C."

Nick was about to remark on the nickname when the push-to-talk radios they held beeped. Both turned down the volume to a barely audible level, and the incessant beeping ended. A voice thick with cold menace said, "Deputy Director—or should I just say Mr. Brandon Harper—how are you this fine evening? I *believe* you have something that belongs to me. You know what? Before we go any further, tonight is no night for formalities. I think I'll just call you 'boss' for old times' sake. You have a lovely neighborhood, and unless you do exactly what I say, it's *all about to burn.*"

The sound of the man's voice set Sam on edge for reasons she couldn't explain, like an "irrational" fear of a boogeyman that turned out to exist.

"Do you know who that is?" Nick asked, concern in his voice.

Sam shook her head, as she hadn't heard that voice on the hand-held radio until now.

Nick nodded. "I don't like the sound of him, and whatever's happening, it's going to happen fast. We need to move. Like I said, when we get close, I'll motion for you to stop and remain in place, and I'll do what needs to be done. Are we clear?" There was no humor in Nick's voice. It was all business, which Sam found both comforting and disconcerting.

"Understood," Sam said, inhaled deeply, and started jogging as quietly down the path as she could, followed by a trained killer hell-bent on protecting his older brother. *This is what families do. This is what Ben would do*, and the thought comforted her.

CHAPTER
TWENTY-EIGHT

Zack had reached the far side of Forest Edge Court, and unbeknownst to him, he'd been less than a third of a mile from his brother before Nick and Sam had left the main path to move back toward Hidden Refuge Drive.

The backpack weighed on him, not just physically, as he wondered what could be so valuable that the intern son of a retired deputy director would be intentionally placed at risk over. As Josh Harper had stated, the entire Intelligence Community leaked like a sieve at times, and Zack had been following it out of a sense of professional curiosity. He despised those who'd betrayed their oath to the Constitution, and it was for that very simple reason that he'd left the agency. He'd found himself bitter to the point of resentment, distracting him from his mission. The fact that the senior executives on the seventh floor were aware of what had transpired with his team and refused to act because the mission had been deemed "a success" had been the straw that broke Zack Chambers's back. He'd resigned more than six years ago and never *once* considered returning.

He'd been dating his wife at the time, and he'd told her he worked for the State Department, which was amusing to her when she'd met some of his "coworkers," actual paramilitary teammates in Special Activities Division. She'd commented to him that they looked like they belonged on a battlefield and not in an office. He'd only kissed her, laughed, and told her that foreign policy was a full-contact sport. She hadn't believed a word of it, and both of them knew it.

When he'd finally decided to pull the proverbial trigger, the first day after he'd returned from Malta, he'd informed Steph before doing it. The beautiful blonde with green eyes that would become the mother to his two children had known what he was leaving, and she'd asked him to be sure it was the right thing for *him*, not her. That selfless response had been the final nail in his government coffin, and he'd walked into his boss's office the next day and walked out of the agency two weeks later. They'd given him a choice, but it wasn't one that he could accept. The irony that his boss had been Brandon Harper and that the man he'd once respected and served was now back in his life was not lost on him. *Maybe it's some sort of twisted karma, everything coming full circle like some kind of dysfunctional family reunion.*

Zack kept moving, wondering when Barrett Connolly would reach out again. As if the radio were reading his brainwaves, a voice that Zack Chambers prayed he'd never hear again spoke. He stopped abruptly and nearly tripped over his own feet as Griffin Huntsmen, his former team leader and a certifiable sociopath, whispered not-so-sweet nothings to Brandon Harper.

"Deputy Director—or should I just say Mr. Brandon Harper—how are you this fine evening? I *believe* you have something that belongs to me. You know what? Before we go any further, tonight is no night for formalities. I think I'll just call you 'boss' for old times' sake. You have a lovely neighborhood, and unless you do exactly what I say, it's *all about to burn.*"

Zack's blood ran cold because he knew in that instant that Griffin Huntsmen would do exactly what he said he would, even if it meant killing every last resident of Hidden Refuge.

Zack changed directions completely and stepped off the path into the woods toward Founder's Circle. There was enough ambient light to guide him. He'd moved through much thicker environments while training in Virginia. All that mattered was reaching the pavilion. *With that evil monster on the board, your chances of survival just dropped, my friend. As good as you are, that lunatic is better.* And then, as an after-thought: *Thanks for the pep talk, Freud.*

"Boss, did you hear me? Or do I need to make my point by executing a hostage? I won't ask again. You have until the count of three, and then some unfortunate soul gets removed from this mortal coil. Don't *make* me do it." A brief pause, followed by, "Okay, then. Here we go. One . . ."

"I hear you, Griffin. Don't kill anyone. I hear you loud and clear." There was an audible sigh, and Zack imagined what was running through Brandon's mind, as he thought the same thing. *How the hell are we going to get out of this?*

As Zack moved back into the lion's den, he listened intently to the exchange unfold on the push-to-talk radios.

"There you are," Griffin said, emphasizing each word like a south-ern gentleman greeting an old friend. "The ironic part is that I didn't know you lived here, which I have to say, makes me wonder how and why you came into possession of that which I seek."

* * *

Sitting at his kitchen table, Brandon loathed the quirky mannerism and organizational structure of Griffin's phrasing. He talked like someone trying to elevate his own intelligence through clever sentence construc-tion. Brandon had no patience for it.

"Yes. I have 'that which you seek,' but there's no way you're going to get it, not unless you let the hostages go, at least back to their homes. You've cut off communications to the outside world. What are these people going to do? They're not like you, Griffin. They're civilians, through and through, and if you recall, you once swore an oath to protect and preserve their way of life, not destroy it." Brandon knew his words were futile, but he had to buy time to give Zack a fighting chance. He figured Zack was listening, and he was grateful both for it and for the fact that Griffin hadn't discovered Zack Chambers was also a resident. He knew that fact alone might have changed the entire calcu-lus for Griffin—and not for the better.

"You always had a way with words, Brandon. You knew just when to say the right thing, and you always made it sound sincere. I respected that . . . once. Unfortunately, that time is gone, and I don't live by that oath anymore. The agency chose sides, and it chose incorrectly when it refused to let me off my leash. There is an endless supply of evil men, terrorists, cybercriminals, and foreign agents, and all you had to do was let me do my job. But instead, you and the agency chose to reign me in, to force me to take a position at headquarters, a job not in the *field*, where I belong. Your words are hollow, and you never get to tell me what to do again," Griffin ended, the seething rage he still felt at his perceived betrayal by the CIA festering like an old war wound that never healed quite right and chronically became inflamed and infected.

"It wasn't my call. I told you that. The political environment was no longer permissive. After the ridiculous review of our enhanced-interrogation efforts, we no longer had a say. The politicians put the handcuffs on, and you know it. There was nothing I could do. It was way above even my pay grade."

Griffin knew what he said was true, but he didn't care anymore. He only cared about results. "It's irrelevant, and quite honestly, it's exhausting and a waste of my time to rehash old disagreements. We have more important things to talk about. Let me rephrase that—I just have to tell you what you're going to do, and then maybe, we walk away and allow you and the rest of your neighbors to live."

"And what is it you want me to do?" Brandon asked in resignation.

"Easy. You have five minutes to bring me the laptop. I'm at the pavilion. If you're not here, I'm going to light the biggest bonfire this neighborhood has ever seen, and I'm going to do it with your neighbors as live kindling."

Brandon's head fell forward, as if the weight of what Griffin would do were bearing down on the back of his neck. *You only have one option, now. No point in delaying the inevitable.* "I'll see you soon, Griffin," he said, and stood up from the kitchen table as his wife and son stared at him with fresh terror in their eyes.

"You don't have to do this," Emily said, although she knew he did.

"I have to buy Zack some time to escape with the laptop. Once he's gone, Griffin will have no choice but to leave. He's a lunatic, but he won't kill an entire neighborhood—no matter what he says. He knows we'd hunt him down to the ends of the earth for something like that," he said, sounding more confident than he felt. "But to buy that time, I have to go to the pavilion. While he won't kill everyone, he might execute someone, and I can't let that happen."

His wife reached out to him, and he hugged her fiercely. "You and Josh have to stay here. You're safe here. Keep listening and get out if things go sideways. I love you."

Emily stared hard at him, her eyes acknowledging the gravity of the situation, expressing it in a way that only the two of them understood. "You make sure you come back. Do you hear me? I love you."

"I will," Brandon said, uncertain if he'd be able to keep that promise. He stepped over to Josh and grabbed his son by the shoulders.

"You did nothing wrong. In fact, you did all of the right things. This is not your fault. Sometimes—and you'll learn this—operations, like in life, go horribly wrong for reasons beyond our control. No matter what happens, this is *not on you*. This is all on them. Do you understand? I *need* you to understand."

Josh stared at his father, knowing that what his dad had said was true. "I know, Dad. But I still hate that this is happening. It's like this physical repulsion I have to this whole situation. I can't stand it. It's just not right, and it's just not fair. I want to *do* something about it. I *need* to."

Brandon smiled for the first time that night, a genuine, proud smile. "What you're feeling—I felt it before. People refer to it as a calling, a purpose, whatever you want. The bottom line is that it's the innate desire to right the wrongs in the world. It's what drives men and women to join the military, to join our agency and others like it. It's what drove me when I was young, but you're experiencing it before I did because of tonight. What you do with it—that will determine the man that you become."

Josh hugged his dad instinctively. "Like father, like son."

Brandon felt the enormity of the moment, a combination of love, pride, and sorrow threatening to overwhelm him and prevent him from facing his fate.

"I love you, Josh, always," Brandon said, and broke the embrace, knowing there was likely only one way this would end for him.

* * *

Zack knew his former team leader would follow through with his threat. It was a veritable certainty, just as the sun rose in the east and set in the west.

God help me. I do not want to have to do this. But Zack knew he was the only one who could. If there was a fighting chance that his neighbors could be saved, he had to give it to them. He had no idea how many hostiles remained, and given the addition of the most dangerous man he'd ever met, psychological status notwithstanding, he had to try. He owed his neighbors that much.

One M4, three magazines; one Glock, three magazines; one Kevlar vest . . . and one bad attitude, Zack thought, and smiled to himself. *Time to get your game face on.*

As he moved silently through the woods, he thought of Griffin, Malta, and a promise he'd privately made to himself the last time he'd set eyes on his old team leader, a promise he'd spoken clearly and loudly.

"If I ever see you again, I'll kill you, no matter what the agency says about it."

Griffin had grinned that arrogant smile of his, his hair hanging down near his shoulders like a Harlequin Romance cover. "I look forward to it, Zachary."

As he approached his reckoning, Zack hoped he'd be able to fulfill that promise.

CHAPTER
TWENTY-NINE

The wind intensified, pushing Zack forward through the woods as he neared his final approach to the hub of Hidden Refuge. The cold front approached quickly, the temperature drop imminent, the blast of cold air denuding the trees of leaves the way that the voice of Griffin Huntsmen had wiped away the past six years. *There's no point in wondering why or how. For whatever reason, he's here, and you have to deal with him, once and for all.*

After the way their last encounter had ended, he wasn't eager to face him. But he also wasn't going to allow Brandon Harper to politely hand himself over to face certain death once Griffin realized the retired deputy director didn't possess the laptop.

Zack's plan was simple, as the best-laid ones often are—an assault from the woods in the northwest quadrant of the neighborhood, on the other side of the main drive from where he'd violently announced his presence in the earlier phase of the siege. He just hoped that he'd be able to kill Griffin and Barrett first, before the remaining contractors and hired henchmen counterattacked and overwhelmed him. The wildcard was his neighbors, the hostages. He prayed that once the shooting started—and it would start; it was a guarantee—they would run the right way. He'd been briefed on too many hostage situations that *always* ended with civilian casualties, either from bullets from the hostage-takers or stray rounds from law enforcement. It was the ugly nature of the business of hostage rescue.

Zack had once trained for two weeks with the FBI Hostage Rescue Team, executing in extremis hostage rescue missions under the most intense conditions—pitch-black darkness, blaring music that would make a heavy metal band proud, smoke, lasers, and even government-grade tear gas. The one thing that had stuck with Zack was that no matter how good they were or how precise their shots were, innocent civilians died nearly every time. *Well, you better have a perfect run, then, because no one else should have to die because of Griffin Huntsmen.* He'd stopped the madman from causing collateral damage before, and he knew that with a little luck, he could do it again.

As he drew near, lights from the hub in the middle of Founder's Circle began to flicker in the dark, solidifying in the widening gaps through the trees. His internal clock notified him that he had less than two minutes before Brandon Harper offered himself up as a sacrificial lamb to provide time for Zack to escape with the coveted computer. Zack just wasn't good with that plan, even though he'd remained resentful toward Harper for what he'd done, for it had been Harper who'd conveyed the agency's position to him regarding Malta.

Everything that Griffin had enthusiastically thrown in his face on the USS *Carney* had come to pass *exactly* as he'd predicted, and there was nothing Brandon Harper could do to prevent it. Zack knew Harper had likely tried to advocate on his behalf, but it hadn't been enough to keep Zack from resigning and walking through the door past the Memorial Wall and great CIA seal on the floor. The fact that Director Hartnett had retired and was on the speaking circuit, as well as appearing on cable news as a political and national security pundit, provided no solace to Zack. The damage had been done. *But you can fix it, at least partially, right now.*

Zack tried to soften his footfalls and prevent his weapon and gear from snagging on the surrounding branches even though the wind masked his movements. He found himself less than fifteen feet from the edge of the woods, the picture clearing with each step forward. He paused for a moment, less than five feet from the tree line, and waited with a clear line of sight to the pavilion, the vans, and the remainder of Griffin's assault force.

Three gunmen stood on the pavilion, M4s pointed at his neighbors, who'd been forced into a small section along the back of the pavilion. Another two enemy combatants were between the vans, which were still parked on the hub at the mouth of each street. *They die first—they're the closest.* And just north of the pavilion stood Griffin Huntsmen and Barrett Connolly, staring toward Windy Tree Way, waiting for Brandon Harper's arrival as if he were the honored guest at the Annual Hidden Refuge Gala.

It's almost time. He glanced at his watch, acutely aware of the weight of the laptop on his back, somehow heavier than when he'd first shouldered it. *Zero three thirty-two.* He thought of Steph, Ethan, and Addison, asleep in their beds at her sister's place in Richmond. As much as he longed to be with them, to hold them tight, to inhale the intoxicating scent of his wife, feel the warm embrace of his children—the way Ethan patted him on the back when he hugged him, mimicking Zack's movements, the way Addison curled her head under his chin—he was relieved that they weren't here on this night. They were safe, and that was all that mattered.

And then Zack Chambers did the hardest thing he'd done that night and forced them out of his mind, breathing deeply, allowing the calm before the storm to infiltrate every fiber of his being and focus his mind on one simple thing—*to prepare for violence.*

PART VI
SPY VERSUS SPY

CHAPTER
THIRTY

Pain, sharp and throbbing, split the back of Zack's head as if trying to chisel its way into his brain. Awareness dawned on him slowly, a recognition that he was in a sitting position with his hands bound behind his back. *I'm on a chair*, was the first lucid thought he had. His predicament flashed into his consciousness, snapping him alert, and he opened his eyes to see Noah watching him intently. His teammate was already adorned in full battle gear, his HK416 resting across his lap.

"How's your head, brother? He hit you with the butt of his Glock before we could even object. Say what you want about that man, but that fucker is *fast.*"

"I'll live," Zack said, fighting the panic as he felt time spiral out of his control. "Has it happened yet?"

Noah only shook his head.

"How much time do I have?"

Noah checked his watch. "Nine minutes." He stared at Zack, waiting.

"I need to give them a chance," Zack said earnestly, desperately pleading with his friend and teammate. "You have to cut me free, brother. They don't *deserve* to die," he said, reminding himself of the classic Clint Eastwood western, *Unforgiven*, where Eastwood's character says at the end, "*Deserve's got nothing to do with it.*" Yet in this case, it was everything.

"I already did," Noah said matter-of-factly. "Just pull your hands apart. Do you really think I'd let him kill innocent women and children, no matter what Langley says? You should know me better than that. I was a cop, remember? Protect and serve. I took that oath seriously, hombre, and I still do."

A wave of relief washed over Zack as he realized what Noah had done while he was unconscious—cut through the connecting piece of zip-tie between his hands. He twisted and pulled, and his hands snapped free. He brought his wrists forward and saw that Noah had also sliced through each binding encircling his wrists, and within seconds, he was free and moving toward the table, where his weapon and gear lay untouched.

Zack felt the seconds tick by as he secured the grenades and magazines for both the HK and the full-size Glock 17 9mm pistol secured in his thigh rig. The pistol was a backup weapon for last resort or very tight spaces, but the G17 was as reliable as any weapon manufactured in the last thirty years. He grabbed the team's internal Motorola push-to-talk radio, attached it to his vest, and wound the microphone through a loop in his Kevlar vest before clipping it to another loop near his shoulder.

The pounding in his head subsided with each beat of his heart and the surge of adrenaline, and he turned back to Noah. "You got the keys?"

Noah smiled a wide Texas grin and held up his right hand, dangling the keys to the second black Range Rover. "But I'm driving. He hit you hard, and you may have a concussion, no matter how tough a sonofabitch you are."

Zack smiled. "Fair enough. Let's go."

Both men jogged through the open front door, left ajar to allow the ocean breeze to permeate the farmhouse. Once inside the Range Rover, Zack and Noah pulled down their tan balaclavas and Noah started the SUV and slammed the vehicle into gear. The tires gripped the tan dirt and gravel, and the Range Rover shot down the two-hundred-foot driveway toward the main road. As soon as they hit the worn asphalt, the SUV accelerated left out of the driveway, rocketing down the old road.

"Just under seven minutes. This is going to be close," Zack said. "If Griffin and Charles are already in position, we need to get below them to head off the convoy before it reaches the kill zone." They knew from reconnaissance and following Belyakov's security detail that his driver had scouted the southern coastal approach via Triq tal-Prajjet. Not only was it a straight shot to the village, it was also the most scenic drive, and while there were roads dissecting the entire island, most people preferred the sweeping coastal vistas. Zack understood that it was human nature, and he prayed the drivers had stuck to the plan. The team had devised an alternative if the convoy traveled a different route, but it required a second vehicle, and at the moment, the elite team of operators had been broken into two independently operating teams pursuing different objectives. The only advantage Zack and Noah had was that Griffin didn't know they were back in play.

Zack glanced at his watch as the arid plains passed by on the left at dizzying speed. *Although in less than six minutes, he's going to find out with a rude awakening. And then all hell is going to break loose.*

But Zack didn't care. Both Griffin and Langley were *wrong*, even if they were too egotistical to realize it. *It's all up to you and Noah.*

The SUV approached an intersection, Noah slowed the Range Rover, turned, and slid through the middle of it, accelerating and allowing the vehicle to naturally regain its traction. The SUV roared down the coastal road that approached Popeye Village from the north.

It's going to be close, Zack thought, and watched the crashing waves batter the rocky coastline on his right, wondering what kind of storm they were driving into.

CHAPTER
THIRTY-ONE

Griffin and Charles lay hidden behind an outcropping of rocks thirty feet above the road, a two-lane unmarked stretch with no visible traffic in either direction. The IEDs had been buried the previous night in two large potholes sixty feet apart. The road had been neglected, and the two holes had been enlarged by the team under cover of darkness. They'd placed the canister-shaped weapons of war under two feet of gravel in the middle of the left lane, since the Maltese drove on the left side of the road, a fact the team had adapted to within days of their arrival. They were confident that both vehicles would get struck by the destructive force of the explosions.

The EFPs were powerful enough to disable and destroy the engine compartment of any vehicle, but the survival of the occupants depended on the timing of triggering the devices. Zachary had initially volunteered to operate the radio-controlled detonator, but after his sudden betrayal, Griffin had assumed responsibility for launching the attack. *And I'm not risking failure, no matter who's inside the lead vehicle.*

Griffin Huntsmen was a complex, ambitious, and driven sociopath—the last, a fact that the CIA had failed to determine during his screening, which included a lengthy background investigation and a full psychological profile complete with an interview with a psychologist. Unfortunately, the assessment tools had failed to illuminate the dark inner workings that drove him because he'd become an expert in compartmentalizing that part of himself off from the world. Ultimately, the same character trait that made him a valuable asset was also his greatest vulnerability, but he failed to see it that way. To Griffin, it was a strength, hiding one's true emotions, desires, and intentions. That alone would not have raised the red flags, but the fact that he felt no empathy toward others and successfully disguised it would have.

But it was too late by the time he'd applied to the agency, as the emotional and psychological abuse that he'd sustained at the hands of his father had shaped his worldview and distorted it beyond repair. When he failed to take the trash out *exactly* when his father wanted it, he suffered a beating. When he got anything other than an A in any subject in school, he suffered a beating. When he asked the wrong question, he suffered a beating. Years later, in college, after his father had died, Griffin would describe him as the world's greatest practitioner in negative reinforcement.

By the time he entered the agency, he was beyond salvation, and the only lens he looked through was one of cause and effect. The effect was always defined by his unspoken ambition—to be the youngest director of the National Clandestine Service in the agency's history. The cause was anything—mission, task, or other—that brought him closer to achieving his objective, which was why he'd entered SAD and quickly become a team chief, running missions with little to no guidance other than headquarters' desired end state. He described his philosophy to Zachary, Charles, and Noah with one brief statement: "They tell us what they want done, and we do it." Simple as that. And his team had, mission after mission, from Afghanistan to South America, from insurgent HVTs to cartel leaders. Some enemy of the great American republic always had to be captured or killed, and it was his sworn oath to fulfill that requirement. More importantly, to the compartmented core of Griffin Huntsmen, each mission was an incremental step toward *his* end state. The trick was to make the agency see it that way, especially when the powers that be were notorious for their determination to remain unsatisfied at the expense of their workforce.

But Malta was different. Deputy Director Harper had told him directly, "No matter what you do, those two do not leave Malta alive. Do this job, and I guarantee that one day, sooner rather than later, this chair will be yours." Griffin hadn't shared that insight with his team, as it was his cross to bear, albeit on their backs.

What made it all the more infuriating as he stared through a military-grade pair of tan binoculars was that it was so *simple*, so *easy*. Trigger the EFP and kill the remaining targets. But instead, due to the arrogance of Zachary Chambers, he was at half strength, with only Charles, whom he trusted only slightly more, by his side. *Fucking Chambers. Always has to be the white knight.* Zachary Chambers had a better chance of swimming home than preventing Griffin from eliminating the targets. Come hell or high water, as Noah would say, there would be death on the road below.

Griffin glanced at the IBM Toughbook, the image tracking the two-vehicle convoy as it navigated the desolate plains beyond the western outskirts of Valetta. The two SUVs were just south of the Santa Maria Estate and Ta' Bragg areas. "They'll be here within minutes. Let's get ready."

Griffin held the remote control in his right hand, waiting to flip the metal switch upward to arm the weapons. The button below would send a radio signal to both IEDs, simultaneously detonating them. While he didn't want to kill the women or children, if he were being honest with himself, he didn't care if they died. But Moretti and Belyakov *had to meet their fate.* His career depended upon it.

"There has to be another way," Charles said, inhaling deeply as the warm sea breeze poured over their position. He scanned the horizon, a vast flat table of blue that stretched endlessly in all directions. *This place is too goddamn scenic for an assassination. But what can you do? He's the man, and we've got orders.*

Not you too, Griffin thought, but suppressed the anger he felt surging at Charles's doubts. "Listen. I know this isn't ideal, but these two have to be brought to justice for what they did." He smirked internally, amused at invoking the catchphrase his government brandished to justify questionable actions. *You're sounding more and more like a senior executive at Langley every day.* "And we're the ones entrusted to do it. It's the job, Charles. You know that. Now cowboy up, as Noah would say, and get ready to do your job."

Charles remained silent for a moment. *Listen to your moral compass,* he heard his father whisper to him. *It's the only thing you can rely on to guide you through this life.* He sighed, placed his hands on the HK416 assault rifle, and said, "I understand," although he wasn't sure whom he was responding to, Griffin or the ghost of his father.

CHAPTER
THIRTY-TWO

"Drive faster, Noah. We only have four minutes," Zack said, and gripped the handle above the window as he felt the speeding Range Rover accelerate. The end of the road that ran parallel to Triq tal-Prajjet raced toward them, and Zack wondered if Noah would kill them both before they even reached the ambush site.

"One more right turn, a short straightaway to the main road, and we're there. We got this," Noah said with more confidence than Zack felt.

The SUV decelerated rapidly, and Noah navigated around the corner at forty-five miles per hour. The weight of the B7-level armor, which could stop 7.62mm rounds, kept the SUV on all four tires. Zack looked past Noah and through the driver's side window and felt a brief moment of triumph.

Due to the relatively flat landscape and barren plains on this part of the island, Zack was afforded an unobstructed view of the road adjacent to them. Two black SUVs moved quickly along the main road, Triq il-Mellieha, which intersected Triq tal-Prajjet and the dirt road they were on more than three hundred yards ahead.

The relief was replaced by a slight sensation of panic as Zack realized the two-vehicle convoy was going to reach the coastal road ahead of them. "I hope your PIT-maneuver skills are current. This is going to get ugly fast."

"Already on it. Just sit back and enjoy the ride," Noah said, his Texas accent rising to the surface.

As the Range Rover raced toward the intersection, the other two vehicles grew closer as the three SUVs reached the point of convergence. *Jesus Christ. They still don't see us*, Zack thought, and prayed for several more seconds of situational unawareness on the part of Belyakov's security detail.

The two Mercedes SUVs reached the intersection, barreled through while maintaining their speed, and raced up Triq tal-Prajjet. Seconds later, the Range Rover replicated the maneuver only fifty yards behind the second black Mercedes. A short zig to the left, followed by a short, straight patch of road and then a zag to the right led to the final straightaway that stretched all the way north to Popeye Village and the kill zone before it.

The two SUVs slowed down as they hit the first turn, and Noah accelerated, taking advantage of the convoy's deceleration. The Range Rover gained ground as the two Mercedes moved away to their left, traveling the short distance to the next turn to the right. Noah slid the Range Rover through the first turn, straightened out, and accelerated once again.

"Nice driving, Tex," Zack said, as the second SUV was only twenty yards ahead of them and halfway through the final turn onto Triq tal-Prajjet, where its doom lay a half mile ahead.

The adrenaline had dulled the pounding in the back of his skull, which made it slightly easier for him to concentrate on solving the biggest problem they faced: how to stop two SUVs with one in less than half a mile.

Noah considered the same tactical dilemma. "Brace yourself. I'm hitting the second vehicle as soon as we make the turn. We know that one has Belyakov. The security team won't abandon their master. Just get ready for the gunfight. Time to work," Noah said, grinning under his balaclava.

"I knew you were going to say that," Zack said, and gripped the handguard rail of the HK416 assault rifle, ready to engage. *Do or die, Zack. It always comes down to this.*

The Range Rover covered the remaining distance to the final turn, shot around it at perilous speed, and rocketed forward. Noah was the best tactical driver on the team, and Zack was thankful for it as he braced himself for the impact.

As the Range Rover closed the final feet, two young faces appeared in the rear window of the SUV, expressions of confusion and dawning fear apparent. In that frozen moment, Zack felt the terrible weight of what they were about to do, but as bad as it was, it was better than allowing Griffin to blow them up in a fiery death. Sometimes, there were no good options. *The kids. God, please let them be okay. It's not their fault their father is a monster.*

And then they were gone as the Range Rover accelerated and moved left toward the shoulder and the low rock wall that separated the road from the sea below. Noah yanked the steering wheel to the right, the distance between the Range Rover and the Mercedes providing a space in which to increase the SUV's momentum.

The right front quarter panel slammed into the left wheel well of the Mercedes with a tremendous crunch and potentially disastrous consequences for the occupants of the SUV. The rear of Belyakov's Mercedes was shoved to the right, exposing the left side of the vehicle to the front of the Range Rover. Unfortunately for Zack and Noah, Belyakov's driver was experienced and worth the extremely high salary he was paid.

He spun the wheel *into* the tailspin, even as the Mercedes suddenly shot toward the rock wall on the left, scraping across the front of the Range Rover. At the last second, the vehicle straightened itself out, and the driver regained control. Rather than slam into the low, rugged wall of rocks head-on, the Mercedes turned to the right and delivered a glancing blow, grinding along the rocks for several feet before detaching itself miraculously and then accelerating away.

"You've got to be kidding me," Zack said. "Who is this guy?"

"Shut it, Zack. I got this," Noah said, and raced forward for a second strike.

Explosions of big glass spider-webs suddenly appeared on the windshield as the passenger in the wounded SUV leaned out and opened fire. "Motherfucker," Noah said through clenched teeth. The two vehicles roared down the road, the Mercedes in front and to the left of the Range Rover.

Zack grabbed his HK and vaulted over the middle console into the back seat. He hit the window button on the left rear door, and the glass immediately began to lower, wind rushing in violently. "When I tell you, floor it, and sorry for the noise. It's going to be loud. This chase is about to be over."

Zack ensured the selector level was on semiautomatic and raised the weapon. He exhaled partially, said, "Hit it," and steadied the barrel on top of the door's windowsill.

The Range Rover shot forward like a malevolent mechanical predator running down its prey. More starbursts appeared on the Range Rover's windshield. *Wrong target, asshole*, Zack thought, and adjusted the red dot in the middle of the holographic scope so that it lay transposed on the shooter in the Mercedes's passenger window. He opened fire while the SUV was still slightly behind the Mercedes, the explosions of the gunfire deafening inside the Range Rover. The bullets struck the man in the black suit in several places, including the chest and side of the face. The black submachine gun he'd been firing clattered to the pavement and disappeared between the vehicles. His body slumped forward across the open window, arms and head hanging out, just as the Range Rover pulled up directly adjacent to the vehicle. Zack had a perfectly clear line of sight to the driver at near-point-blank range and pulled the trigger four times in quick succession.

The driver never had a chance and was struck in the side of the head and neck, his head slumping against the driver's window covered in dark red blood.

Zack thought he heard the screams of the children over the roar of the rushing wind, but he wasn't sure, as he was more concerned with what was about to happen next. With no driver, the Mercedes, traveling at more than fifty miles per hour, turned lazily to the left, moving closer to the rock wall it had previously struck.

Zack wasn't fond of movie theatrics, which didn't always abide by the real laws of physics, but he aimed the HK at the right front tire and opened fire. Sparks flew off the inside of the wheel well, and several ragged holes appeared in the body, but he managed to strike the tire. The tire exploded under the vehicle, discarding large chunks of rubber like a lizard sheds its skin. He prayed it would be enough to slow the Mercedes before it completely lost control and crashed or flipped.

Noah was one step ahead of Zack, and yelled, "Get back inside and brace yourself!"

The two teammates had operated together for so long and were so fully synchronized in their movements that Zack had already cleared the window with his HK by the time Noah had finished barking the order. "Clear!" Zack yelled, and the SUV moved to the left as the Mercedes struck the rock wall one more time.

The Range Rover smashed into the Mercedes, making contact along the entire length of both vehicles, pinning the ruined SUV between it and the rock wall. *Smart man*, Zack thought as he felt the Range Rover press against the Mercedes. Explosions of glass and the loud sound of wrenching metal erupted from the left side of the Mercedes, but the Range Rover pushed harder, and both vehicles began to slow.

Zack looked into the back seat of the Mercedes and was greeted by the surreal sight of Aleksei Belyakov staring back at him with hatred and fury on his face. His wife in the driver's side rear seat was turned around, holding the hands of her two children as they cried in terror. Zack returned the stare, mouthed the words "only you," and pointed at him simultaneously. For a moment, Belyakov glared at Zack, hidden beneath the tan mask, but then he nodded slightly and turned toward his wife to calm her and his children down.

The two vehicles ground to a halt, the noise and vibration ceasing as quickly as they had started. Noah pulled the SUV from the side of the Mercedes, moved forward a few feet, and angled the Range Rover slightly to the left in front of the incapacitated vehicle.

"Second vehicle is stopping," Noah said as both men opened the doors on the Range Rover, feet away from the Mercedes.

"I got it," Zack replied. "Can you secure Belyakov? Change in plans. No one else is getting killed today." He stepped out onto the pavement and moved around the back of the Range Rover, concealed from the second Mercedes, which was halfway through its turn thirty yards away.

"What about the security guys in the other vehicle?" Noah asked.

Good point. "Fine. Other than them, no one else is getting killed. We're capturing both Moretti and Belyakov. Langley and Griffin can go fuck themselves."

"My man," Noah said in his native accent. "Going *way* off the reservation. I love it. I got Belyakov."

The two men switched positions as Zack covered the second SUV by resting the HK416 on the hood of the Range Rover. As the second Mercedes came to a stop thirty yards away and faced them, Zack flipped an invisible coin inside his head. *Which one of you is going to die? Left or right?*

He heard Noah scream at Belyakov, the sound of a door being wrenched open, and then louder voices of Belyakov's terrified children. He forced himself to ignore the sympathy he felt for the two children, innocents who were being terrorized because of their father. *And you, Zack. You're a part of this, like it or not.*

Both doors on the Mercedes abruptly opened, catching Zack momentarily off guard. *Fielder's choice. I can roll with that.*

If the two security personnel had jumped out simultaneously, it might've made Zack's decision a little harder. Instead, the profile of a man appeared behind the clear glass on the open passenger door, holding a black submachine gun. Zack waited and adjusted the red-dot sight on the moving figure, operating under the assumption that the Mercedes's glass was bulletproof. Unfortunately for Belyakov's personal security guard, he wasn't as patient as Zack.

He brought the submachine gun up and around the edge of the door, exposing himself slightly, which was all that Zack needed. He pulled the trigger once on the HK416, the report ricocheting off the low rock wall to his left. The round struck the man in the head, and he collapsed to the concrete, falling to his side, the submachine gun still clutched in his hands. Zack shifted the red-dot sight to the driver's side of the vehicle and waited for the driver to decide his fate. Zack watched him, his hands on the steering wheel, and imagined the internal deliberation with which the driver was struggling—come to his boss's aid or flee.

The Mercedes suddenly lurched forward, and both doors slammed shut from the sudden momentum. For the briefest of moments, Zack thought the driver was aiming the Mercedes at him and the Range Rover, but then the SUV turned to the right, squealing its tires. *Wonderful.*

Zack turned to shout at Noah, who had already yanked Belyakov out of the vehicle and was shoving him into the back of the Range Rover. His family was screaming as their husband and father was yanked away from them, and Zack felt his heart break for them, but immediately quashed it. "We need to go, now!" he shouted as he threw the HK into the passenger seat and slid into the driver's seat, the engine running.

"Go! Go! Go!" Noah yelled, and Zack shifted into drive. Instantaneously, the Range Rover rocketed forward, and Zack heard Belyakov swear in Russian.

"Sit back, Mr. Belyakov," Zack said emphatically in proficient Russian. "You're not going to die today—not if I have a say about it. But from here on out, speak English. I know you know it, just as I know your native tongue." The surviving Mercedes had a head start, and Zack floored the accelerator. "And you might want to buckle up. It's going to get a little bumpy."

CHAPTER
THIRTY-THREE

Griffin was livid, his pulse pounding in his head as he watched the mutiny unfold at the beginning of Triq tal-Prajjet. He cursed himself for believing Noah would never turn against him, not out of loyalty, but out of fear for what Griffin might do. He'd made an error in judgment and been forced to watch the cost of that error play out before his eyes. *I'm going to kill Zack for this, one way or another*, he promised himself.

Once Belyakov's SUV had been disabled, Charles had packed up the laptop and slung the black Oakley backpack across his back. The two men knelt behind the boulders on the short, steep rise above the road, preparing to move once the IEDs were triggered. "What now?"

The two vehicles raced toward them and the ambush site, and Griffin realized instantly what Zack intended to do. *He's trying to capture both of them alive. Oh no you don't.* "We stick to the plan. We trigger the IEDs and make sure Moretti and Belyakov are dead. And then we get back to the farmhouse and wait until the commotion from the day's events dies down before we leave this lovely island."

Charles Davis stared at his team leader, comprehension and anger forming as one. "You can't be serious? We *cannot* trigger the ambush, not with Zack and Noah in the kill zone."

Griffin looked away from the approaching vehicles to confront Charles. He was finished masking his feelings and intentions, and his conviction shone through from within like a dark sun. "Of course we can. *They* betrayed us. *They* betrayed the mission. And *they* betrayed our *country*. I won't let that stand."

He turned back to the road. The Range Rover had closed the distance on the remaining Mercedes, but Griffin wasn't sure there was enough pavement left for Zack to dodge his fate one more time. In less than fifteen seconds, he'd know for certain.

"I'm not going to let you do this. They're our teammates, no matter what," Charles replied, resolve in his voice.

Griffin turned back one more time and was greeted by the barrel of Charles's Glock, inches from his face.

"We never kill our own," Charles said.

I'll give you that one. There'd be too much paperwork, Griffin thought, and lashed out before Charles could react. Leaving the detonator on the ground, he brought his two hands up and together, simultaneously striking the Glock hard with his left hand and Charles's wrist with his right one. The gun was knocked out of Charles's hand and sent spiraling to the dirt and rocks several feet away.

Before Charles could respond, Griffin struck him in the left side of his jaw, delivering two powerful punches with all the momentum he could muster on his knees. With his size and strength, the blows landed squarely, violently pushing Charles's head to the right. The movement caused his brain to shift inside his skull and shut down all motor activity to the rest of his body as it defended itself. Even as Charles slumped to the dirt, Griffin turned back to the SUV chase on the road, which had nearly reached their position. He knew Charles would be unconscious and then disoriented for at least the next fifteen to thirty seconds, which was all he needed to flip the switch and press the button on the detonator.

Time to pay for your sins, Zack.

* * *

Zack concentrated on the Mercedes, acutely aware of the two buried IED locations in the middle of the left half of the road less than a hundred yards away. The problem was that he needed to force the SUV to the right side of the road away from the blasts of the EFPs. The only thing he was grateful for was that they'd calculated the amount of explosives and copper slugs needed to disable the vehicles, unlike the ones in Iraq and Afghanistan, which were designed to kill and maim as many Americans as possible.

He glanced into the rearview mirror and saw both Noah and Belyakov securing the seatbelts across their shoulders. "This is going to be dangerous, and while I said I wasn't going to kill you today, if we get into a bad crash and all die, that's not on me. So hold on."

Belyakov's fear and anger sent a feeling of satisfaction coursing through Zack. *A bit of your own medicine. Good. Savor it before this gets worse.*

Zack unholstered the Glock from his thigh rig, shifted it to his left hand, and moved the Range Rover as far left as he could without striking the rock wall. He kept his right hand on the steering wheel as he stuck the Glock out the window and cocked his left wrist at an angle, the pistol aimed toward the Mercedes. He opened fire, praying the loud reports would have the desired reaction. He kept firing until he saw a starburst appear on the rear passenger window, the bulletproof glass absorbing the slug. The barrage of bullets had the intended effect—the Mercedes jerked to the right to avoid further fire, which was all the room Zack needed.

He floored the accelerator once again, and the Range Rover lurched forward into the space between the Mercedes and the low rock wall. *Fifty yards, Zack. Running out of pavement.* He turned the wheel to the right and slammed into the left side of the Mercedes, driving the vehicle into the right half of the road where oncoming traffic would normally be.

Belyakov mumbled in Russian, and Noah said, "Better pray for all of us, Aleksei. We might need it."

The right half of the road transitioned into a small shoulder and a dirt landscape beyond that sloped upward steeply. Zack knew Griffin and Charles were close and that his former team chief was likely losing his mind with fury, but he didn't care. He had bigger problems—the two IEDs were only twenty yards ahead, directly in his path.

While Noah was technically the best driver on the team, Zack was no slouch behind the wheel. Rather than panic, he acted, shoving the Mercedes once more to ensure the driver remained on the right side of the road. He felt the two vehicles separate, and he tapped the brakes of the Range Rover, instantly decelerating. Like a NASCAR driver who realizes at the last moment that he can't pass the leader, Zack waited until the Mercedes passed by him, and then he twitched the steering wheel to the right, sliding behind the Mercedes close enough to draft on him. And then Zack braced himself for the explosions.

"Nice move, Ricky Bobby!" Noah exclaimed somewhat manically, just as they reached the IEDs.

As the two vehicles passed the ambush site, the world exploded in thunder and rock as small chunks of pavement were propelled upward in two clouds of dirt. The windshield of the Range Rover was instantly covered, and the SUV was moved even further to the right by the concussive blast of the IEDs. Zack held on to the steering wheel as the right tires moved from the pavement onto the dirt, and the SUV started to vibrate violently. He flipped the windshield wiper switch upward and pulled the Range Rover back onto the road. The wipers smeared the dirt away, and Zack was relieved to see the Mercedes intact in front of him. *Guess that driver really is worth his weight in gold.*

As the explosions reverberated across the road, the two vehicles sped northward, the vehicular game of cat and mouse once more underway. *Step one—survive. Step two—capture Moretti alive.* A bend in the road lay just ahead, followed by a short straightaway that led to Popeye Village. *And more innocent civilians and potential collateral damage.*

* * *

While his sociopathic tendencies were a liability that often controlled his emotions, it was his methodical and relentless pursuit that dictated his actions. And for Griffin Huntsmen, as he watched the perfectly planned ambush literally go up in a flash of flame, smoke, and debris, it was the latter that urged him forward. *Okay, Zack. Let's see what you do next. I'll play.*

It was obvious that his soon to be former team member was intent on capturing Moretti alive, which meant that the alternate extraction plan might come into play.

He grabbed an encrypted Motorola handheld radio off his vest, and said, "Maintain ISR. Also initiate and standby for alternate exfil. I say again, standby for alternate exfil."

A young female communications officer in the USS *Carney*'s combat information center replied, "Roger, Hunter Actual. Moving alternate exfil into position. Standing by for further orders."

"Roger. Hunter Actual out." Griffin slid the radio back onto his vest and looked at Charles, who shook his head groggily as he regained consciousness. Griffin viciously slapped him on the right side of his face, and Charles's eyes flew open, searching for the source of the fresh pain.

"You're alive. And so are Zack and Moretti. No more *Caine Mutiny* stunts, or I won't just knock you out next time. I will *kill* you. We're getting the Range Rover and following our former teammates. We may be using the alternate extraction point." He paused for the briefest of moments and then added in a genuinely menacing tone, "Am I going to have any more problems with you?"

Charles Davis, former Navy SEAL and operator, stared at his boss and knew the man could've killed him, probably wanted to, but didn't. While his head was still buzzing from the knockout, he was thankful he was still breathing, but more importantly, that Zack and the targets were still alive with no civilian casualties. He remembered the SEAL creed and thought about the legacy of his teammates, the ones who'd fallen in classi-fied missions and locations, and he knew that his actions, while threatening his career with the agency, had honored his brothers. "No. I'm good."

"Okay, then," Griffin said, the cloud of dirt still rising into the air in front of them. "Then like you SEALs say, Charles, embrace the suck and move. We still have a job to do, even if Zachary just changed it."

PART VII

WINDS OF WAR AND FLAME

CHAPTER
THIRTY-FOUR

From the dark of the woods, Nick and Sam watched the Falling Rock PD impersonator that had turned him away earlier at the gate. They'd been forced to tread carefully into the underbrush since the series of light posts that lined Hidden Refuge Drive illuminated the last twenty feet of the path before it joined the sidewalk on the north side of the road. They'd moved forward, careful with each step not to crush a branch or rustle leaves more than the wind, which masked their movements with each gust.

For Sam, the fifteen feet they'd navigated through the trees toward the road until they'd had a clear line of sight to the guard was the most harrowing two minutes of her life. Her heart had pounded in her chest as if she were sprinting in a race in which the loser would be shot dead at the finish line, and the fear had threatened to incapacitate her until she'd pictured Ben clearly in her mind, encouraging her to move forward. Once they'd reached their vantage point, Nick had stopped in front of her, and she'd followed suit immediately, relieved that the moment of potential compromise had passed.

The guard stood next to a Ford Explorer parked in the middle of the road in front of the sliding gate, facing the inner sanctum of the neighborhood. Stenciled on the side was Falling Rock Police, and had she not known differently, she would've believed this was a legitimate police vehicle. *In fact, had they not killed poor Mr. Flores, you would've believed everything.*

The guard's back was to both of them, and he spoke into a handheld radio, although the words didn't carry to them through the wind and ambient noise. He paced back and forth in a tight pattern—two steps to the right, two steps to the left—over and over, as if he were penned inside an invisible cage, waiting to be freed.

Nick looked at Sam, the suppressed Glock in his left hand, pointed at her with his right finger, and then pointed at the ground, the order to remain in place easy enough for a toddler or puppy to understand. Given the circumstances and the level of fear she felt, Sam wasn't insulted. Her thought processes seemed to have slowed to the point that she couldn't have formulated a sarcastic response even if she'd wanted to, and she knew it was the fear that had partially paralyzed her. *Get it together, Sam. Stay calm and let Nick do what Nick apparently does.*

She nodded in response, and Nick nodded back, silhouetted against the streetlights. She braced herself for what she knew came next—a violent death for another human being, albeit one that wanted to cause the residents of Hidden Refuge harm. She'd never believed in a purpose for violence until now, and the merciless realization slightly sickened her. *The world should not be this way.*

Nick glanced right and left and confirmed that the street was still deserted. Satisfied, he raised the suppressed Glock, sighted on the back of the guard's head, exhaled, and fired.

CHAPTER
THIRTY-FIVE

Brandon Harper felt like a condemned man as he reached the end of his street, walking quietly down the middle as if he were the sheriff on the way to confront the evil outlaw who'd been terrorizing the town. *Which is kind of what you're doing, old man.* He pushed the vision out of his mind and allowed the weight of the Kevlar vest that he wore and the M4 that he carried to comfort him. A Glock was tucked inside his waistband near the right front pocket, the handle protruding visibly.

He knew this was likely the last time he'd travel down this street, as he'd calculated his chances of survival to be near zero. But he'd resigned himself to whatever fate lay ahead of him because he knew that he was partially to blame for the events of the night.

When Griffin and his team had returned from Malta, Brandon had personally and individually debriefed each one of them. Once he'd been sure that he'd had all the information available and an accurate picture of what had transpired, he'd met with Director Hartnett for two hours in the director's office. While Brandon cared about both the operation and the internal team dynamics that had nearly ended in blue-on-blue fratricide, Director Hartnett had viewed it through the additional lens of politics. And as with all things political, the facts had morphed into an alternate reality, one that was briefed to the president, the DOJ, and the rest of the

IC. Because of the presence of civilians, the mission had changed from kill to capture, which *had* been true. The why and the how were the key elements of the story that were conveniently left out of the official version.

But it was his meeting with Zack that he regretted most of all, for it would become the exchange that he replayed over and over in his head in his moments of retirement solitude. He'd thought he'd been doing the right thing, toeing the company line, protecting the image of the agency. But over the months and years that followed, the flicker of doubt had intensified into a full-blown conflagration of shame. What exacerbated the guilt was that he'd never had the chance to come clean and ask Zack for forgiveness, and with the way things were going, he realized regretfully that the chance would likely never come. He would go to his grave without making amends to the only person who'd done the right thing during the entire operation, a man who'd been sacrificed at the altar of politics for it.

As he crossed through Founder's Circle to the grass, the sounds of the terrified residents grew louder, but it was the sweet, pungent smell of gasoline that chilled him more than the gusts of wind. *Jesus Christ, he's going to do it. You know he will, especially once he knows you're bluffing. He'll kill you, and then he'll kill them as punishment.*

Brandon gripped the M4 tighter as he marched toward Griffin, who waved to him as if he were an old friend joining him for a midnight stroll. With every step closer, he felt the tension increase exponentially. The wind, the vans, the hostages, the gunmen, and the gasoline all combined to create an invisible level of electricity that threatened to explode at any moment. If that happened, only one thing was certain—there would be blood, and a lot of it. But he had no choice, and he kept walking, his Nike running shoes gathering dew like absorbent sponges.

Less than a minute later, he walked his final steps and stood before Griffin, waiting for the psychotic former operator to take control of the conversation, the way Brandon knew he wanted to, *needed* to. If that bought Brandon extra time, he'd gladly let Griffin have his way. A leaner, younger, shorter man stood next to the former SAD team chief, carefully scrutinizing Brandon with a mixture of hostility and mistrust. *You're smart not to trust me, young man.*

"Let's go, Brandon," Griffin said, as if it had been days and not four years since they'd last spoken. "You look good. Different but good. I guess retired life suits you."

"I was enjoying it, at least until you decided it would be a good idea to stage an assault on my quiet community and take the entire neighborhood hostage," Brandon said politely.

"It was unavoidable. But more importantly, it's the job, and you know how I am about seeing a mission through to the end, even when the means are less than desirable. Now please, hand my assistant your M4 and the Glock in your waistband before we get to the formal portion of tonight's ceremonies."

Brandon did as he was ordered and stood still, forcing the buzzing voices of his neighbors out of his head. The conversation he was about to have required every iota of concentration he could muster.

"Next, open that Kevlar vest and show me what's underneath."

Brandon pulled the Velcro flaps near his left side apart and opened the Kevlar vest like a perverted flasher, turning for Griffin to see his exposed stomach and sides.

"Are you satisfied? Can we talk now, like two former agency men who once swore an oath to protect this country and innocent people like the ones you've taken hostage, like the one your men killed? I know you feel betrayed, but this? Is this what you want to be known for?" Brandon pleaded.

Griffin smiled and shook his head slightly. "You just don't get it. You never will. I'm going to explain this one time, and one time only, and then we're going to have a serious chat about the laptop that I *don't* see in your hands or under the vest. But out of respect for who you once were, I'll grant you this wasted breath, as it may be your last."

The swirl of commotion and chaos had created a small vortex in which the two men spoke, oblivious to the world just feet away. Brandon readjusted the Kevlar vest so that the opening under his left side was only a few inches all the way down, a narrow strip of vulnerability if—no, *when*—Griffin decided to shoot him.

"You speak of legacy as if it's something tangible, something you can

hold, feel, touch," Griffin said, looking at Brandon with arrogant condescension. "But it's not. It's just what people like you tell yourselves at
the end of your careers to justify your existence, all those years of sacri-
fice doing the bidding of a bunch of politicians who have less honor
and integrity than our enemies. At least with them, we know exactly
who and what they are. With the politicians, their moral codes shift
more than these winds. They *don't care* about you, me, or the Constitution, and you know it. The system is broken, and until it changes, it
will continue to chew apart and destroy those that serve it. I consider
myself fortunate in that I had my epiphany sooner rather than later. I
almost felt bad for poor Zachary after Malta. Almost. But the agency
had my back in that debacle, as it should've. Even you had my back. I
often wonder what happened to him, but in the end, it doesn't matter.
The agency cut him loose and promoted me. But then things changed,
quickly, with a new administration."

Brandon struggled to retain his composure. *He has no idea Zack lives
here too. Good God. How could he not know? Stay focused and keep him
talking. The longer he talks, the farther away Zack gets from here.*

"You didn't have to go, Griffin. We *needed* you. You were a force to
be reckoned with. Think of all you could've accomplished. You would've
had my endorsement to replace me."

Anger flashed across Griffin's face. *Careful*, Brandon thought. *You
need to be ready. When he lashes out, it will be fast, and you'll only have
one chance, if you even get it. If you don't, you won't even know it because
you'll be dead.*

"That's a lie, and you *know* it, if you're being honest with yourself.
The agency grew soft, afraid to act, even in the face of overwhelming
evidence and intelligence. How many terrorist attacks, cyberattacks, and
acts of corporate espionage by our enemies are supposed to go unan-
swered because of political correctness? As for you," Griffin laughed, a
sound loud and genuine that startled the hostages, "I heard you were
no longer in favor with the seventh floor. In fact," Griffin taunted, "I
heard your retirement wasn't really a retirement. You were urged to retire,
rather than force the agency to put you out to pasture."

Jesus Christ. How does he know this stuff? He'd thought that only a handful of the most senior executives, including the director, knew the circumstances of his retirement. While Malta had been the end of the line for Zack, it had also been the beginning of the end for Brandon. The new administration wanted to focus on policies and negotiation, not intelligence and action. Brandon had been a casualty of that school of thought. He sighed, deflated. "It's true, but that doesn't negate all that I did during my career. We're all just cogs in the big intelligence machine, and my time was up. It's just that simple."

"That's my point—others made the decision for you. I saw the writing on the wall, and I made my choice before it was made for me. *I* am the only one responsible for my destiny, not some headquarters dweller on the seventh floor who never gets his hands dirty." His voice was filled with resentment and disgust. "I'd rather make a fortune my way than spend a life serving a thankless, soulless bureaucracy. I took my fate into my own hands, and I have *no* regrets. None."

And there it was, the unblemished truth—Griffin Huntsmen was a narcissistic, delusional, self-centered sociopath who only cared about one thing: himself. *Are you ready to do this, truly? You have to provoke him and hope for the best.*

Brandon exhaled and cocked his head as if he were studying an exotic animal for the first time from behind a thick pane of glass. "You really don't see it, do you? I guess it really is true what they say—crazy people *don't know* they're crazy. You're living proof of it, right here, right now. You're brilliant, highly functional, and one of the most dangerous people I've ever known. But you literally have no idea that you're out of your fucking mind," he finished, smiling and shaking his head in amusement, seemingly oblivious to the threat in front of him.

Griffin's eyes hardened, and he let his hands, which he'd held clasped in front of him, fall to his side. "This conversation is growing tedious. I only have two questions for you. One, how do you even know about the laptop? And two, where is it?"

He really doesn't know. Whoever is paying him didn't tell him. This gets better and better. "Have you considered why you don't know that critical piece of information? Your buyer really didn't tell you, did he? It's amazing to me how naive you are, but quite honestly, I find it rather amusing."

Griffin clenched his jaw, his entire upper body tensing as his aggravation increased. "You know, I won't hesitate to kill you and the rest of your neighbors. You should realize that, which is why I don't understand why you won't answer my questions. You're making this much harder than it has to be."

"Your *buyer* is making this much harder than it has to be, *you idiot*," Brandon shot back. "I know about the laptop because someone at the agency put it in my son's box of personal belongings after he finished his latest intern rotation. It came home with him and sat in his room until he discovered it today. But you didn't know that, did you?" His voice picked up steam, fighting the wind, which seemed to grow stronger as he spoke. "You know, I just now realized that I've been giving you too much credit all these years. You're not nearly as smart as I thought you were, because there's no way a smart man would get played so easily."

He stepped closer, cutting the distance between himself and Griffin in half. A roar built in the distance, and Brandon recognized that the approaching front was nearly upon them. *Time to take the plunge. Please watch over my family, God.*

"Someone has an agenda, and I *guarantee* that it doesn't include you. You're just a tool to be used," he spat. "Nothing more. You did the agency and the country a favor when you resigned. You were *never* going to be the director of NCS. You—don't—have—it—in—you."

Griffin's eyes narrowed slightly with each verbal blow, his entire body tensing with the rage and frustration that coursed through him. His former boss's words cut to the core of his belief that he had deserved the position, the throne that he'd actively sought, driving every decision for every moment he'd been employed at the agency. While he'd walked away from the CIA voluntarily, Brandon Harper's admonishment transported him back to a time when he still served the master standing before him. It made him feel small and inadequate, which only enraged him further. His voice was a low hiss, barely human. "Where is the laptop?"

Brandon ignored him and played the last card he had, one that had just appeared in his head, a verbal arrow that he knew would be near fatal to Griffin's psyche. *This is going to be bad*, he thought. "It's gone. Zack Chambers left the neighborhood with it as soon as your henchmen showed up. All of this has been a delay just to give him more time, but I guess you're not smart enough to see that either."

Griffin's jaw clenched as he ground his teeth in outrage at the insult and the knowledge that his former subordinate had been the one upending every phase of the operation and killing his men.

"And I'll tell you something else, something I realized after Malta." *And here it is.* "Zack should've been in charge of the team. He was always better than you because he had the maturity, heart, and the right mentality for it. In fact, *he, not you*, would've made an outstanding director of the National Clandestine Service."

The cold front fell upon them, the roar building in a crescendo, the trees bending and swaying, branches cracking in the dark woods all around the neighborhood. With the arrival of the sudden windstorm, Griffin Huntsmen snapped and lost the control that he valued above all else.

Brandon never saw his hand move, but he heard the explosions and saw the flashes as the Glock roared twice in his direction. The 9mm slugs struck him in the chest, nearly simultaneously, and he fell to his left, facedown on the damp grass.

The temperature dropped as the wind roared through the center of the subdivision, mixing with the screams of the terrified hostages in the pavilion that had begun at the sound of the shots.

"Griffin, what do we do now?" Barrett asked quietly, having borne witness to his friend's sudden explosion of violence. "What do we do about the laptop?"

His friend and partner ignored him and stepped closer to the fallen former deputy director of the CIA, the Glock pointed at the ground. "It's not over," Griffin replied, more to himself than to Barrett.

Brandon Harper lay in pain, still and quiet, struggling to control his breath without moving. The bullet impacts had felt like someone had struck him full force with a hammer, but the vest had worked, exactly as he'd hoped, and he was still alive. More importantly, his right arm was pinned under his chest, his hand inserted in the opening of the Kevlar vest, gripping the Glock he'd duct-taped to the *inside of the back* of the vest. He just prayed he'd have enough time to extract the weapon and fire. He tightened his grip and pulled, peeling the gun away from the Kevlar, and steadied himself for what came next.

Brandon Harper would've died had it not been for the screeching of tires followed by the explosion of more gunshots. While a breaking branch had condemned and startled Kevin Oliver into murdering the charging Esli Flores, the new diversion had the exact opposite effect, saving Brandon's life. Mother Nature had been ruthless, but unbeknownst to him, human nature in its desire to preserve life had saved his.

In one quick move, he rolled to the right, yanked the Glock from inside his vest, and pointed it at the looming figure of Griffin Huntsmen. His former operative had turned away to look back over his shoulder, exposing himself to the new threat that lay several feet in front of him.

Barrett Connolly had also been distracted by the sudden sounds of combat, but unlike Griffin, his focus was always on the tactical situation, which was why he'd quickly glanced at the figure on the ground just in time to see the Glock move into position, duct tape attached to its side. *Smart bastard*, Barrett thought, and raised his own Glock. "Move!"

The sound of Barrett's voice spurred Griffin into action, and he lunged to the left, but not quickly enough, as both weapons fired simultaneously.

Brandon Harper's bullet struck Griffin Huntsmen in the right shoulder, tearing through cartilage, ligaments, and tendons. The Glock Griffin held fell from his right hand to the grass.

Given the circumstances, it was a worthy shot and a valiant effort to end his former protégé's life. He would've been satisfied with the result, had it not been for the more precise fire from Barrett Connolly that struck him in the side of the head. Brandon Harper—legendary clandestine operative, retired deputy director of the National Clandestine Service, husband, and father—was no more.

CHAPTER
THIRTY-SIX

Killing the guard hadn't been the hard part. The shot had been a question of aim, and Nick, an expert marksman, had had the luxury and the time to exhale, expelling all breath as he slowly caressed the trigger backward until the suppressed Glock had bucked and coughed loudly in his hand. The guard had been standing one moment and in the next had collapsed to the pavement, motionless.

The act of killing the gunman, as easy as applying six and a half pounds of pressure on the trigger, troubled him, as it was more of an execution than a straight-up gunfight with an enemy combatant, but it wasn't as troubling as the thought of these men terrorizing his brother's neighborhood.

The hard part had been finding the keys to the Ford Explorer. They'd assumed, incorrectly, that the key fob would be in his pants or in the vehicle. After a panicked minute following a fruitless search of the vehicle and the dead man's pants, Nick noticed a small coil attached to a loop on the Kevlar vest that disappeared inside a magazine pouch attached to the front of the vest. He'd yanked the coil and pulled out the keys to the SUV.

He pulled the dead man to the side of the road and removed his Glock, although Nick didn't think anyone would be looting bodies for weapons if things spiraled out of control. A minute later, they were through the gate and had approached Founder's Circle. The plan had been to circle the hub and hope that they weren't spotted while trying to get a better layout of the battleground, what his command J-2, the intelligence officer, would call "preparation of the battlespace." More importantly, he needed to find his brother. He knew his brother wouldn't let this travesty go unpunished, and he absolutely would not abandon his neighbors to their demise.

As soon as they'd turned right onto Founder's Circle, Sam had gasped in horror and pointed, and Nick had turned his head just in time to see a big man with a ponytail in a Falling Rock Kevlar vest near the backside of the pavilion point a pistol at another man in a similar vest and pull the trigger.

Sam inhaled sharply as the second man collapsed, and she immediately knew that whoever the killer was, the much older man he'd shot had likely been a resident.

"Sam, get down now!" Nick ordered, yanked the wheel to the left, and accelerated.

The Ford Explorer leapt over the curb and onto the grass, barreling straight for the pavilion and the three guards that held the remaining residents hostage. Nick scanned the rest of the area. *Three in front of me, Ponytail and another in the back of the pavilion, and two others near one of the three vans, fifty yards away. These three are the priority.*

Two gunmen on the pavilion had descended the short steps to the grass at the appearance of the SUV, and as the vehicle tore across the grass toward them, they raised their M4s and fired in unison.

The slugs impacted the windshield and created a patchwork of starbursts in Nick's field of view. Sam shrieked in terror at the sound, as if baseballs were being thrown in rapid-fire succession by the world's angriest pitcher.

"We're fine," Nick said calmly. "Bulletproof glass. I thought the glass looked a little thick."

The men continued to fire, but for reasons only they could explain, they remained fixed to the ground, even as the SUV closed the distance.

"You *thought*?" Sam yelled at him angrily from below the dashboard.

"Relax. Now, hold on down there. You're going to feel a bump or two," Nick said, and floored the SUV. When the Ford Explorer was less than ten feet from the two gunmen, Nick turned the wheel to the left, and pumped the brakes, putting the SUV into a slide on the wet grass. The SUV struck both shooters simultaneously, as if they were bowling pins set slightly apart.

The front right corner smashed into the legs of the first shooter, who screamed upon impact, although his scream didn't last long. The force placed on the lower half of his body caused the top half to smash forward face-first onto the hood of the SUV, breaking his nose, jaw, and cheekbones.

The second man received a slightly less painful but no less lethal impact as the passenger mirror slammed into his chest and shattered his sternum with blunt force.

As the SUV skidded to a halt almost immediately upon impact, both men were flung off the Explorer. The first man, whose legs had been shattered and face ruined, was propelled backward into the steps, and the base of his head struck the edge of a step, crushing his skull and vertebrae, leaving him to die unconscious. The second shooter was flung backward and upward, as if he'd been shot out of a cannon. He flew up and over the stairs, spinning to his right from the blow to his chest. He nearly cleared the landing, but his right foot caught the lip of the top step, violently ending the flight of the gunman. Temporarily anchored to the pavilion, he slammed down to the surface as though pushed from above and behind. Unfortunately for him, he hadn't released the M4, and as he struck the pavilion floor, his throat slammed down on the top of the red-dot scope with enough force to rupture his trachea and obstruct his airway. He convulsed on the floor as he began to suffocate, spasming in unspoken agony during the final moments of his life.

Sam sat up in the seat and looked out the window at the pandemonium inside the pavilion.

As the two gunmen had opened fire on the SUV, the residents had stood up as one and inched closer to the sole shooter who held them at bay. The crash and violent deaths of his two partners in crime had caused him to look away from the throng just feet from him. The last shooter turned toward the SUV, swinging the M4 down and around toward Sam, which was when Sam saw Ben for the first time that night, and her heart leapt at the sight of him.

He was just behind the shooter, creeping forward. She realized his intent, and her mind panicked in fear for him. She grabbed the handle to open the door, to shout at him to stop what he was about to do, and pulled the release just as her boyfriend launched himself at the gunman.

CHAPTER
THIRTY-SEVEN

Once the man in the ponytail had arrived, a new sense of dread had fallen over the crowd, as they all recognized that he was the real man in charge of the operation, not the arrogant, wild-eyed Irishman. To the horror and shock of them all, he'd taken the huge gasoline cans from the back of the SUV and emptied their contents around the entire base of the pavilion, until the stench of gasoline hung over the crowd despite the wind whipping around them. But even then, the residents didn't truly believe he'd light a fire that would incinerate all of them. They figured it was just a bluff, a threat to obtain whatever he was looking for from whoever had it.

But Ben hadn't thought it was a bluff. There was something *sinister* about the man, and it disturbed Ben greatly. It was also why he'd hadn't been shocked when one of his older neighbors he didn't recognize—he assumed he was a neighbor, although he was dressed like Ponytail—had been shot point-blank in the chest and then executed by the Irishman as he lay on the ground after shooting Ponytail. He was reminded of an old movie called *True Romance*—where everyone shot each other at the end in one final blaze of glory—and forced the recollection out of his mind.

The crowd had stood up, even as their three captors yelled at them to stay seated. The shooting had initiated an invisible tug-of-war for control, with the residents resisting. Some of the men, including Ben, knew their captors couldn't kill all of them, but the residents had waited, at least until the SUV crashed the party.

Once the first two shooters had been killed or incapacitated—Ben didn't know which—he'd made a decision: attack the last gunman, no matter what. He felt confident he could disarm him, and he stepped closer, only feet away, when he saw Sam in the passenger side of the SUV, staring in his direction.

He knew the vehicle was bulletproof, as he'd just watched the two other men hit it dozens of times without penetrating the windshield. But Ben didn't know enough, or anything, about vehicle armor to know whether the passenger door's glass was also bulletproof. As the remaining gunman brought his black assault rifle up toward the SUV and Sam inside it, Ben instinctively leapt forward with hostile intent.

While he wasn't a football player, he'd spent hours mastering various takedown maneuvers, and he slammed his left shoulder into the man's side as he struck out at the rifle just under the barrel in front of the magazine. As the gunman was knocked forward off his feet, the barrel rose a few inches from Ben's blow just as Sam opened the door.

The burst of fire struck the hood of the SUV, leaving a trail of dents across it before additional rounds sailed away into the woods across the street. Sam, recognizing her nearly fatal mistake, dropped flat to the grass, just below the steps and out of the line of fire.

Ben's only thought was simple—*Have to get the rifle away from him.* An expert in judo techniques, he clambered up the back of the man and snaked his left arm around his throat. He torqued his legs around the man's torso and pinned the rifle to the floor of the pavilion, locking it in place with his right heel and calf. He squeezed his left arm, and screamed, "Someone, get the gun! Please!"

The man bucked in his grasp and managed to pull the trigger one more time, sending another hail of bullets into the open area, shattering the back window of one of the vans. As Ben held on, there was a great commotion all around them, and he felt the chill from the temperature drop caused by the wall of wind.

A loud *whoosh* erupted from behind him, just as dark brown hiking boots appeared out of nowhere and stomped on the gunman's wrist and hand. Ben heard and *felt* the impact as several bones in the man's hand and wrist were shattered. The gunman screamed in agony, and Ben heard the owner of the hiking boots order, "Let him go, quickly!"

Ben had spent years taking instruction and responding to orders from his sensei. The tone of the command was no different, and he released his chokehold just as the butt of a gun struck the screaming man in the jaw. His body went limp, and he collapsed to the floor, unconscious.

Ben rolled onto his back and looked up to see a man with a serious expression staring down at him. "Thanks," he said.

"Get up. There's no time," the man said.

Screams exploded from behind as a wave of warmth reached him, and he realized that what he'd known was not just a bluff had erupted into a fiery reality. Ben scrambled to his feet as the newcomer who'd helped him yelled for the residents to move as quickly as possible out of the pavilion.

The flames raced from the back of the pavilion around both sides with malicious intent to meet at the front steps. Ben heard Sam scream his name, but he had to ensure his parents and the rest of the residents escaped the building conflagration. Smoke began to billow over the railing into the pavilion, but the flames hadn't reached the front steps.

"Come on, son. Let's get off this deathtrap," his father said, appearing beside him with his mother. His father yanked the unconscious gunman by the back of his vest where the soft handle protruded and began to pull his dead weight across the floor.

Fewer than ten people remained on the pavilion, when more gunfire erupted from the north part of the hub, striking the crashed SUV and the steps to the pavilion. More screams, fire, and smoke rose into the night, and the newcomer fired his pistol at an unseen target.

He must have missed, as more gunfire peppered the front of the pavilion, just as Sam leapt up onto it and the twin flames closed in a circle of warm embrace behind her.

CHAPTER
THIRTY-EIGHT

Before Brandon Harper had approached Griffin and Barrett, the two men on patrol had moved to the northeast side of the pavilion, and Zack had lost sight of the shooters behind the gigantic playground. He'd had to work his way to the right, slowly, through the edge of the woods, until he'd found a clear line of sight. By then, Brandon Harper was already engaged in a heated conversation with Griffin, which only heightened Zack's concern, which was also when the SUV appeared. Zack had decided to break cover but held his position until the Explorer had passed.

When the SUV had reached Founder's Circle and turned right, Zack had glimpsed the driver and was shocked to see the profile of his brother, Nick. He'd smiled at the knowledge that his brother, a formidable warrior in his own right, had been shrewd enough to realize that something unusual had happened at Hidden Refuge when all communications had been lost.

As Nick turned the Explorer right, Zack had no idea what his little brother was planning, and he didn't care. His presence alone was a force multiplier on the suburban battlefield. That fact was enough to propel Zack into action, and he broke from the tree line just as Brandon Harper was shot in the chest. Zack skidded to a stop as he leapt off the curb onto the street. He estimated he was eighty to ninety yards away, and even with the howling winds, the odds favored him in the standing position to take Griffin down.

He might've had a chance to save Brandon, but the two combatants who'd been between the vans appeared in the EOTech scope, obstructing his view. He held his fire, as the two men hadn't seen him and kept walking toward the pavilion, their heads turned to the drama playing out with their leader. If Zack fired, he'd be compromised, and he'd likely lose his shot at Griffin.

The two men cleared his scope, and Zack was afforded a view of Brandon Harper's final act of valor and defiance as his former boss shot Griffin and was subsequently killed by Barrett Connolly. Zack's mind recoiled in outrage and horror, and he prepared to fire, when the sound of more gunfire from the pavilion distracted him. *So that's your plan. Not very subtle, Nick.*

His brother's SUV raced across the grass toward the three shooters, who in turn unleashed a stream of gunfire at the attacking Explorer. Zack instantly made a tactical decision—assist his brother and deal with Griffin and Barrett afterward. *Family first, always.*

He shifted the scope to the right and reacquired the two men who'd walked through his field of view. They'd both stopped walking and were in the process of bringing their M4s to bear on Nick's vehicle. Zack placed the red dot of the EOTech on the man closest to him and pulled the trigger.

The first round went wide, and Zack cursed under his breath, but the second and third shots caught him in the right shoulder and the side of the neck. Even as the first gunman began to fall, Zack adjusted the sight and placed the dot on the head of the second shooter, who, to his credit, had spotted Zack and was moving to return fire. There just wasn't enough time for him.

The sounds of carnage continued, and he forced himself to ignore the two loud thumps as his brother stopped the Explorer near the steps of the pavilion. *First things first.*

A single shot to the man's head ended his futile attempt to engage

Zack, and he fell to the grass, already dead, beating his friend into the afterlife as the blood and life still flowed from his friend's ruined neck.

A flash of light flared from behind the pavilion, and flames bloomed up from behind the structure as if the gates of hell had been opened beneath it. The flames spread quickly, encircling the structure. Zack ran toward the chaos, when more gunfire erupted from his left. *What now?*

He scanned the hub, his eyes moving across the abandoned vans, the playground, the two dead shooters, and the Falling Rock PD Ford Explorer that had been parked behind the van at the mouth of Forest Edge Court. *Bingo.*

The driver's door was open as a man—*it's Barrett; has to be*—fired at Nick's SUV, striking the hood and the steps of the pavilion. Unfortunately, Zack had no clear shot since the door provided cover, and Barrett appeared to be sitting on the edge of the driver's seat, facing the pavilion as he fired with an M4. There was enough light for Zack to see a passenger in the right front seat.

Zack glanced at the pavilion as he ran toward the Explorer, praying that Barrett's fire would find no innocent victims. *It's a diversion. The fire and the suppression. They're just trying to buy time to make their escape.*

He didn't need to kill Barrett. He just needed him to stop shooting. Zack slid to a halt, aimed the M4 at the door, and opened fire. Rounds struck the roof, the door, the door's window, and the left front quarter panel, sending sparks showering across the grass and starbursts across the driver's window. The gunfire had the intended effect, and Barrett stopped and ducked back inside the vehicle.

The weapon emptied, and Zack rotated the M4 slightly to the right, ejected the magazine, and inserted with his left hand a fresh one from a pouch on the front of the Kevlar vest. He slammed the charging handle backward with his left hand, and the bolt slid forward, a fresh round in the chamber.

The tactical reload had taken less than two seconds, but in that time, Barrett had closed the door, leaving Zack no target to engage.

Zack sprinted to the pavilion as the Ford Explorer slowly pulled off the grass and onto the road. A group of ten or so residents were trapped inside the ring of fire, and the wooden railing had begun to burn, sending smoke swirling into the windy night.

Several of his neighbors stopped and stared as he ran to the open door of the SUV that Nick had crashed. *Here comes Mr. Chambers with a Kevlar vest and an assault rifle. Don't mind him.* He would've been amused at the shocked expressions under different circumstances, but the wind was accelerating the fire.

"What the hell is going on, Zack?" Josh Davidson—an African American former college and professional football player for the Washington Redskins, one of the few neighbors Zack occasionally ran with—asked.

"No time, Josh, but can you please get everyone away from the pavilion. Thanks," Zack said as he slid into the seat and slammed the door shut.

Fortunately, his brother had left the SUV running, and Zack shifted the vehicle into reverse. *If they thought me running with an M4 was an attention-grabber, wait until they get a load of this.* He glanced right through the burning steps and saw the small group of residents, including Sam and his brother and the unconscious gunman, huddled in the middle away from the smoke and flames. The engine roared as the vehicle shot backward, tearing up the grass and dirt.

* * *

"We're going to be fine. Trust me," Nick said to the neighbors who hadn't had time to evacuate the pavilion before becoming trapped. "My brother won't let anything happen to us," he said, looking sincerely at Sam.

Sam nodded, and squeezed Ben's hand fiercely.

Their reunion had been short-lived once she'd run into his arms, gunfire still sounding behind her. She'd kissed him fiercely on the lips, and for the briefest of moments, everything had fallen away. "Are you okay? Your family?" Percy jumped up on her, barking in joy.

"We're fine. What about you?" his eyes shimmered with emotion as he stared at her, studying her face. "I was so worried."

At that moment, she'd felt her heart well up inside her until she'd thought it would burst from the intensity of her feelings for him. "I'm fine," Sam had replied, and then she'd blurted out uncontrollably, "except I killed a man earlier in my house. It was awful."

Ben had looked at her, seen her for who she was and who she would become, and hugged her fiercely. "That seems to be going around tonight," he'd whispered into her ear. "But it doesn't matter. All that does is that we're back together. And I mean what I said on the walkie-talkie earlier."

She'd felt tears in her eyes, and she knew in her heart that she felt the same. "I know. I feel it too." Sam was once again just a teenage girl, like the day she'd first met Ben, fiercely gripping the hand of the boy she loved, and all was right with the world, even as it burned down around them.

CHAPTER
THIRTY-NINE

Zack's solution was straightforward—break through the fire barrier with the SUV without bringing the entire flaming structure down upon the heads of his brother, neighbors, babysitter, and one unconscious enemy combatant. As he pulled away from the burning pavilion, he'd considered driving straight up the stairs, but he didn't know what kind of load the floor could bear. The second option was slightly safer, if there was such a thing when crashing an SUV into a building inferno.

As the SUV shot backward, he glanced to his left and saw the other Explorer with Griffin and Barrett slowly move around the circle toward Hidden Refuge Drive. He forced himself to turn away and kept the vehicle in reverse. Once he was approximately fifty yards away from the pavilion, he slammed the brake, and the SUV dug into the wet grass. He shifted into drive and floored the accelerator, glancing left one last time, shocked to find the SUV had stopped in the street. *Bastard is probably watching to see how this will end. Stick around, and you'll find out. I promise.*

His neighbors had cleared a path and stood on both sides, watching in awe and fear as they'd realized his intentions. The SUV rocketed forward, gaining speed as he aimed at an area ten feet to the right of the steps. The pavilion grew larger in his windshield, and he braced himself for the impact. Malta flashed through his head. *You and SUVs don't seem to end well.*

The Explorer hit the circle of fire with a tremendous crash, and splintered pieces of wood and flaming railing exploded up and out from both sides of the Explorer. The SUV tunneled forward for several feet into the pavilion, chewing up floorboards like a hungry mechanical monster. And then the damage ended as the Explorer ground to a halt, and Zack saw the group of stunned and frightened people—Nick, Sam, and her boyfriend in front—just feet away.

The fire had reached the roof of the pavilion, and time had nearly run out. Zack made eye contact with his brother, beckoned for them to come toward him, and waited for the understanding to appear on Nick's face. Once it did, Zack reversed the SUV one more time and raced backward out of the pavilion, leaving a gaping, fire-free hole the width of the Explorer.

Before he'd even stopped, the last of the hostages leapt down or were helped by his brother and Sam's boyfriend, Ben. Ben's father dragged the gunman off the pavilion to safety several yards away.

Zack jumped out of the driver's seat and shouted, "Let's go, Nick! We have unfinished business!" Zack looked left and saw that Griffin's SUV had left the hub and turned onto Hidden Refuge Drive.

Zack absorbed the sights of the carnage before him—the funeral pyre that nearly was, the dead bodies strewn about the lawn and pavilion, the discarded vans, the smoke, and the people looking around in disbelief that the horrors of the night had just ended. *At least for you*, he thought, unsure if it was the wind and cold air that sent chills up his spine.

Sam ran over to Zack, Ben right behind her, and said, "I knew you'd come back. *Thank you*," she said sincerely, and then added, "and your brother's not too bad either. See you afterwards, Mr. C. You still owe me that conversation," referring to his promise to fill her in on his history.

"You got it, Sam. It's a date," Zack shot back. "No offense, Ben." Ben's parents had reached them by now and had overheard the conversation. "Okay, home team. One last job at hand—there are communications jammers inside each of those vans. Please assemble teams with some of the neighbors, find them, destroy them, and then call for help. You'll know them when you see them. They'll look like horizontal computer towers. Now, I got to go." He smiled and hopped back in the Explorer.

His brother grinned at him, an unbelievable look of energy and excitement on his face. "So, this is what married life is like in Suburbia on a Friday night? This is fucking awesome, man. I need to hang out with you more often."

"And give up that harem of women of yours? I don't think your constitution could take it," Zack shot back. His eyes softened. "You okay? You have no idea how glad I am to see you. This has been a real clusterfuck."

Nick adored his older brother and had worshipped him most of his life in the way that younger brothers had done since time immemorial. "Your babysitter told me what you've been up to all night, mounting your own suburban counterinsurgency. I have to admit, it's pretty impressive, even for you. I love you, man."

Zack controlled the well of emotion that threatened to overtake him as he shifted the Explorer once more into drive. He reached out and grabbed his brother's left shoulder and said, "I love you too." He let the words hang for the only second he could spare, and then he asked, "How did you link up with Sam? I sent her out of here to get help."

The Explorer sped away from the pavilion, navigating a clear path around the survivors and wreckage. The taillights of Griffin's vehicle were still visible. *Bastard hasn't left the gate yet. There's still time.*

"She made it out to the main road, like you told her, but they had a guy waiting, and I had to neutralize him," Nick said apologetically. "Sorry. I had no choice."

"How? That poor girl—who's tough as nails, by the way—had to kill one of them. With a shotgun, no less."

"Knife, although I made it as quick as I could," Nick said.

Zack sighed. "Okay. Changing subjects. Remember that lunatic I told you about, my old team chief at the agency, the one who looked like he belonged as an angry extra in Point Break?"

Nick paused. "You mean the one who you said you didn't think you could beat if it ever came down to it? *That* one?"

"Yup. To quote Doc Holliday, he's my Huckleberry," Zack said.

"Do me a favor, Zack. *Never* say that again. It just doesn't sound right, at all."

The SUV had torn a path straight for Hidden Refuge Drive, and both men had a perfect view of the fleeing SUV and the gate that slowly closed behind it. The Explorer bounced from the curb onto Founder's Circle and accelerated.

"Fine, but let me tell you one thing. No matter what happens tonight, that monster is going to die. You hear me? He is a malignancy on society that needs to be eradicated. He's responsible for the death of an innocent man and the death of the retired deputy director of the Clandestine Service. That's who he shot back at the hub," Zack said.

"Oh, man. Your old boss?" Nick asked.

"The one and the same, but we can talk about it later. For all that's happened tonight, Griffin Huntsmen and his psychotic Irish helper, Barrett Connolly, the other guy in the SUV, get to die," Zack declared. It was an easy decision. There was no chance of civilian collateral. It was simple—they were going to hunt down two very dangerous men and kill them both.

"Well then, I recommend you pick up the speed a little bit so we can get to the killing," Nick said, automatically transitioning into the same state he'd experienced before every mission with Special Forces. *The battlegrounds may change, but the battles remain the same. Time to put on your game face, Nick.*

As the SUV barreled toward the gate, each man took comfort and confidence in the knowledge that there was no one better on the planet to fight alongside than the other.

CHAPTER
FORTY

The pain in Griffin's arm was excruciating, but it was no comparison to the fury he'd experienced at the sight of Zachary Chambers moving tactically across the street and grass, eliminating the remainder of Griffin's forces. First Brandon Harper, and then Zachary. He didn't believe in coincidences, but he also didn't know enough to come to an informed conclusion about it. He'd hoped that after Malta, Zachary Chambers had died in a ditch somewhere or contracted an extremely painful type of cancer that guaranteed a slow demise. But he'd been disappointed once again.

While his blood ran down his shoulder, he checked the range of motion, and he could still lift the arm as well as flex his hand. *Not totally useless.*

"That man right there, that is none other than the arrogant bastard who disobeyed my orders in Malta, the one the agency kicked to the curb, the infamous Zachary Chambers. He believes he's a crusader, when in reality he's just an arrogant, small-minded man. He is good, though. I *will* give him that," Griffin said, his voice trailing off, mixed with seething hatred and respect for his former subordinate. "Stop the SUV. I want to see what he does."

Barrett was livid with himself. It was his job, his *responsibility*, yet he'd somehow missed both a retired deputy director of the CIA *and* a former SAD operator living in the same community. *How did this happen? How could I have failed Griffin?*

"When I looked at the list of residents tonight, your background check had Harper listed as retired from the State Department. It should've raised a red flag and caused you to do a deeper dive into his background," Griffin said accusingly. "But it's not all your fault. I missed Chambers because he must live on a different street, which you'd organized the list by. Once I saw Harper's name. I stopped looking and came right here. You had no context about Chambers because I never talked about him, but Harper's on *you*."

Barrett knew his boss was right. In the rush to plan the operation, he'd completely forgotten how often agency personnel tell other people they're with the State Department—it's easy, and everyone accepts it without question. *You screwed up, royally, and you and Griffin may pay for it.* "I'm sorry," was all he could summon. Even though he'd never worked at the agency, he knew that even deputy directors tried to hide their identities. If he'd been agency personnel, like Griffin, he'd have spotted it immediately. But he also knew Griffin didn't care about his excuses and had punished others for much lesser errors. He just prayed the merciless man next to him, a man he called his friend as well as his employer, would accept it.

Griffin glared at him momentarily, the contempt for the oversight rising to the surface until Barrett felt like it would explode from beneath his skin. But just as quickly, it dissipated, and Griffin turned away. "Hopefully, it doesn't cost us our lives," Griffin said as the SUV slowed to a halt.

Before Barrett and he had jumped into the Explorer, Griffin had tossed a flare off his vest toward the back of the pavilion, which had ignited the structure instantly. He figured no one would actually die, but he wanted to see how they'd escape, and with the appearance of his old team member, he needed to watch. The physical compulsion, a trait of his psychopathy, demanded that he stay, but not too long. He needed to escape the range of the jammers and contact the buyer, who was not going to be pleased, to say the least.

"Are you sure about this? We need to get out of here, or our chances of survival dwindle by the minute."

"I'm sure," Griffin said, even as Zack crashed the SUV into the pavilion. "He is decisive. I'll also give him that."

"I wish I'd known who he was and that he lived here. I would've killed him before this even started," Barrett said, waiting for his friend to give him the order to leave the neighborhood.

Barrett had had enough of this accursed suburban battleground. All their operators were dead or missing, and by the time the sun rose, he and Griffin would be the two most hunted men in North America. Griffin had arranged for safe passage to South America through Mexico, but Barrett was not looking forward to his face plastered across every TV station around the globe. The next few days were going to be a nightmare. But in order to begin the nightmare, they first had to escape their current predicament.

Moments later, the residents had been rescued. Griffin had ignored Barrett's spoken regret, and said, "Let's go. This gunshot wound is throbbing like hell." The Explorer turned down Hidden Refuge Drive and made its final approach to the gate.

"What about the school?" Barrett asked. There were still several men and the large group of hostages in the gym, unaware of the violence and failure that had just transpired.

Griffin picked up the long-range handheld radio that Barrett had used to communicate with him back at the school. "I left mine back at the gym." He pressed the talk button. "School base, this is Hunter Actual. The mission is an abort. I say again, the mission is an abort. Leave the hostages and get out of there as fast as you can. Execute the E&E plan, and we'll link up in forty-eight hours," he finished, referring to the escape and evade plan that he'd arranged for all of them.

There was a pause, and Griffin thought his message hadn't been received, when the voice of Thomas, his point man for reconnaissance as an Amazon driver, finally responded. There was an air of relief in Thomas's voice, which piqued Griffin's curiosity but not enough to mention it. Griffin had more pressing matters at the moment. "Roger, Hunter

Actual. Abort order acknowledged. We'll close up shop and be gone in ten minutes." A pause. "Good luck. Contact us when you're at the safe house in two days. School base out."

Griffin let the handset drop to the floor as the SUV triggered the motion sensor and the gate began to slide to the right. "*Now*, we can get the hell out of here."

Griffin lowered the passenger window and inhaled the fresh, crisp air. He still loved the woods, even after his father had nearly ruined the outdoors for him. He'd taken him fishing and camping for the weekend, when he was ten, but what had been planned as a bonding trip had turned into a weekend blackout binge for his father, who'd never left the tent, let alone taught him to fish. But Griffin had left the tent and the campsite, and he'd wandered the surrounding hills, exploring the trails and developing an instant obsession with nature. He didn't realize it at the time, but it was because it had provided an escape for him from his father, from the self-destructive cycle of alcoholism. *But that time was long ago, and you're not that little boy. Most importantly, your father is long gone, decomposing in the ground.* The thought comforted him, and the wind blew harder, as if responding to his momentary contentment.

The Explorer had reached the halfway point to the main road, and Griffin glanced in the passenger mirror, spotting headlights near the hub. "Pick it up. I think Zachary has decided to pursue us, in which case, we'll find someplace to ambush and kill him."

"Are you sure?" Barrett asked.

"Trust me, for him we can make the time. Just knowing that Zachary Chambers has left planet Earth forever will almost make this debacle worth it."

A deep rumbling slowly vibrated through the floor of the SUV, and Griffin looked at Barrett. The vibration intensified, and both men looked at each other as they recognized the sound.

"I just hope it's not a police helicopter with FLIR," Barrett said, referring to the police department's forward-looking infrared capability. "If it is, we're more screwed than a blue-eyed blonde on Saint Patrick's Day in Southie."

"There's no way it's the police. The county aviation division is twenty miles from here, and even if they just disabled the jammers, help is still several minutes away. No. This is something else," Griffin said, and leaned his head out the window. The wind ripped through the trees, and he saw nothing but black woods all around and a canopy of dark sky above. "I don't like this—at all."

The sound intensified, but the SUV rolled on, at least until the entire front of the vehicle was suddenly awash in a bright, garish white light that blinded both men. Barrett slammed on the brakes, and Griffin raised his hands instinctively, sending a jolt of pain through his wounded shoulder.

A bright flash erupted from the hovering, black helicopter less than fifty feet above the ground, and a second later a flaming streak shot downward at them as the shoulder-launched RPG warhead was unleashed.

Barrett swerved to the left, which was just enough to avoid a direct hit, and the RPG struck the road. The explosion shook the vehicle, and the right tire disintegrated. The Explorer turned to the right in a big arc, even as Barrett tried to regain control. The only thing he managed to do was accelerate the destruction, and a second later, the SUV slammed into the base of a light pole, which disintegrated under the impact. The top half of the pole smashed onto the roof of the SUV as the Explorer fell into the ditch on the side of the road and buried its nose in the ground in an explosion of dirt and grass.

As Griffin faded into blackness, he thought, *Things haven't gone this poorly since Malta. I should've known this would happen someday.* And then, temporary nothingness.

CHAPTER
FORTY-ONE

"Jesus Christ, Zack, with all of this chaos and suburban combat, I totally forgot about the real reason we were supposed to get together this morning," Nick said as the brake lights of the SUV lit up several hundred yards ahead of them.

"Funny how that happens," Zack commented, and then added absentmindedly, "What the hell is he doing?"

The gate was less than twenty yards ahead of them when the ground began to vibrate. "What the . . ." Nick muttered, realization dawning as he spoke.

Zack accelerated, and Nick said, "I hope your homeowner's association is going to pay for this."

"It's got to be good for something," Zack replied as the Explorer exploded through the gate, which was constructed to be more of a deterrent than an actual security barrier. The gate was torn off its rails and flung to the side of the road.

"Do you see it?" Zack asked, referring to the helicopter both knew was hovering somewhere close by.

"Not yet, but it can't be far away," Nick said, just as the brilliant white beam on the hovering helicopter illuminated the fleeing SUV like an alien ship spotlighting its next abductee. A moment later, the RPG raced toward the SUV and exploded near the vehicle.

As the destruction unfolded in front of them, Nick couldn't resist, and added drily, "Hey, I see it."

"No kidding. You must have eyes like a hawk," Zack said. He aimed the SUV at the wreckage of Griffin's Explorer, and with less than a hundred yards to go, he said, "Get ready. You can have Barrett, Griffin's right-hand man, but the big guy is mine."

"Roger that, but what about our new friends up in the sky?" Nick asked, referring to the black Bell UH-1 Huey helicopter that had slowly come into view in their headlights.

Zack accelerated and cut the distance in half as he realized that the helicopter had begun to descend. The Explorer covered the remaining distance, and Zack slammed on the brakes, the SUV skidding across the pavement toward the spot Griffin's SUV had left the road. "Ignore them. They're either with us, or they'll kill us. Either way, *Griffin Huntsmen dies right now.*"

Nick exhaled and nodded. "Okay, then. Happy hunting, big brother. I've got the Irish sonofabitch." The vehicle slid to a stop, and both men jerked forward with the sudden deceleration. "One more thing—I love you, man. Good luck."

"You too," Zack said, and both men bailed out of the car as if they were fugitives fleeing the police, not hunting domestic terrorists in the early hours of a Saturday morning.

The wind howled as if in rebellion, and the rotor wash from the Huey added to the environmental chaos, whipping up leaves and gravel from the street and sidewalk in big swirls.

Zack had drawn the Glock, the suppressor still attached to the barrel, and jogged toward the edge of the street. He glanced at the helicopter and saw that two men in black tactical gear, including balaclavas that covered their faces, had stepped out of the open cargo section and were watching him, black assault rifles in hand but not pointed at him. *Screw it. They can join the adventure later,* Zack thought. Nick was less than ten feet away, a Glock in his hands, and

Zack nodded at him. The Chambers brothers shuffled forward and looked into the ditch.

From his vantage point, Zack saw that the driver's door was wide open, which meant that Barrett Connolly had already escaped the ruined vehicle. "Barrett's gone. Must be in the woods, running."

"You better get over here, brother," Nick said urgently.

Zack hurried over and saw the source of Nick's concern. Griffin Huntsmen sat on the ground with his back against the bottom of the doorframe, the door hanging open like a book cover. His head was slumped forward, and blood had soaked the shirt on his right arm. His right hand was empty, but his left lay concealed on the other side of his body.

"I got this. How do you feel about a walk in the woods?" Zack asked his brother, the Glock trained on Griffin as he spoke.

"See you soon," Nick said, and bounded down the ditch into the woods as if he belonged with the deer and foxes that inhabited them. Within seconds, the sounds of breaking brush had disappeared, over-shadowed by the roar of the rotors. Zack didn't know what the men in the helicopter had planned, and he didn't care. The man before him was his only priority.

Zack crept down the slope, the front sight resting on the side of Grif-fin's head. There would be no second chances, no quarter given. Even wounded, he was dangerous, and Zack suspected the slumped head was just a ruse, like everything else with Griffin had been.

As he inched forward, a feeling of dread fell over him, as if he were stalking his own destiny, one that had been determined years ago, one that was welcoming him home. He'd known, deep in those dark spaces of his former life, it would always go back to Malta. The reckoning was upon him.

PART VIII
STRONG TO THE FINISH

CHAPTER
FORTY-TWO

MALTA

SIX YEARS AGO

The Mercedes's driver had regained control faster than Zack, and the SUV pulled away from him at more than seventy miles per hour. With each moment lost, the possibility that Zack might lose Moretti was becoming a reality. *Don't think Griffin's going to like that too much.*

The Mercedes was about to reach the blind bend in the road, when it suddenly swerved to the left, off the shoulder and onto the dirt and rocky ground interspersed with shrubs and faded patches of grass. The SUV bounced across the landscape like a mechanical bull, bucking back and forth but barely slowing down. And then it dropped behind the backside of a hill and out of sight, leaving Zack to stare at the spot the SUV had been a moment before.

"Better follow the man. We're in for a wild ride!" Noah shouted with more enthusiasm than Zack Felt.

"Always the cowboy. I'm not looking for my eight seconds," Zack shot back.

Noah just laughed and grabbed the handle above the window.

As Zack raced to catch up to the vanished SUV, he saw what had forced the Mercedes to veer off the road—a white, double-decker tour bus, heading straight for Zack *on the right side of the road*, where the Mercedes had remained after the explosions. Zack fought the natural urge as an American to remain in the right lane and swerved to the left, removing the Range Rover from the path of the charging bus.

He spotted a dirt road that turned off and sloped downward, toward Anchor Bay and Popeye Village. From his reconnaissance, he knew the road had a few turns before it sloped down through the rocky wall of the cliffs that lined Anchor Bay across the water from the film set. But he also knew that the Mercedes had taken a straight path down the slope, and Zack floored it off the main road and along the dirt road, following in the Mercedes's path. *There's nowhere to go*, he thought, as the Range Rover bounced across the ground for twenty yards before plummeting down the back of the hill toward the opening in the cliff wall.

Noah shouted like a raging lunatic, and Belyakov screamed in fear, as Zack fought to control the steering wheel.

With a full view ahead of him, Zack saw the opening through which the dirt road sloped and wound its way down toward the water, the black SUV at the entrance between a towering wall of rock and earth on each side. A scattering of people, no doubt tourists looking for sweeping panoramic shots of the village several hundred feet across the water, were on the side of the road, looking up at the charging SUV. *Oh, Zack. What are you doing? This is not going to end well.*

Zack, relieved he'd put on his seatbelt before the second chase had commenced, was jerked up and down inside the Range Rover as it tore across the ground. He faintly heard the screams of people as they ran from the two SUVs, but he couldn't see them, as the ground rose and fell with each bump, the images initiating a slightly vertiginous feeling inside the car.

What felt like a jarring eternity later, the Range Rover slammed onto the dirt road and settled on all four tires. The road was empty of people, and the Mercedes was nowhere to be found. Zack floored the accelerator, his senses heightened by the knowledge that the pursuit was almost over.

He sped down the gentle slope, aware that he was nearly at sea level, and the Range Rover passed through the gap as if the tan walls and rock were swallowing the SUV, never to be seen again. The Range

Rover came around one last slight curve, and Zack was greeted with the exact sight he had envisioned in his mind's eye moments before—the concrete breakwater that stretched from the end of the road 250 feet into Anchor Bay, the deep blue hue of the water, the wooden village on the other side of the bay, and the black Mercedes, which had slid to a stop before driving onto the breakwater that had been collapsing in sections for years and looked like a series of slabs arranged in a straight line, uneven and unpassable by any vehicle. Zack pumped the brakes, and the Range Rover ground to a halt, fifteen yards away from the back of the Mercedes.

"What now, chief?" Noah asked with anticipation.

"What now is that I think you're really going to enjoy this part," Zack said.

The SUV's red lights shone in the daylight, and Zack calculated his options, none of them appealing due to the proximity of civilians if stray rounds started flying and ricocheting off the rocks. Not overly prone to swearing—unlike Charles and Noah, a SEAL and a cop— Zack muttered, "Fuck it," and pressed the accelerator all the way to the floor one more time.

"Oh yeah!" Noah exclaimed, and held on.

Belyakov's muttering began once again as the vehicle shot forward.

The Range Rover sped across the road as the tires gripped the loose surface, kicking up dirt and small rocks as it accelerated. The last surviving member of the security detail had no time to react, and the Range Rover crashed into the back of the Mercedes, shoving it forward over the edge of the road. The front end dropped from the road and crashed onto the first slab of concrete ten inches below.

Zack kept the pedal to the floor, and the Range Rover pushed the elevated end of the SUV forward like a sumo wrestler intent on forcing his overmatched opponent out of the ring. The engine of the Range Rover roared as if in outrage as the driver tried to engage the brakes, with no impact except to delay the inevitable.

The Mercedes turned sharply to the left, and Zack gripped the steering wheel, held on, and waited. The back end of the Mercedes plummeted off the edge with a tremendous crash as the SUV bounced and came to a rest, its nose suspended in the air off the left side of the ruined concrete over the deep blue water. Any farther, and Ray-Ray Moretti and his girlfriend would've been swimming in the manmade paradise.

"Keep him inside until I wave you out. I've got this. I don't want them talking to each other just yet," Zack said.

"You got it," Noah responded. He turned to Belyakov, and said, "You heard the man. We're going to sit here and enjoy the show. Understand?"

Belyakov was still breathing hard from the gunfight and car chase, his adrenaline surge still commanding his body's physiological response. He nodded and wisely chose to remain silent.

Zack opened the driver's door and stepped out into the sunlight, brandishing the HK416 at the driver's window. He heard gasps of terror behind him, and he imagined how he looked. *Which is exactly the point. Easier to manage people when they're afraid.* Several people whose features weren't discernible stared at him from the village across the water. He looked left and saw a small boat with a cabin approaching from the mouth of the bay, and his pulse quickened. *Too many people. You need to get this done.*

"Mr. Moretti, you literally have nowhere to go," Zack said loud enough so that he was certain the driver and Moretti could hear him. "If you come out, you have my word that no one else will die, and that includes you. If you make me come and get you, that guarantee is off the table. I want the driver out first, hands up, back to me, on his knees. You have five seconds. I won't ask again."

Zack counted internally. *One one thousand, two one thousand, three one thousand, four one thousand—Are you really going to make me do this the hard way?* He grabbed a smoke grenade from his vest.

The driver's door opened, and a black Uzi submachine gun clattered to the stone slab. Its owner emerged a second later, a tanned male with dark brown hair, his back to Zack. His arms were raised over his head, and he knelt on the ground as instructed.

"On your face, hands behind your back," Zack ordered, and the man complied. Zack let the HK hang from his neck on its tactical sling and unholstered his Glock. He moved forward and jumped down to the breakwater slab. "You move, you die. You understand?"

The man nodded in acceptance of his fate, and Zack reached him. Like a cowboy hog-tying a rogue calf, Zack secured the man as the rear doors of the Mercedes opened.

Zack spun on his heels, the Glock's sights coming to rest on the beautiful, tanned face of Ray-Ray Moretti's girlfriend. Moretti himself stood on the other side of the vehicle, watching Zack with interest. In his early forties, he was fit and handsome, with a dark complexion and slicked-back hair like a character out of the Sopranos, except that he had a look of bright intelligence that set him apart from the cast. *He's not afraid. How is that?*

"What now? You going to execute both of us right here?"

"Weren't you paying attention a few moments ago when I said that was exactly what *wasn't* going to happen? I thought you were smart, other than your choice of friends," Zack shot back. "Unless you want to die. If so, save me the time and tell me now, and I'll oblige you. Your call."

"No thanks. Not today," Moretti replied in the defiantly sarcastic tone particular to New Yorkers.

"Good. Now, I need you to follow my instructions, which goes for you too, miss," Zack said, directing his comment to Moretti's stunning companion. "Please get back in the Mercedes and just wait there. I'm sure the Malta police are on their way. I'm sorry, but your boyfriend is coming with me."

The woman looked across the top of the SUV at Moretti, who smiled at her, a genuine broadening of his face in warm relief and regret, and nodded. A moment later, she reentered the back of the SUV and sat stoically facing forward.

"Now what?" Moretti asked, looking around him as if waiting for more gunmen or a helicopter. "There's nothing here, and like you said, nowhere to go."

"Start walking toward the end of the breakwater," Zack ordered as he circled around the rear of the SUV to join his captive.

"Are you serious?" Moretti asked with more skepticism than a man in his position should have.

"Listen to me very clearly. Our mission was not to capture you. It was to kill you and Belyakov, but for reasons that don't concern you, it changed, and I'm the one who changed it. So do yourself a favor and do what I tell you. Don't make me regret my decision. Now, *move*."

"All right already," Moretti said, and started walking toward the end of the 250-foot stone breakwater.

Zack turned back toward the Range Rover and beckoned for Noah and Belyakov to follow. He heard the doors open and turned back to herd Moretti forward.

The two men quietly moved farther out on the slabs and reached the end of the first chunk of the breakwater. The entire structure resembled a concrete pier that had fractured into several uneven and unequal sections, some above and some below the next broken slab as parts of it had slowly begun to sink within the last decade. There was a three-foot gap, and Moretti stepped across it, glancing at the water several feet below. A warm wind rushed in from the ocean, and Moretti said, "You sure picked a nice day for a kidnapping."

"Well," Zack replied, "you picked a nice day for a lunch. We didn't want to take you in Valetta. Too many civilians."

"How kind of you," Moretti said wryly.

Zack heard Noah urge on Belyakov behind him, confident that his teammate realized what was happening.

He glanced back, expecting Griffin to materialize behind them, but his boss was nowhere to be found. The thought of him triggered another sense of urgency to keep moving.

An older couple in their sixties, shorts and short-sleeve shirts flapping in the wind, stood on the next slab of concrete, staring at Moretti and the masked man who marched him forward. *At least they're not snapping pictures*, Zack thought.

The man put his arm protectively around his wife, and Zack nodded at the husband, as if to reassure him there was nothing to worry about.

"Folks," Moretti said, and managed a smile, appearing calmer than the petrified couple.

They were halfway to the end, and Zack glanced to his left, reassured by what he saw. "Keep moving, all the way. We don't want to prolong this any more than we have to."

"Are you even going to tell me what this is about? Or do I go to my death without knowing what I did that condemned me?"

"You're making me repeat myself, which is *seriously* aggravating. Are you always this much of a pain in the ass? I'm surprised someone hasn't killed you already," Zack answered. "You're not going to die—at least not by my hand, and likely not by our government's, although I really can't speak for the bureaucrats who give us orders. But I'll give you a hint: Africa."

Moretti had reached the next section, which lay submerged just below the surface of the small bay, the water lapping over it and pooling across the surface in puddles. He paused as his right foot landed in a puddle, his brown loafers turning dark brown as they absorbed the saltwater. "I knew that was a stupid thing of him to do. Goddammit. You don't kill reporters," Moretti said in earnest anger. "But he told me that was how messages were sent in Africa."

"Well, in this case, it was the *wrong* message and a *very wrong* victim." Zack wasn't sure whether Moretti was upset that someone had been killed or just that it had been the wrong person. "No more questions. Just keep walking."

The two men splashed across the submerged section and stepped up onto the last slab of concrete, which gradually sloped upward. Seconds later, Zack and Moretti stood at the very end of the breakwater, closer to the other side of the Bay and Popeye Village than to their abandoned SUVs. Zack glanced back and saw that Noah had stopped twenty feet behind them, waiting for Zack to make the next and final move.

"Well, that was fun. What's next on this tour? I mean, this place is really cool, even if the movie wasn't that great," Moretti said.

"Watch your tongue, and don't ever insult Robin Williams again," Zack said, aware that Moretti had no idea that Zack had seen every

Robin Williams film and considered him to be one of the most energetic comic geniuses that ever lived, with a capacity to ad-lib in a manic stream of consciousness that was disturbingly hilarious.

"Touchy subject, I guess. Fine. But again, what now?" Moretti asked, his back to the edge of the concrete.

"Now," Zack said, glancing one more time to the left, raising his left arm while the Glock was trained on Moretti. "Now, you jump."

Moretti turned around, spotted what Zack had waved at, and muttered. "Sonofabitch. You thought of everything, including this." With a sigh of defeat, he took off his shoes, grabbed them with his left hand, and leapt from the breakwater into the warm blue of Anchor Bay.

You got that right, motherfucker. We did, Zack thought and followed his prisoner into the waves, fifteen feet from where the small boat with the cabin had stopped, waiting for their new passengers to climb aboard.

CHAPTER
FORTY-THREE

PORT VALETTA

USS *CARNEY*, OFFICER'S WARDROOM

1500 LOCAL TIME

Zack was exhausted and sore. The adrenaline from the SUV chase and gunfight had drained him, and he was recharging the old-fashioned way, a favorite of sailors worldwide—with a dark, thick cup of coffee that the ship's executive officer had made for them. The XO had cleared the wardroom so that Zack and his team could speak without interruption in privacy. "I promise, this will get that pep back in your step," the lieutenant commander had said, as he'd handed him a mug with "Shellback 2019: The Day of the Shillelagh" written on it. A curved stick with knots in it was under the writing, but Zack had no idea what that meant. Based on the picture, he doubted it had been fun for those on the receiving end of that instrument of hazing.

Charles and Noah sat across from him at the table, and both men looked as worn as he was, although Charles was the worse of the two. He held an icepack on his jaw and kept opening and closing his mouth. "That motherfucker hits hard. I had *no* time to react. I'm good, but psycho or not, that bastard is Money Mayweather fast. I'm just glad my jaw's not broken."

"Just like your head—thick," Noah joked semi-seriously.

"All jokes aside, I'm just glad you're alive. He tried to *blow us up*, and that's unforgivable in my book, no matter what. Whatever loose bindings of morality have been keeping him in check are gone. Griffin is the kind of guy who in Vietnam, Iraq, Afghanistan—hell, take your pick—would've committed a war crime and not thought twice about it."

Charles looked down and then back at Zack, acknowledging the truth of the statement without uttering a word.

"But now what?" Noah asked. "Belyakov and Moretti are in the ship's brig. God knows what Griffin is telling Langley. Honestly, what do you think they're going to do to us? We disobeyed a direct order, even if it was the right thing to do."

All three were silent as they pondered the question, and Zack finally broke the quiet, as they knew he would. "Honestly, I don't care. As far as I'm concerned, when we get back, I'm *out*. Today was the day I told myself that if it ever came, I would walk away with my soul intact. I will *not* become like Griffin, no matter what. We all did the right thing— the only dead guys today were the ones who took a job to protect a very bad actor. They knew the risks when they signed up. That was their job. We just did ours better. But most importantly, Belyakov's wife and kids and Moretti's girlfriend got to walk away. *We* did that, and no matter what happens, that's the only thing that matters to me," he finished with such intensity that the words hung in the air, as if affirming the righteousness of their deeds.

"Such a knight in tan-colored Kevlar armor, you are," Charles said jokingly, but then added in a serious, respectful tone, "and I'll definitely miss you, brother, because like you said, after today, we're done."

"Truth," Noah said, and raised his coffee mug.

Charles and Zack clinked their mugs to his, and Zack said, "It's been an honor."

"It has," Charles said.

The men sipped their coffee as the caffeine worked its way through their systems. "All right, boys. I'm going to go have a chat with Belyakov, and then I'm going to clean up, shave, and rack out in a luxurious stateroom the size of my closet."

Their HK416s and Glocks had been stored in the ship's armory, and the cleanup team had brought their duffel bags of clothing and gear from the farmhouse to the ship. The SUVs were cleaned and would be traced back to a low-level prince in Saudi Arabia, which they knew would only add to the confusion and further contradict the forensic evidence on the EFPs of Iranian origin. The entire world knew Saudi Arabia and Iran would never be allies, no matter what the circumstances. As far as the Republic of Malta was concerned, there was no trace that anyone on their team had been there. They were ghosts, which was something the CIA was actually good at creating.

Zack stood up. "Gentlemen," he said, and nodded, turned away, and then looked quickly back. "Except for you, Noah. You're from Texas."

Charles laughed, and Noah shot Zack a hurtful look. "Asshole."

"Always. See you cowboys in a bit."

"You got it, boss," Charles said reflexively, recognizing the unspoken fact that they considered Zack to be their true team leader.

A chill washed over Zack, and he knew that it was a reflection of the bond they shared, formed in combat, mission after mission. He was humbled by their respect. *I just hope I can live up to it*, he thought as he walked out of the wardroom toward the nearest ladder well that led to the brig three decks below near the stern of the destroyer.

* * *

"I know it's not the Four Seasons, but at least you're alive," Zack said in English, standing outside the small cell that served as the ship's brig. The cell's back and left walls were gunmetal gray, the floor a shiny blue polyurethane. The front of the cell and right wall were constructed of navy-blue bars. A sparkling metal sink and toilet sat in the back corner, and a bed was bolted to the floor along the left wall. On the bed sat Aleksei Belyakov, watching Zack intently, as if Zack were the one behind bars and not the other way around.

Since the destroyer was a smaller vessel, the brig only had one cell. As a result, Moretti had been separated and locked inside a small state-room under guard by two armed petty officers.

"No. It is definitely not a luxurious accommodation, but I'm sure this is nicer than what Russian sailors have. I once took a tour of one of our nuclear submarines, and needless to say, the living quarters left something to be desired. In fact, one of the toilets was at the end of a small passageway out in the open. But a US destroyer?" Belyakov said, sweeping his hand across the space. "Well, this is something special," he said in nearly perfect English, his Russian accent present but not overly dominant. "Now, what can I do for you? Or am I going to have to wait until I speak again to the very big man who stopped by earlier? He's not very friendly, by the way." His tone was affable, as if the two men had been friends for years.

Charismatic for an evil oligarch. Zack suppressed most of the laugh, although his lips curved upward as it escaped as a puff of exhalation. "No. He's not. In fact, if it weren't for me, you, your wife, and your kids would all likely be dead by his hand. That's *not* an exaggeration. And I wanted you to hear it from me, because I honestly have no idea what's going to happen to you, and I doubt I'll ever find out. But just know this—you were targeted by my government because of what you did in Africa. You shouldn't have killed the reporter and the cameraman."

Belyakov didn't respond but just returned Zack's watchful gaze.

Zack snorted and shook his head. "You know, I'll never understand what it is with you guys. You have all the money, power, and women any man can have, and yet you *always* screw it up by killing innocent people. You think our government doesn't know what you've been doing with your private army since you started? We looked the other way, at least at first. But you killed the wrong person, and as a result, your world as you know it, is over."

Belyakov stared at Zack, patiently allowing a silence to build between them before he responded. "Who was he, the man I killed?"

No denial. No pretense. This man is cold-blooded. "Let's just say the cameraman wasn't really a cameraman." Zack offered nothing more.

Belyakov nodded. "This business—it's brutal and hard, and when you don't play by the rules, it gets messy. And messy leads to more death and destruction because human nature is inherently greedy, always wanting more, taking, taking, taking. In order to manage that mess, you have to keep people in line, because eventually, they all *fall out of line.* And things like that—with the reporter and the cameraman—they are intended to send a simple message: Do not interfere in our affairs. But"— he raised a finger and looked directly into Zack's eyes—"it also sends a message to those inside the organization: If the man in charge is willing to kill a reporter and his cameraman, what will he do to me if I screw up, if I step out of line?" He lowered his finger and put his hand back on the bed next to him. "It's never personal. It really is just business."

Zack looked at him, shaking his head. "Unfortunately, in this instance, it was very personal. You just didn't know it." He turned to leave the brig, and Belyakov spoke one more time.

"I don't know who you are, and this may mean nothing to you, but *thank you* for sparing my family. No matter what you may think of me, my family means more to me than my life."

Zack felt the sincerity of the man's words, the weight of them, and he looked back one more time, nodded in silent acknowledgment, and left the room oddly satisfied by the way the day's events had played out. *Your soul is still intact.*

He walked away from the area outside the cell, passed an armed guard who sat at a small desk with a laptop on it, and lifted the lever on the hatch that led to the main corridor on the port side of the ship. He stepped through the opening, careful not to catch his foot on the bottom lip of the doorway, which jutted up several inches from the floor. Zack pushed the hatch closed and turned to his right to secure it, when the first blow struck him in the right shoulder, knocking him backward against the bulkhead.

His head glanced off a steel pipe, even as he fought to bring his arms up to blindly block the second and third blows. He ducked and moved forward as the expected blows struck empty air where he'd been a split-second before. The misses afforded him the time to gain distance from his attacker, and he shuffled quickly forward like a boxer trying to dance away from a rushing attacker.

"You always were a fast one, Zachary," Griffin said, amusement in his tone.

Of course. You knew this was coming. Zack felt confident he was out of Griffin's immediate grasp, and he spun on his feet to face the man directly. Griffin stood in front of the hatch, his arms up in a fighter's stance, front foot forward. But it was his size and his height—at least three inches taller than Zack—magnified by the confined space, that made Zack feel like he was battling some mythological monster in a maze. *He wants you to fear him. Everything he does is calculated for that effect. Don't give him the satisfaction.*

"You know, you really are psychotic, but I doubt you even realize it," Zack said, his eyes burning with anger. "I've seen flashes of it in the time I've been on the team, but I have to hand it to you, you do a really good job of hiding it, just like any closet sociopath. But this time, you've gone too far. You tried to *blow us up*, and there's no coming back from that. When we get back, I'm telling Langley *everything*. I don't care. I'm done, but I'm not letting you off the hook. You don't deserve to be on the team." He paused, feeling his voice grow stronger with each word, firing them like bullets. "You're an unbalanced, arrogant, reckless, amoral danger to *everyone*, and Langley deserves to know."

Griffin stared at him, and Zack braced himself for the onslaught he knew would come, praying he was fast enough to avoid the blows and counterstrikes. But then Griffin smiled, a broad, genuine smile, and it filled Zack with more dread than had the monster lashed out at him again.

"You *really* are a Boy Scout, and you're certainly as naive as a child. Where do you think I've *been* for the last hour, Mr. Morality?" The smile faltered as he saw the realization dawn on Zack's face. "That's right. I've been talking to Langley, and I told them *everything*, including how *you* decided to go rogue, how *you* put yourself and the mission in jeopardy, how *you* disobeyed a direct order, and how *you* have no place in Special Activities."

Zack's anger deflated, as if he'd been kicked in the stomach, his righteous fury replaced by a sinking feeling of injustice and the realization that every word Griffin had uttered was true. *Of course, it is. They're all bureaucrats. They don't care about anyone or anything, other than their own careers, no matter what they say. Griffin is one of theirs, and he knows it. And they always protect their own.*

"How's that righteous indignation and sanctimony feel right now, Zachary? What did you honestly think they were going to do? And I told them everything *I* did as well. Feel free to talk to them when you get back. I'm sure they'll have questions for you," Griffin said, snorting with derision.

Jesus Christ. All is lost, was the only thing running through Zack's mind—lost, not for him, but for the agency and the country. *We've lost our way, and no one gives a damn.* But then something occurred to him, and his tone changed. "I just want to know something. You triggered the IEDs, tried to kill us, yet you *still* activated the alternate evacuation plan. *Why?*"

"Jesus, Zachary. You really do take everything so personally," Griffin said, shaking his head in disgust, his fists lowering slightly. "*Because* it was the best thing for me and the mission. Once I realized what you were doing, if you survived the IEDs, I knew you'd do everything to capture them, and by then, I figured I could make the most of it. And guess what?"

"What?" Zack replied, wary of the answer.

"Turns out Langley has decided to use them both. I don't know how, and I don't really care, but they're just as happy. This truly was a dead-or-alive mission, and do you know what the best part is?"

Zack did, and he dreaded hearing it from his enemy, which is what Griffin had become after the day's events.

"That you *destroyed* your entire career, and it didn't make a bit of difference, one way or another. Either way, I win, and you still lose. This is going to make my career, and now that we're being so honest with each other, I'm thrilled that you won't be there to see it." Griffin's contempt was palpable, but it didn't have the effect he expected.

Zack had already made his peace with the knowledge that his career was over, and the encounter with Griffin, while illuminating about the sad state of affairs at Langley, had only reinforced the fact that he'd made the right decision. "Actually, you're *wrong*. It did make a difference:

to Belyakov's family and Moretti's girlfriend." The anger built again. "Because of *me*, they're alive," Zack said, his voice raised to a shouting level. "You would've killed them because that's what you *are*, a stone-cold killer without a conscience."

Before Griffin could react, Zack leapt forward, his fury spurring him into action, and struck Griffin on the chin with a strong jab that would've made Joe Louis proud. The blow caught Griffin by surprise, and he tried to bring his hands up. Zack slipped to the side and delivered a powerful punch to Griffin's gut just below his ribs. He was rewarded with a grunt, and the big man began to bend forward. Zack brought his left arm up in a short arc, a picture-perfect hook aimed at Griffin's chin—and missed.

Griffin had feinted with his head and tilted it back at the last second, drawing Zack into him. As the punch passed by his face, Griffin used Zack's momentum, shoved his arm away, and stood up to his full height. Before Zack could respond, Griffin reached under Zack's head with his right arm and slid it under Zack's chin, putting him in a brilliantly executed front naked chokehold. With his left arm, Griffin had pinned Zack's left arm against the side of his head, connected his hands, and squeezed.

Zack felt the pressure as his windpipe was cut off, but it wasn't his breath he was concerned about. Griffin had cut off the blood flow to his brain, and he felt the effects immediately. He knew he only had seconds left, and he reached down to his belt with his left hand, unsheathed the black Benchmade fixed-blade Infidel knife, and pressed it to Griffin's stomach with enough pressure to hurt without piercing his flesh.

The blade had the intended impact, and Griffin's grip on his neck loosened, albeit slightly. "Stop," Zack croaked, and pressed the blade harder.

"Fine," Griffin whispered into his ear, and released him from the chokehold just as quickly as he'd applied it.

Zack staggered backward and raised his head to see Griffin once again look at him with that cold, calculating stare. "Not even an A for effort, Zachary. Get it through your head. You *can't* beat me, no matter what."

In that moment that spanned between them, Zack knew with perfect clarity that Griffin was right. But he didn't care. Not anymore. He inhaled, caught his breath, and said, "If I ever see you again, I'll kill you, no matter what the agency says about it."

"I look forward to it, Zachary," Griffin replied, his eyes blazing with menace.

Zack spun on his heels, sheathed the knife, and walked away, acutely aware of the hateful gaze of Griffin Huntsmen stabbing him in the back.

PART IX
SPY GAMES

CHAPTER
FORTY-FOUR

"You know," Griffin started, lifting his head, smiling like a wolf who'd lured a sheep into a fatal trap. "I had hoped to draw you into an ambush after we left this godforsaken place, but here you are, still on home soil. It's rather ironic, isn't it, *Zachary*, that after all of the killing, it comes down to just the two of us, like twin moons circling the same planet but never colliding."

"It's not just the two of us, you psychopath. Who are your friends that just blew you off the road?" Zack asked.

Griffin laughed, shifted his weight, and placed a hand on each side of him as if preparing to stand up. "You'll find out soon enough. After their theatrics, I get the impression that they do not tolerate failure lightly."

"Well, I guess I'll have to deal with them after I deal with you," Zack said with no emotion. "Now get up, carefully and slowly. If I see anything in your left hand, I'm sending you to oblivion. Do you understand me?"

Griffin nodded, used his left arm to support himself, and rolled forward into a kneeling position. His right arm hung at his side, but a moment later, he was on his feet, staring up at Zack. "Now what?"

"Move up on the street because I'm not going to gun you down like a wounded animal in a ditch, although you probably deserve it. I *am* going to kill you. Mark my words. But I want answers to a few questions before I send you off into what I presume will be a very unpleasant afterlife."

Griffin took a few steps toward Zack, who backed up as he kept the Glock trained on his former team chief.

"There's that killer spirit I had hoped for in Malta. Why couldn't you have just followed orders? You make a different choice back then, and maybe none of this happens. Who knows?" he shrugged indifferently.

"I don't believe that for a second. And it's irrelevant. You condemned yourself by orchestrating this entire affair. You're responsible for the death of that old man, and you're responsible for the death of Brandon Harper. Those are unforgivable, and you know it. Just the way we used to take down HVTs who were a threat to our national security, I'm putting you down because you're a *goddamned threat to the entire free world.*"

"All very noble, Zachary, but we'll see how this plays out."

Zack had reached the blacktop of the sidewalk, and he sensed movement around him, although he couldn't afford to look and take his eyes off Griffin. He started moving to the right, so that as Griffin came up the slope, he would be between the helicopter and Zack.

Damn. This just got interesting. He'd been right about the movement. Standing twenty feet away was a line of four men all dressed in the same black tactical gear, except their weapons were now pointed directly at him. From behind the line of shooters, the figure of another man moved from the helicopter toward them.

Griffin turned his head and saw the armed gunmen, and he glanced back at Zack with a genuine smile on his face. "I told you this might not go the way you thought, but you always believe you know better."

Zack's eyes moved from the men back to Griffin. "Before this party really gets started, I just want to know one thing, Griffin. What was on the laptop that was worth all of this?"

"Information, Mr. Chambers," said a voice loudly, a sound that sent a shiver of memories falling through Zack Chambers' mind. *No. It can't be.*

But it was. The four masked shooters parted silently and effortlessly, and through the gap stepped the imposing figure of Aleksei Belyakov. "It's good to see you again, Mr. Chambers, and I mean that sincerely. Now, like that time on the ship, let's talk."

CHAPTER
FORTY-FIVE

As a former 18E, the designation for the Special Forces communications sergeant, Nick was impressed that Griffin's men had been able to truly cut off all communications to the outside world. It was technically possible, as they'd demonstrated for the past few hours, but in suburban America it wasn't sustainable. Then again, as he moved through the wind-whipped Virginia woods in pursuit of one of the last two remaining men who'd orchestrated the night's events, it was irrelevant. He didn't need to communicate with anyone, except maybe his God if the hunt went tremendously wrong.

Nick figured he was only twenty to thirty seconds behind Barrett, and the sounds of crunching leaves moving away, but not too far away, validated his assumption. After endless weeks of training in the woods at Fort Benning, Georgia, and Fort Bragg, North Carolina, like all Special Forces operators, he felt totally at ease in the environment at night. While it had been a few years since he'd gone tracking in the woods, the skill hadn't left him, and his trained mind processed the sounds, differentiating between the ambient, natural noise—the wind, leaves swirling, the scurry of small animals—and the sounds of someone attempting to tactically flee the area. What Nick—and Barrett, he was sure—knew was that there was no such thing as perfect silence, not in the woods.

That was another Hollywood misconception, an assassin stalking like a silent ninja through thick woods. He smiled in the dark and followed the sounds, trying not to disturb too much underbrush. *No need to create more noise than necessary.*

He was grateful for the suppressor, not so much out of concern for the noise, but for its ability to suppress the flash. When the time came to engage, the closer he was to his target, the better. While the suppressor didn't prevent all sound and flash, it did help mask them, making it harder to pinpoint in the dark, windy woods.

The sounds of the helicopter, while no more than sixty yards away, felt much farther because of the trees, which dampened the noise. He stepped—and paused. The sounds of evasion had ceased, and Nick felt the hairs on the back of his neck stand up. *He's waiting for me. Be careful or be dead.*

It was the smart play, and Nick likely would've done the same thing. The "dangerous man," as his brother had called Barrett, wouldn't hesitate to eliminate anyone following him since he must know he couldn't successfully escape until he was alone.

Nick slowed his entire being, willing his body to regain control of his lungs and subsequent breathing. He closed his eyes and focused, waiting. He could force his prey to act, but to do that he needed a diversion. He knelt as quietly as he could, his senses heightened. With the Glock in his left hand, he felt on the ground for something of substance, his hand passing over leaves, twigs, and other detritus of the woods until his fingers brushed the hard surface of a rock. His hand explored it, the small, sharp surfaces, the weight of it, approximately the size of a baseball. *Perfect.*

He lifted the rock, cocked his arm back, and hurled it at a forty-five-degree angle to his ten o'clock position. He stood and waited as the rock soared through the lower branches of the trees, mercifully not hitting any until it was at least thirty feet away from him. The rock landed with a thud and then struck a tree.

Instantly, there was a loud crack of a pistol and the briefest of flashes, distorted by the trees, at least eighty feet away. *Now.*

Nick fired a single shot in the direction of his target and took several steps forward and to his right. His plan was simple, and he prayed that the noise of the winds would distort his actual movements. The shot would give his prey an idea of where he'd been moments before. The trick would be to maintain his momentum moving forward, engaging in a solitary version of bounding movement based on sound.

A shot erupted from less than fifty feet away, and the bullet struck a tree near the position he'd abandoned. Nick fired again in the general direction of the muzzle flash, brighter than the last shot, hoping to score a lucky hit and end his aggressive gambit. But rather than wait, he moved forward once again when the next shot came at him. The impact behind him to his left was closer than the first two. *He's going to figure out what you're doing. You have to close the distance and get a line of sight on him—fast.*

He moved once more, angling slightly away as he closed the distance. Instead of stopping, he fired on the run and changed directions, this time moving to his left. Another shot missed him as Barrett took the bait and aimed to his right.

The flash was bright and unobstructed by trees, and Nick realized he'd misjudged his distance—he was closer than he'd thought, less than twenty feet to his target. He stopped, confident that he had a direct line to where the flash had been, elevated the Glock instinctively, and relying more on his natural aim, fired several shots at the last known flash.

A loud metallic crack followed by an exclamation of pain erupted from the woods, and Nick realized what he'd done—like an archer Robin-Hooding a bolt sticking out of the target, he'd hit Barrett's Glock. *Don't let up. Move.*

Throwing caution to the wind that wrapped around him like an invisible cloak, he rushed forward toward his prey, the amorphous grays becoming defined like a painter's dream turned into reality.

Barrett Connolly was on his knees, crawling through the leaves and sticks, and Nick considered putting a round in the back of his head. Instead, he aimed the Glock at the center of his back and squeezed the trigger one time.

The round flattened Barret to the ground, and he shouted, "Mother . . . fucker!" as he writhed in pain and rolled over to confront his attacker. His right hand was darkened with blood, where either the bullet or a piece of the Glock had struck him.

Nick stared at the man who'd terrorized his brother's neighborhood, a man responsible for two innocent deaths, as well as the deaths of his own entire assault force. The amount of blood on his head was staggering, and Nick had one question for him. "I just need to know, was it all worth it?" he asked curiously, the Glock steady.

The pure expression of rage and hatred contradicted the quiet, condescending level of his voice as Barrett answered. "Who the hell are you? Another resident we overlooked? It's bad enough we royally screwed up and missed that Chambers guy."

"That Chambers *guy* is my brother, and you're lucky he didn't come for you, because you wouldn't be breathing right now. But he's got some personal matters to attend to with your boss, and I'm sure he's making the most of it."

Barrett laughed hard and looked up at the swaying canopy of trees. "Of course you are. That's just fucking tremendous. Why am I not surprised?" His laughter ceased. "So, what's your backstory? I just *have* to know."

Nick considered how to answer, wondering why it even mattered. "Former Special Forces and US Marshall on their Fugitive Task Force. So running through the woods isn't new to me, although hunting domestic terrorists in suburbia is. But it's irrelevant. Question-and-answer time is over. Now, get up. We're getting out of here. While I considered putting a bullet in the back of your head while you were on your knees, I think justice is better served if you stand trial for the entire world to see what you've done."

Barrett stared hard at Nick, his eyes transforming from sparkling malevolence to a flat-black matte, devoid of all emotion, and Nick understood precisely why his brother had referred to him as psychotic. No matter how functional he'd been throughout his life, standing before Nick was a broken man whose apathy was now his driving force, which made him extremely dangerous. *He's going to fight or force you to kill him. You have seconds before he strikes.*

"Don't do it. I won't hesitate to shoot you. You have to know that," Nick said, his voice reflecting the seriousness with which he commanded.

"Oh. I believe you," Barrett said as he stood up from the forest floor. "But I'm wondering if you have the *courage* to face me like a man, without the gun. As a former Marine Raider, I crossed paths with you SF types many times. You guys really put the *special* in *forces*, no doubt about it," he said, mocking Nick as he inched forward. His eyes remained cold, bottomless pits of apathy. "So how about it, friend? What's a little fair fight between two military veterans? You think you have it in you, or are you afraid this Irishman will take you to the cleaners and *then* take your life?" The words echoed with pure malevolence, as if speaking them could conjure an evil entity that could strike Nick down.

Barrett inched forward again, and Nick pointed the Glock at his face. "Hold on a second there, *friend*. I'm going to tell you something, and I need you to hear it. I promise it will be worth the extra seconds of your life."

Barrett stopped his minute forward momentum, his hands at his sides, poised to lash out.

"I don't know how much time you personally had to share with my brother tonight, but I want to tell you a story, something that happened to us some years back, something I learned from him. And you being Irish—hell, you being you—I'm pretty sure you'll appreciate it. My brother and I were in a bar outside Fort Bragg after I'd finished Q school, and we were doing a bit of celebrating. He came down from the agency to join me, and we were having a good old time. It was a bit more of a local place than a military bar, as the soldiers tended to avoid it. But we didn't care. At some point in the night, two beautiful blondes who had no business being in that place started talking to both of us. We weren't looking for trouble, but four locals took particular offense to outsiders talking to these girls, as if we were there on some kind of quest to strip them of their masculinity and steal their women. It was absurd, and my brother, always the smart one, told them there was no offense intended, and he pulled me out of the bar. Of course, those Neander-thals followed us out to our car, which did not go well for them. And as the four of them lay battered and bloody, three of them with broken bones—I'm pretty sure I broke one of their arms and dislocated a knee; it's all a little hazy—I vividly remember what my brother told me," Nick said in a hushed, sincere tone.

"And what was that?" Barret said.

"He said, 'Nick, always remember that there's no such thing as a fair fight. All that matters is who's left standing when the fight's over.'"

Barrett's face contorted into a mask of frustration and rage, under-standing dawning as to what the story portended for his next moments. The knowledge that the confrontation wouldn't play out the way he intended infuriated him, but as Nick had discerned, Barrett didn't care. All that mattered to him was the pain and fury and the desperate release of it that he craved.

Barrett lunged at Nick, a whirling form of violent intent and hate, and Nick pulled the trigger.

CHAPTER
FORTY-SIX

For the first time that evening, even more so than when the bullets started flying and bodies started dropping, Zack was stunned at the sight of the man whose capture had directly led to the end of his career at the CIA. Perhaps it was the combination of adrenaline and exhaustion, but as he turned to face the Russian directly, the Glock he held trained on Griffin drifted slightly toward Belyakov. The four faceless operators reacted immediately, and before Zack realized what had happened, four dark earth-colored Belgian-made FN Mk 16 CQC assault rifles with holographic scopes were trained on his face. *Jesus. You're not winning this one.*

"Now, now, gentlemen. Please lower your weapons, at least slightly. In fact, please put them on Mr. Huntsmen, as he's the *real reason* for all of this. Unfortunately, he just couldn't do his job, just like in Malta, could he?" Belyakov said with amusement as the muzzles of the assault rifles left Zack's face for Griffin's.

The expression on Griffin's face reflected the same disbelief Zack felt, but as Griffin spoke, his shock transformed to anger. "It was *you* all this time. You were Gregory's buyer. Where is he? I know he's GRU," he said, using the common acronym for the Main Intelligence Directorate of the General Staff of the Armed Forces of the Russian Federation, Russia's premier foreign military intelligence agency.

Gregory had been the facilitator for the operation and was stationed at the Russian embassy in DC.

"He's been called back to the motherland. Sadly, you won't be seeing him anymore."

"Motherfucker," Griffin muttered, and took a step toward Belyakov. The four armed men took a single step forward in unison, the sound of their boots pounding on the pavement clear even over the sound of the rotors of the Huey behind them, which had continued to slow since it had landed.

"If you move, my men will kill you, and then you'll have no chance out of this. Do you understand me? Now *stand still or die.* Am I clear?"

Griffin remained silent but stayed in place.

Belyakov nodded and looked back at Zack. "Please. We need to speak, and we don't have much time. You can hold on to your Glock. I assure you my men will not harm you. You have my word, as a father— something I know you value." Belyakov started walking to the other side of the street, and Zack followed, his desire for answers a physical compulsion he could not deny.

Once the two men stood out of earshot, Zack started in with the questions. "What the hell are you doing, Belyakov? Are you trying to start a war? Are you some kind of terrorist leader, now? And what the hell is so goddamned important that you had to lay siege to a neighborhood—*my* neighborhood—on US soil? Have you completely lost your mind?" Zack shook with the building rage, controlling it before it slipped off its leash.

"Those are all fair questions, but first, let me tell you what happened to me after that day in Malta, since it's the most important piece of the puzzle that you don't have. And then, I'll get to the rest, although the clock is ticking." He paused, taking a breath for what was to come. "After you and your team left that ship, I stayed on, all the way back to the US. I have no idea where we docked, but once we did, I was blindfolded, escorted off the ship, and driven for three hours to some kind of facility in the middle of the country. I also had no idea what happened to Moretti. I thought that while you had spared me, it was only to suffer torture and execution at the hands your masters. I was wrong. Instead, your government made me a deal, and I took it."

Zack's mind reeled at the revelation. *All that work, all that effort, the dead security personnel—all for nothing?* "But why? We thought they wanted you dead for what you'd done in Africa. I'm sure you saw that the US tried and convicted Moretti and sent him to prison for twenty-five years."

Belyakov shrugged indifferently. "I did see that. He played this game and lost. As for me, honestly, I thought they did want me dead, at least initially, but someone very high up overruled them, maybe the highest." The implication was clear: the White House. "And the deal was simple: I would be freed to return to Russia and my private security business if I gave your government compromising information on all of the countries I had dealings with."

"Unbelievable," Zack said in disgust, although he was unsurprised that the bureaucrats running the country would shift allegiances so easily with no moral compunction.

"Not really, considering that I have contracts with several presidents of countries in Africa, the Middle East, and even Europe. And I gave *everything* to your government to do God knows what with. It was the price for my life, and I don't regret it." Belyakov stared hard at Zack. "You should be relieved. What you fought for in Malta, preventing innocent blood from spilling—I'm still alive and here because of it."

"But that's not justice for what you did to that reporter and his cameraman, who, as I'm sure you figured out, worked for the CIA. You should have *paid* for that crime," Zack argued.

"Zachary, in the world in which we operate, justice is a complicated, convoluted thing. I don't believe in it the way you do. But if it makes you feel better, I did find out who those men were, and needless to say, their families received anonymous trust funds soon after Malta, and they shall never ever want for money. I know it doesn't bring them back, but after the small mercy you showed me, it was the least I could do for them."

Zack finally grasped the complexity and sincerity of the man before him. He was a killer yet compassionate, ruthless yet merciful, a monster yet a benefactor. The gray area where modern-day warfare intersected with politics bred this kind of man. *And at least he tried to make amends, even if it was on his own terms.* "Okay. But what about tonight? Seems like your transgressions and wicked ways have continued."

Belyakov was quiet, as if gathering his thoughts. "You have to believe me—this was not my intent. But for reasons outside of my control, the situation changed. The laptop wasn't supposed to be here. It never was."

"What?" Zack asked incredulously. "That laptop has been the source of death and destruction *all goddamned night.* One last time, what's on it?"

"You have it, don't you?" Belyakov said, ignoring the question.

Zack hesitated for the slightest of moments, which was all the confirmation Belyakov needed. He turned toward his armed fireteam and shouted in Russian, which Zack still understood, "Check the SUV. The laptop is in there, probably in a backpack or something."

Zack raised the Glock as two of the gunmen jogged to Zack's abandoned and running Explorer. Another turned his FN Mk 16 rifle on Zack as the other kept Griffin in check.

"Zack, please. There's no need for any more violence. Because you don't know what's on the laptop and you've risked your life to protect it, I'm going to tell you, since it won't make any difference in the long run. I'm sure the CIA will be scrambling to repair the damage once they realize what's happened. Now, put the gun down so my men don't shoot you. I really do not want your blood on my hands."

Zack was torn. A part of him yearned to put a bullet in Belyakov's head, but he knew that the second he pulled the trigger, his life was forfeit. The thought of Steph alone and the kids growing up without a father was unfathomable, a reality he could not bear for them to endure. He'd once heard it said that a man with a family was hostage to the world, and at that moment, he truly understood the depth and accuracy of that statement. He lowered the Glock and waited for Belyakov to continue. There was no point in resisting, and both of them knew it.

Belyakov continued as one of the operators emerged from the backseat of the Explorer with the prized backpack. "I thought so. No matter what you think, no one else is going to die because of what's on that machine."

Zack sighed, the contradictions from Belyakov almost as frustrating and exhausting as the gunfights. "Explain."

"Do you remember a few years ago there was a story about how all of the spy agencies and countries of the world—yours, mine, the Chinese, Iran, and even the Cubans—were recruiting college students to develop as sources and assets for long-term operations? It grabbed your national headlines for a brief time, but like all things in your country, the people lost interest and moved on to the next item in the news cycle. It's truly amazing to me how short the attention span of the average American is. In Russia, we *never* forget old grievances. Ever. Regardless," he said, waving a hand as if urging himself forward, "that story spooked some senior people in Moscow, as well as the president himself. The thought was that if we and everyone else could recruit in America, the Americans could recruit our students in Russia. The realization shook the halls of our FSB, and as a result, an effort was launched quietly to uncover how your former employer and other agencies might recruit Russian students to one day use against us."

Zack's mind spun at the implications of such assets recruited and developed at an early age. The amount of intelligence they could provide, the damage they could do, for any country, was worth the investment.

"But what the hell does that have to do with that psychopath over there, a man who wanted you dead, who *would've* had you dead had it not been for me?"

Belyakov smiled, a mixture of appreciation and amusement, tinged with the slightest regret, which Zack couldn't decipher. "Do you believe in fate? Better yet, if not fate, then karma? It was never a concept I much considered, but after the events of the last few weeks, I'm beginning to reevaluate my position." He kicked at the ground, as if shoving something aside that only he could see. "Three weeks ago, a Russian source inside your agency informed Moscow that the Americans had compiled a list of Russian students from our most prestigious universities. I was brought over on a diplomatic mission, as were my friends over there, with official documents and support to expedite the retrieval of that list. I was never told who the source was, but once the source had secured the list and relayed all of the information to Gregory at our embassy, I was tasked with devising a plan to receive it."

"But how does that involve Griffin Huntsmen? I still don't get it," Zack said.

"My revenge, Zack. It was all because of my desire for revenge," Belyakov answered honestly, tinged with shame. "As a man who takes professional pride in knowing his international competitors, Mr. Huntsmen's name was provided to me, and I could not resist the temptation. I decided that I'd use him to obtain the laptop, and then when he delivered it, I'd kill him for what he wanted to do to me in Malta," Belyakov said, and looked Zack directly in the eyes. "And just so you understand, I *still plan to*."

No matter how Zack tried to think his way out of the predicament, there were no moves he could make. He realized—and accepted—that Belyakov would have his revenge. Griffin Huntsmen would die, just not by his hand.

"But how did it all go so wrong, Aleksei? Have you seen our neighborhood? I've left a trail of bodies, and our goddamned neighborhood gazebo just burned to the ground," Zack said accusingly, his words like venom expelled from inside.

"The source was supposed to bring it out of the agency himself. I have no idea what happened or what went wrong. Maybe he got spooked. Maybe he realized that while he himself was a traitor, he could place the blame elsewhere. All I know is that two things happened: the source disappeared, and the laptop's beacon was triggered—both on the same day. We tracked it via GPS all the way here, but then we lost the signal, which is when the plan changed. I had Gregory retask Huntsmen to devise a plan to evacuate the neighborhood, search house-by-house, and obtain the laptop." He sighed, an admittance of defeat and guilt. "No one was supposed to get hurt."

"But people *died*, Aleksei, and like it or not, you're partly responsible. What a goddamned mess you've made." Zack said exhaustedly.

"I know. Remember when I asked you about fate and karma?"

"Of course. It was just a minute ago. I don't think I've taken a blow to my head, at least not one that's damaged my short-term memory."

"Good. Here's the kicker, Zack. I had *no idea* that you lived here. Had I known, I never would've sanctioned this. In fact, I would've ordered him to do something else, find some other way. That monster told Gregory that he'd vetted the residents and that there were no 'unknown variables,'" Belyakov said, and scoffed. "But that's *exactly* what you are, an unknown variable, one who spared my life, and one who saved all your friends and neighbors. As I stand here before you, Zack, I swear on my children's lives, I believe you were meant to be here. I believe *all of us* were meant to be here as some sort of cosmic reckoning. One which, I'm sad to say, has nearly come to its conclusion."

Zack felt as if his world, his stable, suburban environment, had been violently wrenched apart, pieces and lives permanently destroyed. What had started as a typical Friday night had turned into an international spy game played out on a suburban battlefield. The irony that he'd been an unwilling participant who'd guided the events of the night weighed down on him. He'd done what he'd thought was right at every step of the violent game, but he wondered if he'd caused more harm than good. He wasn't one for guilt or self-reflection, yet he couldn't help but speculate as to what he would've done had he known what Belyakov's plan had been from the beginning. He might've just turned over the laptop and walked away. *But you couldn't have known, and you'll what-if yourself into damnation and madness if you go there.*

"So that's it? You just take Griffin, the laptop, and disappear? You know, in the spirit of this new glasnost between us, once you leave, I'm telling my government you were here. You know that, right?"

The smile on Belyakov's face was broad and genuine. "Of course, I do. I would expect nothing less from you. But fear not, my American friend, your government won't find me. In fact, I'm willing to bet they won't even try, because they won't want to, not with what I know about them. They would never compromise themselves that way. You and I both know that to be true about both of our governments."

That was the truth of it all, the realization that had painted him into a corner inside his own mind until he had no choice but to fight or flee—men of power only cared about retaining that power at all costs. And those costs usually came with repercussions that lingered like lost dreams and hopes, things that reared their ugly heads years later, as they'd done tonight.

"Zack, it's been"—Belyakov cocked his head, searching for the right word—"an honor. I am forever in your debt, even if you don't want it." He stuck out his hand toward Zack, suspended in midair, waiting for acknowledgment.

This is what it comes down to. A handshake between adversaries. You may hate him for what he's done, but in his own mind, he's a man of honor, and like it or not, he's not completely wrong. Zack shook his hand firmly, and Belyakov nodded approvingly.

"You better get your men out of here before law enforcement arrives. That Huey isn't exactly inconspicuous. I'd say there's no way you can escape, especially if they call a chopper or try to get you on radar, but then again, I'm sure you have a plan," Zack said as the two men walked back to Belyakov's protection detail.

Zack stopped a few feet from Griffin. Griffin still stood on his own two feet like a battered boxer, blood dripping down his right arm where he'd been shot. Something had been unloosed inside his mind, and he no longer pretended to contain his emotions. Seething hatred for Zack poured forth from his countenance like a physical manifestation. There was a part of Zack that would be relieved when the psychopath before him was out of his sight, and even more relieved when Griffin no longer walked the earth, which he figured would be soon.

Zack returned the hateful gaze and finally broke the silence. "You're a psychopath, and you're about to reap the reward for all of the pain you've caused throughout your life. Part of me wishes I could deliver justice, but after what you tried to do in Malta, I'm pretty sure Belyakov won't be denied."

The four armed gunmen stood still, Belyakov in the middle, where he'd first appeared, waiting for the exchange to end.

"God, I really wish I had killed you years ago, you sanctimonious sonofabitch," Griffin spat at him.

"Well, you seem to have made a habit of making really bad decisions. So I'm not surprised. But you can submit your complaints to them." Zack said, turned his head, and nodded at Belyakov's detail. "They seem receptive to that kind of thing."

The headlights of a vehicle suddenly flashed across the group, distracting the four gunmen for less than half a second, which was all the time Griffin needed to act. Had Zack not turned to emphasize his insult, he might've seen the blow coming. But his complacency had cost him, and the powerful punch struck Zack on the right side of the head. He staggered forward to his left and bent over, his equilibrium momentarily destabilized.

Sucker punch or not, get distance, Zack, or he'll own you. He fought the vertigo and sidestepped away from Griffin, but it wasn't far enough. As he turned to face his nemesis, the rushing fury of Griffin Huntsmen came at him like a freight train. *Like Belyakov said, karma. It was always going to come down to this*, he thought, and prepared to stand his ground.

The hulking form of his former boss slammed into him like a tidal wave, carrying both men to the pavement with a jarring impact.

Griffin let out a grunt of pain as his right shoulder hit the road, triggering a white flash of agony inside his head. The pain was a blessing that temporarily dulled the raging storm inside him.

For Zack, the only benefit was that the tackle seemed to clear his head by knocking his equilibrium and the tiny crystals inside his ears that controlled it back into place. He found himself flat on his back, and while his mind had cleared, the onslaught had knocked the breath out of his lungs. He inhaled like a stick shift stuck in gear, struggling to get out of first. He glanced left and watched Griffin roll away from him onto his side, seemingly oblivious to his wounded shoulder. *Better get your breath quick, buddy. Round two is upon you*, the voice of his high school wrestling coach urged.

Close by, Belyakov was speaking loudly in Russian to his men, and Zack caught the gist of it, especially "kill him." His lungs suddenly filled with oxygen, and he screamed, "No! He's mine, no matter what!"

Energized, Zack rolled to his left toward Griffin and lashed out with a straight right punch that landed on the back of his injured shoulder. Griffin roared in pain, but rather than writhe around on the pavement from it, he bent forward and kicked backward, striking Zack squarely in the Kevlar vest.

The blow stopped Zack cold, and the bulletproof material absorbed a significant amount of the shock. Unfortunately, it forced him to change tactics, and rather than press forward, he rolled to his right and rose to his feet, hands in front of him. Standing before him like a crazed, wounded maniac was Griffin, ready to continue.

Both men knew the time for talking had passed, and Griffin beckoned Zack forward like a boxer at the end of a grueling twelve-round fight, urging his opponent to engage in combat one last time before it all came to a close.

He's big, mean, and fast. Your only chance is the shoulder. Zack lunged forward and shot a straight left toward Griffin's face. He reflexively raised his hands and winced with the pain from his right shoulder. Zack rapidly switched his feet, placing his right foot forward, and shot a roundhouse kick into the right midsection. The kick was hard, but Zack didn't feel the ribs crack. *Still hurts like a bitch, though, I'm sure.* The big man bent to his right, his elbow coming down as if to protect his bruised ribs.

Zack moved closer and bent his knees. He stepped across the front of Griffin, twisted his hips to the left, and unleashed a savage uppercut that caught him squarely under the jaw. The blow would've knocked out a mere mortal—*hell, it would've knocked me out*, Zack thought—but Griffin was nearly superhuman, even with a gunshot wound to the shoulder. He fell forward to his knees, his left hand striking the pavement to brace his fall and keep him on his knees. His right arm lay at his side, useless.

Zack moved in and brought his right fist backward in a loop, reversing the punch. He raised himself up as he brought his right hand over the top like a fighter ignoring the referee in order to deliver a finishing blow to a wounded opponent on the canvas. He was so intent on the punch that he didn't feel the blade until it was already jutting out of his left leg just above his knee.

Sneaky bastard, Zack thought, even as he tried to deliver the knock-out blow, but before his fist could connect, his left leg gave out, and he fell forward and off-balance. As if fate were taunting him, he landed in the worst possible position—directly in front of the kneeling and grinning madman.

Zack tried not to panic, but he felt the presence behind him, as if a childhood monster had sprung out of the closet of the boy who believed in him, validating its evil existence. He propped himself up with his left arm and threw a right elbow backward, praying to connect with Griffin's face. Instead, a strong arm that reeked of copper, wet with blood, snaked around his arm and secured its hand on the back of his head. A second arm crossed in front of his throat and squeezed. He felt the bitter stench of the man breathing on his neck.

"It's fitting, isn't it? No matter what happens to me, I still get to win, and I finally get to take your life," Griffin hissed, and squeezed harder.

Zack's mind raced at breakneck processing speed, searching for a solution, a way out. He flashed back to the last altercation he'd had with Griffin, when his team chief had ambushed him in the narrow passageway of the USS *Carney*. He'd been vulnerable, but he'd had a knife at the time. *You have one again. You just need to grab it.*

Zack felt his oxygen dwindling and knew Griffin was trying to cut off the blood supply to his head. If he lapsed into unconsciousness, he was dead. Wounded or not, Griffin had the strength to snap his neck. Given the circumstances, Zack regretted having called off Belyakov's men. *You set the rules for this bout, but it's not over just yet.*

Zack's head was held in place, but he reached down and felt the handle of the blade. He grabbed it and immediately began to pull, just as he felt Griffin shift his weight behind him, and a large leg locked his arm to his side.

Full-blown panic settled over him like a cloak, passing into every fiber of his being. He was immobilized, and with every passing second, his oxygen supply slipped away. He struggled and squirmed, but to no avail.

"Sorry, little buddy. I thought you might try something like that. I told you once before, and you really should've listened—you can't beat me. *You never could.* And now, you're going to die for your arrogance."

Zack's oxygen supply ran out as Griffin tightened his arms around his throat. He felt the edges of his vision blur, and he realized he was close to unconsciousness, and then, oblivion. His ego and psyche rebelled at the thought, but he was totally helpless. Images of his wife and children flashed brightly in his mind. *I'm sorry, honey. I'm sorry, Ethan. I'm sorry, Addison. I love you all. I tried. I'll see you again someday.* He thought he heard faint voices in response, but he felt himself slipping away, his consciousness fading, the blackness enveloping him before consuming him whole.

From far away, Zack felt a warm, wet breath fall across his neck, and he thought for a moment it was God's welcome embrace into the afterlife, comforting and intimate. The tendrils of consciousness told him he was floating, but he didn't know where or on what, but one word echoed in his awareness—*acceptance.*

A brilliant pain of a thousand stars exploding in his head bloomed before his closed eyes, and he slammed back to earth as sound rushed in like an avalanche. Voices, English and Russian. A helicopter. Footsteps running. All of it was a cacophony, but then his lungs expanded as he inhaled, and his senses reawakened as if his entire system had been overloaded with adrenaline.

His eyes flew open, and he bolted upright, his mind instantly clear and searching for meaning. He glanced around at the same time as he felt the back of his neck, which was more than just damp. He looked at his hand, which came away nearly black, the color of blood at night. *It's not yours.*

He turned to his right and saw the fallen form of Griffin Huntsmen, who now lay dead in the middle of Hidden Refuge Drive from a gunshot wound to his left temple. Blood pooled around his head on the pavement, and Zack felt a genuine wave of relief wash over him. The fact that he hadn't been the one to take Griffin's life or even defeat him in a fight no longer mattered. He was just grateful to be alive, images of his family lingering on the picture screen inside his head. He had stared down a real-life devil incarnate, stood tall, and survived.

He glanced up to Belyakov, who stood less than five feet away and was looking down at him with concern. Zack opened his mouth to speak and managed to croak, "Thanks . . . Thought . . . you weren't . . . going to . . . help."

Belyakov smiled and nodded in the direction behind Zack. "Don't thank me, my friend. Thank him."

Zack, puzzled, turned and saw the standing figure of Stephen Flores, son of the murdered Esli Flores, holding a Glock pistol, still aimed at the deceased Griffin Huntsmen. His casual clothes whipped in the wind, his dark hair cascading across his forehead. But his eyes shone brightly, not with regret, but with satisfaction for having saved Zack's life, but more importantly, for avenging his father's murder. *It always comes full circle.*

Sam Hawkins stood on his left, and Ben and Ben's father flanked him on the right. No one spoke, the finality of the moment that had ended the cycle of violence for the night hung like a pall over all of them.

Zack nodded at Stephen, who finally removed his eyes from the body of the only man he would kill during his life. His avenging angel nodded in return, lowered the Glock, and stepped backward into his own thoughts.

Zack turned to Sam and smiled, relieved that she and Ben were safe and unharmed. A moment later, she was on her knees, embracing him before he could react. "Thank you, thank you, thank you," she said in rapid fire. "I knew you'd be okay. Come on. Let's get you on your feet." She pulled back, and moments later, she and Ben had Zack upright, albeit slightly unsteady, the knife still lodged in his leg, which now throbbed painfully.

From the edge of the slope where Griffin's SUV had left the road, a voice exclaimed, "Jesus Christ, I leave you alone for a few minutes to catch this sonofabitch, and all hell breaks loose."

The group turned to see Nick Chambers leading a wounded Barrett Connolly, the last remaining survivor of the assault team and the only one who would face life in the notorious supermax federal prison facility known as ADX Florence in Colorado.

When Barrett had charged him, Nick had already made the decision not to kill him, and he'd shot him in the right foot, the least fatal target he'd thought of at the moment. Barrett had collapsed to the ground, and as he fought back the pain, Nick had rolled him over and zip-tied his hands behind his back. He'd forced the wounded man to hobble out of the woods, excruciating pain flaring with each step, and Nick had enjoyed every moment of it, smiling behind Barrett's back. He figured it was the least he could do for all the misery the sociopath had caused in his temporary reign of terror in Hidden Refuge.

Barrett saw the corpse of his friend and looked at the group, including Belyakov and his men, and the finality of his situation set in. He looked at the ground, defeated, and Nick sat him down in front of the bumper of the Explorer they'd abandoned at the end of the chase. "If he moves, anyone has my permission to shoot him in the face."

Nick walked over to Zack and looked down at the small combat knife sticking out of his leg. "You might want to see a doctor. Just saying . . ." he added with a bit of a grin. Both brothers knew from experience that Griffin had missed all vital arteries and veins. The knife had torn through muscle and tissue, but it would heal completely, minus the scar, a symbol to remind him of the day his neighborhood was attacked by hostile forces.

"Here," Belyakov said as he handed Nick a first aid kit in a tan canvas bag that one of his guards had retrieved from the helicopter. "Consider it a token of my appreciation," he said with a straight face.

"Hey Zack, who the hell is this guy?" Nick asked, scrutinizing and assessing Belyakov.

"An old friend from a former life," Belyakov said. "But your brother can fill you in later." He turned his attention to Zack. "Now, I really do have to be going. Your law enforcement should be here shortly, and as much as I'd like to stay for the entertainment, I can't." Belyakov stuck his hand out one last time, and Zack shook it without hesitation.

As Zack gripped the Russian's strong hand, he asked, "Were you really going to let him kill me? I mean, I know what I said, but come on."

Belyakov smiled again. "When I found out you lived here, I made myself one promise before we arrived—that no matter what happened, and I mean *no matter what*, you would not die, not tonight, and not by my hand. In fact, I was getting ready to shoot him myself. But when that man showed up and walked deliberately up to Griffin without hesitation, ignoring me and my men, I knew immediately what he was going to do. And when I saw his face, I understood that whatever Griffin had done to him, it outweighed the grievance I had with him. So I let him do what he needed to do. Minus that knife, you were never in any real danger."

Zack released Belyakov's hand, and said, "They killed his father tonight."

A flash of sadness flickered and was gone before Belyakov spoke again. "Then real justice was served, and the Russian in me is truly glad that he pulled the trigger. His father can rest easy knowing he's been avenged."

Zack nodded, understanding all too clearly the sentiment. The law could never really right certain wrongs, and it took the hard will of a wronged man to do it.

"Zack, until we meet again," Belyakov said. He abruptly turned away and started moving toward the helicopter.

"Aleksei, don't take this personally, but I hope that doesn't happen," Zack said loudly over the rotors, which had started to increase in speed in preparation for lift-off.

Belyakov turned his head, "You never know, Zack. You never know."

Thirty seconds later, the residents of Hidden Refuge watched the black Huey helicopter with its occupants and one US government-issue laptop ascend into the dark night. Sam and Ben were talking to Stephen Flores near the SUV they'd commandeered, and David York held Barrett at gunpoint with the Glock Stephen had used to kill Griffin. Looking at Barrett, Zack recognized that the sociopathic Irishman had spiraled downward into his own compartmented world inside his head.

"You okay?" Nick asked quietly, now that it was just the two of them.

"I am. I'm also really glad you're as smart as you are. If you hadn't suspected something was wrong, I honestly don't know how this would've turned out. Thanks, man," Zack said, and embraced his brother, careful to keep his left leg turned away. "I love you."

"Love you too," Nick said, and disengaged from his brother. "Speaking of the original job we were supposed to do today, is that still on?"

Zack had been contemplating the same thing. "Not today, but if things unfold the way I believe they're going to, it will get taken care of, and we won't have to do a thing ourselves."

"Roger that," Nick said. "I really wasn't keen on torching your place of employment, you know."

"You know I have insurance and that I actually own the building, right?" Zack said.

"I do, but arson never really looks good on a résumé," Nick shot back, sinking into the familiar sarcastic banter that was often the truest bond between brothers. "Now, sit down and let me do my best *Grey's Anatomy* impersonation and get that knife out."

Zack sat down carefully, his left leg straight out before him.

"You know pretty much everyone dies on that show, right?" Zack said. "Except Bokhee. She'll be the last one standing."

Nick laughed. "I didn't think you watched."

"Are you kidding me? I live in suburbia, and Steph loves it. Of course I watch."

"Of course you do," Nick said, and laughed quietly as the first faint sounds of sirens appeared on the cool night air. "Now, shut up and let me work."

As his brother pulled the knife and bandaged the wound, Zack watched Stephen Flores, sympathy for what he'd gone through welling up inside him. Of all of the images that would linger for years as fading memories, it was the one of a son, standing with a gun, having avenged the murder of his father, that would remain with Zack until the end of his days.

PART X
WHAT GOES AROUND

CHAPTER
FORTY-SEVEN

Zack sat in his kitchen and stared out into the backyard, wondering when the first snowfall would arrive. The cold front that had swept through on the night of the assault had ushered in what seemed to be an early winter, although who really knew with the erratic weather in the region. The forecasts for the past three years had been especially inconsistent, so much so that Zack thought his five-year-old, Addison, might make more accurate predictions with her Magic 8 Ball.

Steph walked into the kitchen, perspiration glistening on her toned body, her blond hair tied back in a ponytail. Her lean and hard figure always sent his pulse racing, and he asked, "How was the run?"

"Good. Did a forty-five-minute intervals one. That Olivia instructor is ruthless. She literally looks like she's floating when she runs," she said as she refilled her water bottle from the filtered dispenser on the refrigerator. "But I do love this treadmill, and when that quad finally heals, you will too," she said, referring to the Peloton treadmill he'd purchased the week before the siege.

She came over to the kitchen table and sat next to him, her left hand reaching for his right one. "How's the leg, anyhow?"

"It's good. There's no pain, I can put my weight on it, walk around, whatever I want, but they said to refrain from any physical activity for another few weeks," Zack said and squeezed her hand.

"Good," she said, a physical therapist who'd graduated near the top of her program from the University of Pittsburgh, one of the best physical therapy schools in the country.

"And how's our overachieving young neighbor? By the way, you think she can babysit this weekend? We *need* to go out and celebrate after everything that's happened."

"I'm pretty sure that she'd be willing to babysit anytime we ask," Zack said jokingly.

"Don't you dare take advantage of that girl," Steph said disapprovingly and punched him in the right arm.

"Ow," Zack said, pretending to flinch. "I won't. Scout's honor."

"But you were never a scout, or is that something else you didn't tell me?"

Zack laughed. "No. I was never a scout. I promise. As for Sam, she's holding up well. When I took her out to lunch, I told her almost everything I've told you about my past, but especially about who Griffin was. She deserved to know. That kid is strong, and I mean *really* strong. Most people would've folded under the pressure and fear, but she didn't. She's accepted what she did, and I know her dad has been a big part of helping her cope. God bless that man for preparing her. I also think she and Ben have a very good chance of being one of those couples you hear about later in life, high school sweethearts still happily married thirty years later."

Steph smiled. "That's good. I like her a lot. We'll do whatever we can to help."

"I'm pretty sure she thinks it's cool to have such a badass as myself as her next-door neighbor. She's taken to calling me Jack Bauer."

"Oh, good Lord," Steph said, mocking him. "I need to have a chat with that girl."

Zack laughed. "I promise I won't take advantage of my newfound pedestal . . . too much."

In addition to honoring his promise to Sam, he'd visited the

Flores residence after attending Esli's funeral. He'd told the Floreses everything he could as well. More than anyone, they deserved the truth, as the siege had cost them dearly in family blood. Stephen Flores had no regrets or guilt, and Zack respected him for it. He'd done what Zack would've had he been in the same position. Zack had offered to help, to listen, to talk, or whatever Stephen and his family needed.

He'd had a similar conversation with the Harpers after an incredibly large funeral procession and burial at Arlington Cemetery. Brandon Harper's reputation and relationships were global, and in addition to senior leaders and the president, several former adversaries from multiple countries showed up to pay their respects and honor the legendary spy, which Zack knew Brandon would've appreciated.

The majority of the residents, especially the ones who'd been held hostage at the pavilion—which still lay in ruins—had been provided a version of the facts, including Zack's background and the motive. But a full accounting of the details had been reserved for those with the greatest need to know.

"Well, since that's settled," Steph said playfully, her green eyes dancing in the sunlight that poured into the kitchen from the backyard, "does that physical activity include joining me in the shower before I head to the grocery store? The kids won't be home for another hour from their playdate at the Thomases'."

Since the summer, Ethan and Addison had been having playdates with the Thomas children next door. They went back and forth, and today Sherry had the rambunctious group.

"I think I might be up for that kind of physical therapy," Zack said, when the home phone rang.

"Of course," Zack said, frustrated at the interruption. He loathed it when the phone rang, no matter who was calling. His time at home was precious, and every call was an unwelcome disturbance.

Zack walked over to the counter near the refrigerator and picked up the cordless voice-over-IP phone from the docking station. "Hello."

"Mr. Chambers, this is Nick Phillips. I'm an executive for the director at your old employer. Director Jamieson would like to meet with you, preferably today."

Zack had known since the day of the siege that this call would come. It was inevitable. He'd been debriefed twice by the FBI and their joint terrorism task force, but the CIA hadn't reached out to him yet, although he'd known they would. They had to, since the entire affair revolved around them and their actions.

Zack mouthed the words *it's them* to his wife, and she nodded, waiting patiently for the call to continue.

"We have a car ready to pick you up. Will one hour from now work?" Phillips asked.

"The timing will work perfectly, but make it ninety minutes, as my wife will be leaving then for the grocery store with the kids. There's just one thing," Zack said.

"What's that, Mr. Chambers?" Phillips asked cautiously.

"After all that's happened, you have a better chance of getting me to visit Moscow than return to Langley. Please tell the director that if he wants to talk—and I know he does—he can come to my home. I promise it's a low-threat environment. He can even bring two of his personal security detail, but they stay outside. I've had enough gunmen in my neighborhood to meet my annual quota."

Zack was impressed with the executive when he didn't argue, even in the slightest, and said, "Please hold."

There was a short silence of thirty seconds, and Zack smiled at his wife. *He's telling the director right now exactly what I just said.*

"Sorry for the wait, Mr. Chambers," Phillips said. "Director Jamieson understands and said he'd be happy to meet you there. You'll see the black Suburban in approximately ninety minutes. Thank you for your flexibility on such short notice," Phillips said.

"I'll be waiting," Zack said.

"Perfect. If you need to reach me, you have the number on caller ID. It's a direct line to me."

"Understood. Goodbye," Zack said.

"Goodbye, Mr. Chambers." And the line went dead.

"Look at you, commanding the CIA to do your bidding. I'm impressed. It's a total turn-on," Steph said mischievously. "You think we have enough time for that shower before they get here?"

"For you, babe, I'll *always* make time," Zack replied, and stood up from the table to take his beautiful wife's hand.

CHAPTER
FORTY-EIGHT

As the black government Suburban pulled into his driveway, Zack opened the front door and stepped out onto his front porch. Simultaneously, the driver's door and right rear passenger door opened and out stepped Director Matthew Jamison and his driver. Zack noted an additional member of the director's security detail in the front passenger seat. *Security in numbers*, he thought, amused.

Director Jamieson was younger than previous directors of the world's foremost intelligence agency. In his early fifties with a full head of jet-black hair and a lean physique, he was an exception to the usual heavyset and weathered figures of previous directors. A former clandestine officer like most directors, he'd spent his career all over the world in various posts, combating evolving threats in ways that would never be disclosed to the public. Zack had read that the man was smart, aggressive, and ambitious, but that those traits were balanced by an innate sensitivity and thoughtfulness he concealed except from those in his inner circle. He was also reported to be brutally direct, although not with the typical condescension or arrogance that accompanied it.

Zack waved to the director, when he heard, "New friends, Mr. Bauer?" He turned and smiled at Sam Hawkins, who sat on her front steps and studied the newcomers. She was dressed in sweatpants, a teal hoodie, and slippers. Zack vividly recalled the same situation—she sitting on her steps, calling out to him on the afternoon of the siege—and the image sent a chill up his spine. *Don't be jumpy. There's no need for it anymore.*

As the director walked up the driveway under the watchful gaze of his driver and the other member of the detail, Zack replied, "Unfinished business."

"Really?" Sam asked, her curiosity piqued. "They look like spooks. They are, aren't they?"

Zack laughed. "As a matter of fact, they are."

Sam nodded and looked intensely at Director Jamieson, never once averting her eyes from his face. *She's testing him,* Zack thought. *Good God, that girl is brave.*

"Do I have to worry about anyone getting shot?" Sam asked with a straight face.

Director Jamieson stopped in his tracks and looked from Zack to Sam. He raised his eyebrows as if to say, *Who is this kid?* but smartly held his tongue.

"Not today, Sam. I'm pretty sure he's harmless. By the way, why aren't you at school?"

"Oh. Yeah. Touch of the flu. I'm on the back end of it. Mom just wanted me to take it easy today."

"You think you'll be good to go by this weekend? Steph wants to know if you can sit. She wants to go out and celebrate."

"Celebrate what? Is it your anniversary?"

Zack laughed. "No. I think she wants to celebrate our survival."

Sam nodded. "That's definitely cause for celebration. And I should be one hundred percent by then. Can Ben come over while I'm there?"

"Absolutely. Just no hanky-panky," Zack said. "I'll text you the time when I know."

"Sounds good. And I'm pretty sure no one says 'hanky-panky' anymore, Jack."

"Well, I'm bringing it back," Zack said, and then added, "and I'm just kidding."

"I know," Sam replied, and grinned. "It's just still fun to watch you figure out whether or not I'm being serious. Okay. I'm heading back inside from the fresh air. I'll leave you to your new friends. Talk to you soon," Sam said, and disappeared inside.

Her sudden absence left a void, and Zack smiled inwardly. *That girl could rule this country with her mettle.*

Director Jamieson walked up the steps and stuck out his hand. "It's an honor, Mr. Chambers. Believe me. Or should I say Jack Bauer?" He was obviously amused at the moniker Sam had bestowed upon him.

"Please, sir. Call me Zack, and, well, that's just Sam being Sam. I learned a long time ago that people who get into gunfights together can pretty much call each other what they want," Zack said, and shook his hand. *Nice, confident grip.*

"I hear that, and you had better call me 'Matt,' especially in your home," Director Jamieson said.

"Fair enough. Come on inside and get out of the chill."

Once inside the foyer, Matt said, "That girl, she's fearless. I can see it."

Perceptive on top of everything else. Maybe there's a reason he's in charge after all. "She is, more than any of us, including me, can probably fathom. She's going to be truly formidable one day."

"She should come work for us," Matt said.

Zack laughed. "No offense, but she was distrustful of the government *before* the siege. Now, I'm surprised she was that polite to you."

"Well, judging by the FBI report that I read, you do have some rather resourceful neighbors."

Zack nodded and said, "Come on. Let's talk out back on the screened-in porch. Don't worry—it's heated. Before we head out, can I get you something to drink? Coffee? Something stronger?"

Matt smiled. "There was a time when all the executives had stocked bars in their offices, but that time has long passed. I think I'll take one of those Nespresso's, if you don't mind."

"Not at all. They're good, especially with the foam," Zack said.

"You really do have a beautiful home, Zack. It's obvious you've done well since you left us," Matt said as the machine revved up quietly and began to dispense its thick, luxurious brew. "You ever miss it? I know you don't miss the agency, but the work, the *direct action* of it."

Zack handed the director a black mug and considered his answer as the machine dispensed a second one for him. "Before two weeks ago, I would've said yes, but now? I don't know, if I'm being honest."

The Nespresso finished, and Zack grabbed his mug and walked through the open door to the screened-in porch. Two plush tan love-seats and matching full-size couches were arranged in a square around a stone table. Zack sat at the right end of a couch, and Matt dropped onto the left end of the adjacent loveseat. The two men looked at each other, but Zack waited for Matt to initiate the conversation.

"I'm not going to beat around the bush. Whatever you've heard about me is likely or partially true. I'm a bit of a straight shooter, often to my wife's chagrin," Matt started, smiling. "But before I get to the real reason I drove all the way out here, I have one question for you."

"Shoot," Zack said, acutely aware of the poor choice of words as they left his mouth.

Matt nodded. "Okay. You're an incredibly smart guy. You're one of the best operators we likely ever had. I don't say that to set you at ease for something else; it's just the truth. Now, I read all—and I do mean *all*—of your debriefs multiple times. But I'm pretty sure you held one thing back."

"Is that so?" Zack replied, amusement written all over his face as he raised his eyebrows quizzically.

"It is. And *here* it is—do you know what was on the laptop?" Matt asked.

Zack considered for a moment. He had to give the director the credit he deserved. It had been the one detail he'd decided to withhold from the official reports. If what Belyakov had told him was true, then the only agency that needed to know was the CIA, which was why he'd waited for this conversation, knowing that the director or someone who worked for him would come. "You're a smart man, yourself. And yes, I do know what was on the laptop, at least if Belyakov told me the truth of what was on it. The list of US assets you're recruiting at Russian colleges and institutes. But I guess you're going to confirm or deny it for me right now, correct?"

"I thought so," Matt said, seemingly pleased with himself. "But before I do, can you please tell me who else you told that information to?"

"My brother, Nick; that girl next door, who deserved to know, since she had to kill a man in her own house; Esli Flores's family; Claire Simmons, whose husband was executed by Barrett; Director Harper's wife and son; and my wife. Sam may have told her boyfriend, but other than that, no one."

Matt nodded in a way that didn't reveal whether he was content or upset with the answer. "Okay. Here it is, but you're not going to like the answer, not at all. What Belyakov told you was true, at least based on what he *thought he knew.*"

Alarm bells in Zack's mind started ringing, and even before the director said it aloud, he realized for the first time the true nature of the laptop. His heart sank as he thought about Brandon Harper and Esli Flores, and he said, "Oh, please don't tell me, not after all that's happened."

Matt shifted uncomfortably but maintained his bearing, refusing to shy away from the responsibility that was his alone. "There was nothing on the laptop, nothing but a fake list of names. The list was part of a counterintelligence operation to draw out a leaker, one who's been compromising extremely sensitive operational classified intelligence."

Zack closed his eyes and leaned back in his couch. He inhaled deeply to control the fury and frustration that coursed through him much more strongly than the caffeine. All of the dead bodies had been the price of a mole hunt inside the CIA, one that had gone terribly wrong. *It was a false flag from the very beginning.* "How . . . could . . . you?" Zack said, and opened his eyes, his anger subdued to a whisper but directed at the head of the CIA.

"I don't necessarily expect you to believe this, not after what you've been through, but I didn't know until it had already been initiated. By then, it was too late to stop it. Apparently, this traitor has been the one responsible for the news coverage of our covert operations. We thought this would draw him out, plug the leak. No one at the agency had any idea he would try to sell it to the Russians and trigger . . . all of this. On its face, it wasn't a bad plan, but the execution of it, well . . ." Matt trailed off.

"Just please to all the gods tell me one thing—I assume you know who this motherfucker is," Zack said, slipping into profanity once again.

"As a matter of fact, we do. But as of right now, he's in the wind. We think he may have fled the country to Europe—specifically, Poland. He was apparently having an affair with one of the DC political reporters, which is how the intelligence kept showing up in the press. I can assure you one thing—there is a very special group of individuals, a group you'd be familiar with, who are on his trail. And no matter how long it takes, we're bringing justice to him."

Zack noted the order of the words in the phrasing. *Justice to him, not the other way around. They're going to kill him overseas. Good.* He was disgusted, livid, and conflicted. He understood the *why*. But the fact that it had gone so horribly wrong, that no one considered this consequence, infuriated him.

"And he used Harper's son precisely because he *was* Harper's son. Unbelievable. When you find him, send him Brandon Harper's regards," Zack ordered rather than requested.

"We will. I assure you," Matt replied. "Also, I hope you understand that I've compromised myself and the agency by telling you the truth. But that leads me to my second item, the real reason I'm here, personally."

"And what's that?" Zack asked, although he suspected he already knew that piece of the puzzle as well.

"To ask you to come back as the deputy director of the National Clandestine Service. The executives who planned this operation didn't think it through all the way. I can't have people I can't trust. The ones involved with this fiasco are either in the process of being fired or have been moved into positions where they can't do damage like this again. But you? You, Zack Chambers, I absolutely believe I can always trust you to do the right thing, even if it's to tell me I'm wrong. I read what happened in Malta, and I believe you were the only one who tried to do what was right, and the agency let you down by leaving you to the wolves. *That* is a wrong I want to try and right, if you'll let me," Matt said, and waited for Zack's response.

The naked truth lay bare before him. The agency the man in his house was responsible for had royally screwed up, and they—*no, just him; I think this is his idea*—wanted him to try to fix it, or at least to fix the culture that had fostered it. At his core, Zack was still a patriot, but he had his doubts. He had two beautiful children and an amazing wife. He made a significantly healthy living with plenty left over for his kids' college and their retirement. *Are you really willing to trade all of it in for them?*

"I can't give you an answer right now, as I'm sure you figured before you walked in the door. But I have a problem of my own, and maybe you can help me with it," Zack said. Matt looked visibly puzzled, but he said, "Go ahead."

"Did you ever wonder why my brother was here that night? Why he got here so quickly?" If Zack were going to trust Matt Jamieson, what he was about to propose would test that trust.

"Actually, no. You told the police and the FBI that you two were supposed to go running in the morning and that you couldn't sleep. You texted him to let him know, even though it was the middle of the night, to come early if he wanted. He said that when all communications went down, he thought something might be wrong, which is when he decided to come over to check on you, which is how he ended up here and in the fight."

Zack grinned. "It's a pretty good story if I say so myself. Believable, honest, partially true. But no. That's not why he was here."

"Tell me," Matt said, a serious interest having replaced his puzzlement.

"I assume you know what I do as a software programmer who contracts with DOD?"

"I do, and in fact, I know you're currently subcontracted by a major player in DC on some kind of classified project, but I don't know the details. Honestly, I didn't look that hard into it, not with everything else going on," Matt said.

"Well, those details involve a software program that my brother and

I designed that truly disguises the identity of a cyber network actor on a hostile network. My brother is the real genius of the family. In addition to being a former communications expert in Special Forces, he took advanced programming courses and excelled beyond even his instructors' capabilities. But he's always been an action guy, which is why when he left the army, he went into the US Marshals."

"What does all of that have to do with me?" Matt asked.

"You see the value of that kind of program, I'm sure. But like Spiderman's uncle said, with great power comes great responsibility, and I don't trust the company that's already paid me to do the right thing. My brother did some digital sniffing around after I signed the contract, and he's not sure what their real plans are. He doesn't think they're going to sell it to the US the way we were led to believe, but he doesn't know who the real buyer is."

"Good God," Matt said. "I can see why you wouldn't want to do business like this. What do you need from me?"

There was no hesitation on his part, and Zack appreciated it. *He really does want to do the right thing.*

"On the Saturday morning of the siege, very early, my brother and I were going to torch my building in order to destroy our servers, where the software resides. Trust me when I tell you we would've gotten away with it, and I would've rebuilt with the insurance money. I know that's insurance fraud, but for me, committing that crime would be the lesser of two evils. There's no way I'm giving this software to that company. Ever. But instead of burning it, I want you to help me destroy it," Zack declared.

It went unspoken that by doing so, it would increase the chances that Zack would come back into the shadowy fold of the CIA, and it would almost guarantee his silence about what he knew regarding the counter-intelligence operation that had triggered the siege on Hidden Refuge.

"How?" Matt asked.

"Everyone in the IC is working cyber issues these days. It's the hot new thing. I'm sure you have offensive cyber capabilities where one of your young, brilliant analysts could hack into my network, insert a program that destroys the software, and leave no digital trace behind."

"Isn't that the same kind of software you've just developed?"

"Kind of, except ours can also frame another actor in such a way that even NSA's digital forensics people would believe it. Regardless, I need it destroyed within two weeks, when I'm supposed to be providing an update on the project to my corporate benefactors."

Matt absorbed the information and thought quietly for a moment, calculating the risks and rewards. Like the man before him, he knew that sometimes the hard, right thing had to be done, even if that thing was outside the lines of the law. "Consider it done. No questions asked. And you won't know it until it happens. And by the way, I understand that by doing this, it doesn't guarantee you'll come back to work for us. That's not how you operate, and I respect that. This one's on me. It's the least I can do after all that's happened."

He placed his hands on his knees and looked around. "And on that note, I think it's time I got back to my office. Friday afternoons are notoriously busy. People downtown seem to create crises that they think absolutely have to be addressed with meetings and phone calls late on Fridays. No idea why, but it happens every week."

Zack laughed. "I don't envy you that part of your job. DC is no place for someone like me."

Both men stood up, and Matt looked at Zack. "Actually, DC is *exactly* the kind of place for you, if you want to try and change the culture. It's not easy, and it's painful, but it *is* possible."

"I appreciate that, and as I said, I'll consider it. Very seriously. You have my word."

"That's worth more than most," Matt said, and the two men worked their way back through the kitchen to the front door. "You know, Belyakov is going to flip when he finds out that what he has is worthless."

"Actually, I don't think he will, at least not like that. I think he'll content himself with the fact that Griffin Huntsmen is dead and that I'm still here to tell the tale. There's an honorable part of him that is glad he had a role in saving my life. He's like that. He's not an evil man. He's just a man who does both good and evil things, and then he justifies them all."

The two men had reached the foyer, and Matt said, "Don't we all." It wasn't a question. "Okay. I appreciate the coffee, and let me know when you make a decision, even if it's weeks from now. One last thing, when our leaker is finally found, I assure you, you'll know."

"Now, that is news I very much look forward to hearing. Until then," Zack said, and stuck out his hand.

Matt shook it and paused. "I know it's no consolation, that there were so many variables you couldn't control, but after meeting you and reading the reports, I truly believe you did the best thing you could given the circumstances. And I'm sure your neighbors feel the same, especially that one next door."

"I hope so," Zack said, the weight of all that he'd done still hitting him at random moments over the past two weeks. His conscience was clear, but even then, the butcher's bill had been high.

As the director of the CIA walked out the front door of his home, he added, "When it's all said and done, though, there's only one whose opinion truly matters, and he's not talking."

Matt stopped on the porch and turned around. "You're wrong. He just talks in ways that are harder to understand sometimes. Like I said, your neighbors know what you are, and I guarantee they're grateful for it."

Zack nodded, although he still wasn't sure. He knew that in life, his neighbors' actions toward him from the night of the siege forward would tell the real story. So far, he thought it might be a story with a happy ending. *Then again, it's life. Happy endings are never guaranteed for anyone. Ever.*

"I pray you're right. I truly do," Zack said, and closed the door one last time.